C000146707

A Rainbow Round His Ankles

George T Johnson

MINERVA PRESS
LONDON
MONTREUX LOS ANGELES SYDNEY

A RAINBOW ROUND HIS ANKLES
Copyright © George T Johnson 1997

ISBN 1 86106 449 7

First Published 1997 by
MINERVA PRESS
195 Knightsbridge
London SW7 1RE

Printed in Great Britain by
BWD Ltd, Northolt, Middlesex

A RAINBOW ROUND HIS ANKLES

To
ASHLEIGH
daughter and friend

Author's Acknowledgements

Ian and Cyndi Tunstead
Stuart J Darley
Hannah Benton
Peter Darley
Gillian Hind
Helen Banks
Deborah Chaplin
Michael A Townsend
Eric and Joyce Brand
Paul and Christine Anthony

Deborah Setterfield
David A Jordan
Pamela Gavin
Jack Dalton
Ron Blanks
Sarah Benton
Valerie Cummings
Bert and Joan Benton
Martin and Jacinta Rose
Graham and Maureen Benton

my children
Aaron, Ashleigh, Ben *and* James
and
Geoff and Pat Benton
for the practical support which made the publication of this book possible

Mary Johnston *and* Stephanie Symes
for deciphering my abominable handwriting and providing typed copy

Ian Tunstead
*for persistent and unfailing
enthusiasm*

Peter Stavrinides *and* Paul Perry
*for promptly responding to
queries*

Geoff Benton, Gillian Hind, Mark Verity, David Jordan, Peter Darley
and others, for criticizing the initial proofs

Vera Eglinton   Jim Cawthorn   Winifred Findlay   David O' Neill
who encouraged, researched, and welcomed me home after too many years

Barrie Stacey *and* Michael Clow
whose reassurance was crucial

Cyndi Tunstead
for providing initial artwork

Helen Banks
who typed, argued, proofread, enthused, supported – and designed our ostrich

Kate Dale *and* Nicola Theobald *(Minerva Press)*
*whose unshakeable calm, whilst unnerving, added so necessary a touch of
professionalism to my efforts*

and
Shirley
who lived the book with me

Main Characters

Malcolm Birstin	*A local government auditor*
Archie Carrigan	*An alderman of the borough*
Jacob S Cracker	*The theatre manager*
Emlyn Cruddle	*The town officer, mace bearer and chauffeur*
Fenwick Fancourt	*A car salesman*
Jules Federman	*A theatre company manager*
Elton Fish	*A newspaper reporter*
Horace Goodenough	*A sergeant of police*
Mary Kean	*A barmaid*
Paddy Kean	*Her husband, a retired local government officer*
Gloria Lessingdale	*A star*
Arnold Locock	*Our hero*
Midnight Masomi	*Head moulder at the metalworks*
Giuseppe Mescolare	*An Italian by profession and Midnight's workmate*
Ernie Moon	*A damaged youth*
Florrie Moon	*His unfortunate mother*
Harry Moon	*His terminally unfortunate father*
Dodie Ochiltree	*A television presenter*
Christopher Oates Postlethwaite	*A creative local government accountant*
Mrs Postlethwaite	*His wife, yearning for something or other*
Ethel Robinson	*A local government officer*
Willie Rumley	*A bus driver with a grudge*
George Sammen	*The chief constable*
Stan Scrimshire	*Another local government officer*
Doreen Slater	*Another local government officer*
Nora Slattery	*Sister of Florrie Moon, and the mayor of the borough*
Jimmy Slattery	*Her husband*
David Smith	*Another local government officer*
The Town Clerk	*The town clerk*
and	
Bill And Karen	*Actors*
Rodney	*'Friend' of the star*
Brigid	*Theatre press officer*
with	
Chocolate	*The ghastly result of a chance meeting between an Alsation/Great Dane cross and an Irish wolfhound*
Jess	*Large, fluffy sort of dog*
Winston	*A circus-trained toy poodle, so cute*

ix

PROLOGUE

Early in his professional life Paddy Kean had found the most direct route to the office and since then he had stuck to it. His smart, sprightly figure was as familiar, regular and unnotable as a milk cart, or a coal-wagon, or one of the battered blue buses that ground through the town's dingy streets.

He knew there were other places to live; he was well-travelled. He knew there were places where a red sky at night might mean a sunset rather than the poisonous outpourings of an ironworks' chimney-stack, but he also knew that he was where he was best placed. Just as in the fields of France the peasant labourer seamlessly joins the surrounding countryside, so Paddy fitted the sheer monotony of Mankley, with its slag-heap, pit-head and acres of dustily nondescript heavy industry. He blended naturally into the background, in keeping with his public position.

Few of the townsfolk were aware of his public position, and those who were thought no more of him for it. The deputy borough treasurer did not rate highly on Mankley's social scale – he was merely known to be there, not a real person like the pork butcher or the priest.

Yet in his chosen profession he had done well. Thanks to inherent caution he had slid unobtrusively up the rungs of the departmental ladder: clerk, rating assistant, wages clerk, rating officer, accountancy assistant, senior accountancy assistant – every job except the typing. His promotion to deputy borough treasurer had been as inevitable as it was deserved.

But it was a step short of his goal. He craved the treasurership itself, and his name black-printed at the bottom of every rate demand.

A morning came when it seemed that this ambition, and Paddy's one conceit, would be realised. He entered the office to find the old borough treasurer gently dead among a heap of ledgers.

Naturally enough, once the news broke – which took all of an hour or two – the denizens of the town hall anticipated yet another unmeteoric rise for Paddy; a last, well-deserved, upward progression to the status of chief officer, with ultimate control of the department, and of what the elected members would ever learn about the town's finances. Paddy's promotion was presumed more positive than the product of a penny rate.

The town clerk encouraged him to take on the role of 'Acting Borough Treasurer' and the Council RESOLVED that, in accordance with standard local government procedure, the placing of an advertisement be considered by an appropriate subcommittee – a formality which caused Paddy no distress. He was used to and approved the processes of civic decision-making.

But that week Great Britain declared war on Germany, and in a fussy display of administrative activity the calling together of the subcommittee was DEFERRED.

Once it was discovered that hostilities might last a bit longer than a term of office, it was SUSPENDED, and when bombs began to fall and rationing began to bite and councillors' preoccupations turned towards granting planning permissions only to extending their own gardens, it was forgotten altogether.

"We'll just have to muddle through," puffed the mayor defensively.

"Makes no difference," the town clerk purred, "you'll be paid an increased salary for the extra responsibility."

Mild, reticent Paddy politely accepted these assurances, finding it beyond his nature to explain that money was the least of his considerations; it was the satisfaction of reaching a life's ambition that mattered.

So he muddled through the war with a depleted and ageing staff while, as the years passed, his face gained a few wrinkles and his black hair distinguished itself into rich silver.

His name, of course, never appeared on a rate demand.

*

The war ended. A much-changed council, guided by the town clerk, somewhat eager to please, reviewed the situation, and the long-vacant post of borough treasurer was finally advertised.

Applications poured in. A shortlist was prepared. But without Paddy's name on it.

"He's too old!" exclaimed a newly-elected councillor.

"Always looks a bit tired to me," muttered another.

"Gentlemen!" the town clerk protested, "Mr Kean has worked for the borough since leaving school! He has faithfully devoted his entire working life to administering the town's finances..."

"Too long in one place!" was the flat response.

Sighing at the realisation that these brash new councillors could make life for him too run less smoothly, the town clerk put Paddy's neatly hand-written application slowly to one side.

"Perhaps, then, gentlemen, you're looking for a younger man, one with experience in another local authority, someone qualified..."

"Exactly!" interrupted the chairman, who vaguely approved an element of logic to back up council decisions.

"After all," the town clerk continued, "theoretically... er... conceivably, I suppose, the appointment of a deputy to a chief's position might be seen as a means of allowing a malpractice to continue unchecked..." His voice faded to an ashamed mumble. "... not that I would dream of suggesting that Mr Kean..."

The sentence was drowned by rough protestations of support for Paddy's honesty. But a point had been made. There was little further discussion.

Nobody explained that Paddy had been treasurer in all but name for the past seven years, or troubled to detail his record of devotion to the town. Nobody gave him another thought. The council members had got from their town clerk just the kind of policy guidance they paid for, understood and liked; just the kind of principle to hide behind if questioned. Clever fellow, the town clerk – you can't beat a legal mind.

Paddy received a letter in which he was thanked for his 'interest in the post' but advised that 'on this occasion' it had been inappropriate to include his name on the shortlist.

Christopher Oates Postlethwaite, A.I.M.T.A., got the job. That was the name to appear black-printed at the bottom of the rate demands. A younger man than Paddy, qualified too, with experience in other local authorities and, coincidentally, a Yorkshireman like the town clerk.

Paddy, numb with disappointment but too well-trained to do otherwise, continued to work as 'Acting Borough Treasurer' right up to the day the new man started; but the Yorkshireman was quick to alter that.

From the town clerk he had learned of Paddy's lifelong aspirations to the senior position, and from experience had gleaned that peace of mind came easier without competition from others. This was Postlethwaite's début as treasurer. Mankley was to be the niche from which he intended to make his mark on the world of public finance. He didn't want a deputy who sought power, or who might consider himself more than dispensable.

It took only a day or so for Postlethwaite to assume full control of, and responsibility for, all the duties carried out by Paddy; a day or so in which to take over every record, file and account – all meticulously kept and presented.

Paddy, in what he considered a proper professional manner, attempted to explain whatever might not be obvious, but his words were pooh-poohed by the new man, sniggered at, derided; and when Paddy suggested that the workload might prove more than Postlethwaite appeared to anticipate, the new treasurer laughed, cutting dead all further discourse – and whatever hopes his deputy might have had of a viable professional future.

So Christopher Oates Postlethwaite encumbered himself with not only the work that was properly his, but that of his deputy as well. Paddy hadn't thought to replace himself at the beginning of the war, he'd simply absorbed the duties of both posts. Now, unwittingly, Postlethwaite had got the lot. Lock, stock and barrel.

14

Paddy reassumed the mantle of deputy borough treasurer, but without anything to do whatsoever, and for a time the suspicious, insecure Postlethwaite was too enrapt with power to notice.

Paddy's initial numbness gave way eventually to outrage and hurt. It was bad enough to have failed in his ambition, but to be left without the dignity of daily work was cruel. He felt he had been scurvily treated. He began to drink. Not excessively. Just sufficient to dull the frustration. And no one knew. He chose a pub well away from town. But he had nobody to keep him company. He had made few friends in his lifetime and had lived alone since his parents had died in the early thirties.

He was fifty, friendless and futureless.

There was only the barmaid on whom to unburden himself; a chummy, talkative lass called Mary, and she listened sympathetically to his tale as she set many a pint before his sad eyes. Within a few weeks she had learned a lot about the fastidious little man who came into the pub so often, and she warmed to him.

It was a matter only of time and alcohol absorption before Paddy asked her to marry him. She agreed at once. Why not? Any life with anyone had to be better than what she'd had up to now. Born illegitimate, tender years spent in the hellish care of the county children's home; pregnant at fifteen, again at seventeen, and both times abandoned, her overriding obsession was to ensure that her daughters would enjoy a better life than her own. There was no other way to that achievement than by working hard at whatever casual jobs nobody else wanted, and in the huddled-up northern corner of England during the depression of the mid-thirties that meant a degree of privation unimaginable by those in happier places.

In a sense the war meant salvation for the murdered towns. Their populations, skilled in heavy engineering, coal, shipbuilding and steel – all basic to effective warfare – had again become valued by the nation, and for Mary came her first steady job, in the bomb factory, and regular wages to bring ballast to a tumbled life. But the preceding years of poverty had taken their toll.

Love, ambition, social acceptance, hope – all had passed her by, the pretensions of other people.

The war over, unemployment again rife, Paddy came along as a protector, an escape from desperate insecurity. She didn't love him. Nor did he love her. They simply found a need satisfied, each by the other.

Paddy reacted favourably to discovering that his wife-to-be was less than half his age, and quite stoically to the existence of her daughters. Anyway, he married his barmaid and, together with the girls and a suitcase, she moved into his house at Mankley.

His outward habits were unaffected. He told no one he was married, and nobody asked – nobody knew him well enough to care – and Mary, with intuitive respect for his habit of privacy did nothing to excite curiosity. The newly-formed Kean family was left to forge its bonds without distraction.

Paddy adapted quickly to his altered domestic circumstances. He papered walls, fitted carpets, bought Mary clothes and delighted in her joy at having them. He took the girls away from the state school to enrol them in what he termed a 'more suitable educational establishment' in the nearby city.

Cooked and cleaned for, with Mary's chatter in the evenings and the youngsters to entertain at weekends, he began hesitantly to enjoy life. There was freshness around him and contentment hammered persistently at his heart.

By unspoken agreement Paddy and Mary, while sharing a bedroom, had occupied separate beds. Paddy had not presumed a physical aspect to the marriage, and Mary, coldly seduced at fifteen and virtually raped two years later, was more than normally demanding in the subtleties of sexual arousal.

It was a long time before the two beds were pushed together and Paddy came to cuddle her through the night, even longer before he was met with more than an affectionate response. But, to his surprise, a night came when he found himself being eased gently towards his wife. Warm and soft her arms enfolded him, and Paddy – courtly, tender, respectful, overawed, seeing Mary's face glow and soften in the half-light of a summer dawn – made love.

Next morning, while he ran off to the Co-op to buy a double bed, Mary sat in an armchair, with a cup of tea on her lap, staring thoughtfully into the fire. She pulled her dressing gown around her and hugged herself close, enriched by Paddy's gentility. She loved him. Hard. And with the love came a longing to see him fulfilled.

Ideas came quickly and some took shape. Her view ahead was clear by the time Paddy returned. It was obvious that she had been pondering – Paddy could tell from her eyes. They had about them a translucence seen normally only in the newly pregnant.

Irish eyes are generally beautiful. It's a fact. They were to be seen everywhere in Mankley, though the town's Irish were mostly third generation. Mary's eyes were particularly engaging, magnetic, and loquacious enough to make her face redundant. They could laugh when she was serious, cry without a tear falling, emasculate those who crossed her, and enslave those she loved. As she knelt by his chair, their blue was turned on Paddy, and quietly, slowly and persuasively she told him her thoughts.

"We can work on it, darling," she concluded. "I know it'll take time and effort - probably all the twelve years to your retirement. You would never want to leave this town, would you?"

Paddy shook his head, thoughtfully but with decision.

"No, love, I don't want to be anywhere else!"

"Then we'll do it, Paddy!" She took his hand and squeezed it. "Mankley will be the rainbow round your ankles!"

*

Rainbows were not in prospect for Christopher Oates Postlethwaite – more like persistent drizzle. He might have effectively destroyed the prestige and influence he imagined to be Paddy's, but in the process had created for himself an overload of day-to-day tedium. For a time he had hoped that Paddy would resign, leaving a vacancy to be filled by some more productive younger man but, within months, that hope faded.

Paddy, of course, had no intention of resigning. He had applied logic to his situation. In order to bring his plans to fruition it would help to have a close connection with the town hall. To avoid curiosity his respectable lifestyle should continue. His salary was adequate, his superannuation accumulating. He had agreeable working hours, and the fact that he did nothing in them protected him from criticism. In all, Paddy could not conceive a better way to sit out the years. His position was impregnable.

Postlethwaite came to realise it, so turned to the town clerk for advice.

Despite his nominal authority as chief executive of the council, the clerk was not a man of great intellect or compelling ambition. He tended to despise such qualities. By nature he was humble, of an integrity beyond reproach and powerfully attracted to the tried and tested. By nature he would have unhesitatingly had Paddy Kean promoted to the treasurership, but another of his virtues had intervened – scrupulous impartiality. There lay the dichotomy, and the guilt. He had done less than he felt he should to support a loyal, valuable servant of the borough and, instead, had tacitly approved the appointment of a fellow Yorkshireman. He was concerned that his normally sterile administrative judgement might have been subconsciously influenced by ties of kinship. In the town clerk's imagination, therefore, Postlethwaite was a blot – the only blot – on an otherwise unblemished record of impartial service. Somehow this blot had to be erased or, at least, prevented from spreading; and the meeting initiated by the treasurer provided the opportunity.

"You mean to tell me," the town clerk exclaimed after listening to Postlethwaite's tale, "that on the day you took up post you appropriated all Mr Kean's work to yourself? Without knowing how much he was doing?"

"But, Arthur!" whined Postlethwaite. "After you warned me of Kean's ambitions I had to prevent him becoming a threat, minimise his opportunities for revenge!"

The clerk stared coldly at the treasurer. There was no balance to this man, he thought: he was too pompous, humourless – and too damned familiar.

"Did it not occur to you, Borough Treasurer," the clerk suggested through a smile, "that I might have informed you of Mr Kean's interest in the treasurership so that you would have the opportunity to treat him with kindness, respect for his long experience, and give him the benefit of a little understanding after his disappointment at being passed over?"

"No," replied the treasurer. "I thought you were trying to help me by warning me of…"

"I *was* trying to help you! Help you gain the loyalty and assistance of a very able deputy! A little sympathetic thoughtfulness on your part might have given you that!"

Postlethwaite squirmed.

"Well, perhaps you have a point," he muttered, "but how do we put matters right?"

"I don't think it's my problem," the clerk sighed. "I never interfere in the internal affairs of our various departments. I certainly can't assist you in anything Mr Kean might resent. There would be some searching questions to answer if he were to leave us. He has a fine record of service, you know…"

"If I may say so, Arthur," Postlethwaite sneered, thinking he would score a point, "he isn't contributing to that fine record at the moment!"

"Oh, I don't know about that," replied the clerk. "He always dresses smartly, gets to work on time, has regular habits, keeps himself clean. Never heard a breath of scandal about him. Honest chap. Gives the public a touch of confidence in its local administration, and I'm told he's a very hard worker!"

Postlethwaite exploded.

"What? He doesn't work at all! I'm doing it all! Working late every night!"

"Perhaps you should experiment with starting earlier in the mornings," suggested the clerk wryly. "Mr Kean usually gets to work before you do; passes my window as he arrives. Always gives me a courteous wave. Polite man. Perhaps you've noticed?"

"No, I haven't. He never speaks to me..."

The clerk opened a drawer and pulled out a file.

"Yes, as I said, a polite man. Never speaks to his superiors unless they speak first. And I don't suppose he has much occasion to speak to you, seeing as you've left him with no work to speak about!"

The file was placed on the desk.

"Look at this!" the clerk said, "the slimmest personnel file I have. It's Mr Kean's. He's been here for thirty-seven years! Now, I dare say..."

He was about to explain that the slimness of a personnel file was a good measure of the quality of a local government officer, but the treasurer brusquely interrupted.

"You could write formally to Kean, remind him of his duties as specified in his letter of appointment."

The clerk smiled.

"Have you seen Mr Kean's letter of appointment?"

"Of course not!" snapped Postlethwaite.

The clerk removed carefully from the file a thin sheet of foolscap paper and slid it over the desk to where the treasurer could read it. It stated, somewhat ambiguously, that the duties of the deputy borough treasurer would be 'those allocated by the head of department on taking up post'.

"I'm surprised you didn't ask to see that before you removed his work from him," remarked the clerk. "Mr Kean, of course, will have kept his copy. He is precise about such matters. And you don't need me to tell you that in law your assumption of his duties on the day he reassumed the deputyship could constitute a contract."

"In that case," said Postlethwaite decisively, "I'll appoint an additional assistant."

The clerk pursed his lips and slowly shook his head.

"Council won't allow it," he said calmly. "No increase in the workload of your department."

"So I'll spread Kean's work among the people I've got!"

"And have them claiming regular overtime? Might be embarrassing to explain that to the members."

Postlethwaite slumped. He hadn't wanted to be treasurer just to work hard, nor had he studied for years to end up screwing his eyes out over a pile of account books. He had wanted the job for the prestige, the chairing of meetings where he could impress with financial theory. If he'd wanted to work hard he wouldn't have entered local government in the first place. He hated Paddy Kean; intransigent little clerk in his black suit and Hector Powe overcoat. That daft hat. And that deplorable Mankley accent. Got where he was by accident, not talent. It didn't take talent to work hard. Any damn fool could do that. Well, before long Christopher Oates Postlethwaite would ensure that people like that wouldn't be able to get jobs in local government. He would use his influence at the institute and at conferences to so mould opinion that everyone would have to have qualifications before they'd be employed. That was what he'd do.

"There's one little thing Mr Kean will soon be doing to ease your workload," the town clerk cut across the treasurer's musings.

"Really?" Postlethwaite showed only despondent interest.

"Yes. It has been decided by the staffing subcommittee that in order to save the valuable time of chief officers, the appointment of juniors will in future be on the advice of deputies. Mr Kean will be getting his instructions accordingly."

Postlethwaite snorted. Some help that would be. Juniors were appointed to his department only about every five years. He laughed bitterly.

"And I'm afraid you'll be getting a memo too!" the town clerk added, looking sidelong at his watch – he might as well demolish the treasurer before lunch; an appetite is always the better for a completely clear conscience.

"What about?"

"Just a few habits I feel you should correct," the clerk replied lightly as he rose from his chair and went to the window, through which he stared frowning.

Postlethwaite grunted.

"For instance," the clerk's voice floated over the office, "earlier in our conversation you referred to me by my Christian name. We don't do that here. I address you as Borough Treasurer, you should address me as Town clerk."

"Hardly justification for a memo!" protested Postlethwaite hesitantly.

"An equally important matter," the clerk overrode the bumbling objection – he was warming to his subject, these things he understood, "is how we sign letters! Your signature is virtually unreadable. Flamboyant. Offensive really. A signature, in local government, is simply an aid to accountability. We don't require showmanship, simply clarity!"

Postlethwaite shuffled in his seat – he liked his florid signature and had spent years perfecting it.

"But worse than that," persisted the clerk, "you use green ink!" He paused to let the enormity of the accusation sink in. "You realise, don't you, Borough Treasurer, that what you are doing is close to self-publicity? You cannot expect me to remain silent in the face of such irregularities. The public, whose servant we are, is not interested in the personalities employed in official positions. By our careful avoidance of distinguishing characteristics the public is hardly aware that we are here! But, believe me, if the public receives from the town hall letters bearing an unreadable, flamboyant, technicolor signature, its members might begin to take an interest in our activities. You will then learn that self-advertisement is not in the best interests of your career!"

The treasurer remained silent as the town clerk continued.

"Mr Kean, of course, would not need to be told of such matters. I can't recall his ever having been in this office. Certainly, he has never come to me with, or *as* a problem. Always he addresses me in a proper manner, has neat, readable handwriting, and uses black ink. You should have seen his application for your post – an application I supported incidentally – it was a masterpiece of self-effacement."

"None of this is going to solve my workload," grumbled Postlethwaite, almost inaudibly.

"No," responded the clerk as, hands clasped behind his back, his knuckles whitened, "there's only one way to solve that."

"Oh?"

"Mr Kean is a fair man. I suggest you go to him this morning and apologise. Tell him you made a mistake, behaved foolishly. Admit your lack of experience. Flatter him a little by admiring his undoubted expertise in the day-to-day affairs of the department. Tell him you've discussed the situation with me. Beg his help..."

Behind him the town clerk heard the office door crash shut as Postlethwaite stormed out, furious and insulted.

The town clerk unclasped his hands, rubbed them a bit to get the circulation going, smiled, turned from the window and prepared a personnel file headed: "CHRISTOPHER OATES POSTLETHWAITE"; then, with an easy mind, he went to lunch.

No one could say now that he was partial to Yorkshiremen.

He could look the world and his self-esteem in the eye.

*

Postlethwaite's face was still white with anger five minutes later as he sat deep in thought in his panelled office, drumming his fingers on the desktop. He'd made a mistake coming to Mankley. He could have gone anywhere in the country with his qualifications. That was it, of course – in a hick town like this they had probably never had a qualified man. Probably everyone was jealous of his achievements.

It was a full thirty minutes before a degree of rationality returned. With it came a slight brightening of countenance. He was being stupid, he admonished himself, negative. It was early days yet. Give Kean another couple of months of cold war, non-communication, nothing to do, shunned by everyone, why! – Postlethwaite almost clapped his hands with glee – Kean would be begging for mercy, or, better still, off to another job.

But the treasurer's face clouded again as he began to appreciate that even a couple of months of his current workload would be unendurable. What he needed was a clever idea that would push the old fool out of the door; something nasty, but not sufficiently blatant for the town clerk to intervene.

Optimism returned. There'd surely be plenty of scope for the head of a department. It had to be easy. All the weaponry of power was his. There must be dozens of ways to give Kean a taste of hell.

Smiling mirthlessly Postlethwaite stepped to the filing cabinet. Slowly he thumbed through the thick brown folders within it. The smile faded. Black despair clogged his veins. There weren't dozens of ways to torture Kean. Nothing like it. Everything in the town hall was too circumscribed by precedent, union agreement and bye-law. Only one aspect of power emerged as the treasurer's sole prerogative: staff holidays – but Postlethwaite took little joy in allocating November and February for Paddy.

Oddly, that didn't seem to trouble Paddy, so for the next twelve years Postlethwaite was forced to thrash his pedantic way from crisis to crisis, weighed down with indecision and worn out with trivia. Deprived the benefit of a deputy's assistance, his only relief was attendance at committee or council meetings. The longer they lasted the better he liked it, for when he was in a meeting he was not in his office, and that meant less possibility of contact with Kean.

He rarely saw his deputy anyhow, and never spoke to him. A thick wall separated the treasurer from his staff in the outer office where Kean, sphinx-like, dominated the atmosphere.

But Paddy's aura of inactive brooding made little of bricks and mortar. It haunted Postlethwaite, an invisible disciplinary presence preventing his ever risking a mistake, misjudgement or indiscretion, or doing anything other than that which might be deemed appropriate for a man of his position. Overworked, puffed up with pride and obstinacy, shackled to the limitations of his profession, terrified that Kean might be planning revenge, without support from beneath or approval from above, Postlethwaite became the most apt of local government officers – just like the town clerk wanted.

Meanwhile, through the years, Paddy Kean sat at his desk with a pencil – the same pencil – held between the forefingers of each hand as he stared blankly down the long bit of the L-shaped room for seven and a half hours each working day, like a scrutineer at a finals examination – expressionless but dominant.

Discernible movement was rare – the flicker of an eye towards the clock, perhaps, when a member of staff left the room, another as he or she returned. Nobody visited the toilets twice in one day. There was little in the way of idle conversation. The department became one of unmatched concentration.

Only twice a year, in February and November, was the atmosphere in any way different. Paddy's holidays left the staff feeling strangely insecure, unanchored – they were 'on their honour'. Postlethwaite would wander among them as if on foreign soil, stare at Paddy's vacant desk, turn around and walk out looking bemused.

It would be wrong, however, to imagine that Paddy's serene years were entirely without disturbance. It was easy enough at first – most members of staff had been there for a long time; they were on his side – but, as the years passed and newcomers came to the department, serenity became harder to maintain. Even the few juniors Paddy appointed occasionally proved troublesome, despite his typically careful selection.

He found it necessary to build up defences: a number of interesting but fictitious minor afflictions, each calculated to avoid involvement in constructive activity and each accompanied by a doleful tale of its history.

It was not so much the stories that were so bad, it was more their incredible length, inconclusiveness, and Paddy's unique style of delivery. He had developed a voice of undeviating blandness, to which was added a spiritlessness of facial expression and monotony of vocabulary that amounted to genius.

So, were it suggested that Mr Kean might like to assist with some routine bookkeeping task, Paddy would bring to his rescue a rare and incurable eye complaint, one which prevented his looking at columns of figures without an instant feeling of nausea. Or, if he were asked to pass over a file from the cabinet adjacent to his desk, he would hold up his right thumb and wiggle it obscenely while relating an improbable saga involving a maniacal bus conductor who 'bashed me thumb in with his ticket-punch.'

Only one man in all the years stood up to such onslaughts of tedium: Willie Rumley, who had come to Mankley from an authority where it was customary for the deputy borough treasurer to actually work. Every day this unknowing buffoon would ask Paddy to do something or other and, to muffled groans from the staff, another dreary fiction would unfold. The staff got so fed up they chose to act. They went through Rumley's books of account, inscribing single strokes of the pen: an odd ten here, a hundred there. It was not coincidental that the pages they chose on which to wreak this havoc recorded transactions between Mankley Corporation and the firm which employed Rumley's wife – and the district auditor was shortly due his annual visit.

The council was shocked when it received a report of 'inconsistencies'.

Willie Rumley found himself before the treasurer.

Secretly, Postlethwaite was thrilled. This was the nearest he'd been to what might be fraud. In any case, whether it was or not, he had to be seen to be decisive – and such is the stylised innocuousness of local government administration that any deviatory occurrence provides relief from the endless inertia of it all.

Play-acting exaggerated outrage, Postlethwaite reduced Willie Rumley to tears. Guilty or not, the man's career in public finance was over. He resigned and left immediately.

His conscience was clear, he knew he had been wronged – and he placed responsibility for that squarely on the shoulders of Postlethwaite. It was something that Rumley was not to forget during months of unemployment and the beginnings of a new career as Driver 108 of the Trans-Mankley Traction Company.

The staff were happy. Paddy was happy. And, for once, so was Postlethwaite – now there was reason to increase his staff by the appointment of an internal auditor. After all, the council would hardly want to see another 'inconsistency' reported.

So Malcolm Birstin joined the department, giving Postlethwaite the long-awaited opportunity to unload every tedious element of his work on to the unsuspecting newcomer.

*

The years had passed.

Postlethwaite's spirits rose in anticipation of a rosier future. He took holiday for the last of Paddy's weeks in post, thus avoiding a hypocritical, formal farewell and, into the bargain, saving the cost of contributing to a retirement present.

So the treasurer did not see the 'SOLD' notice appear on the building across the road, directly opposite the town hall; nor was he made aware of an unprecedented mateyness between Paddy and certain councillors who visited the office. He remained ignorant of a new appointment in the catering department and he did not learn of the unusual retirement gift Paddy was given by the staff.

*

The deputy borough treasurer's last day at work began as had all the previous thousands: fit as a lop, he marched purposefully down the street of substantial terraced houses in which he lived, through the park, into the decaying alleys near the railway-line, then over the broad, covered bridge to the centre of town where the red, stone town hall squatly dominated the surrounding shops, offices, banks and pubs.

Once in the office he sat at his desk, picked his pencil from his top, right-hand drawer and stared ahead of him.

They were all there: David Smith (senior accountancy assistant, soon to be promoted to deputy borough treasurer), Stan Scrimshire (who had replaced Willie Rumley), Ethel Robinson (accounts clerk), Doreen Slater (wages clerk) and, round the corner, out of Paddy's sight, symbolically placed between the staff and the safe, Malcolm Birstin (internal auditor), muttering to himself while entering totals and checking balances in a fury of unwilling

27

activity, the backlog of Postlethwaite's paperwork scattered haphazardly about his desk.

There was one desk unoccupied, the farthest from Paddy, and as his glance fell upon it he was reminded that today he must, for the last time, appoint a junior accounts clerk. He pulled a folder from the cabinet, unobtrusively extracted from it two letters, and folded them into his breast pocket. Later in the morning he appointed the new member of staff and, on returning to the office, after a quiet exchange with Malcolm Birstin, he placed his pencil in an otherwise empty cabinet drawer and closed it firmly, while the auditor watched.

The mood was of contained excitement as the afternoon drew on. The mayor was to present to the long-suffering deputy a suitably engraved gold watch, and the staff had bought for him a gift which they felt was particularly representative of their regard.

The ceremony was brief and stilted. The gold watch in its purple presentation case was shown around to the approbation of all, but as the staff were disinclined to loiter beyond their properly contracted finishing time, the large box containing their retirement present was left unopened. But hands were shaken, goodbyes said, and Paddy, after a rheumy, unsentimental glance over the office, took a taxi home.

Once there and out of his black hat and thick overcoat, he greeted Mary and the girls who were gathered in the kitchen preparing a special dinner. They casually admired the gold watch but looked on with interest as Paddy began to open the box. Bit by bit straw packing littered the floor as a figure emerged. It was off-white, pitted irregularly with tiny black holes, appeared quite old, and was grotesque.

"Well!" exclaimed Paddy, curiously surprised. "That's a queer-looking thing if ever I saw one!"

"Perhaps it's a Buddha," smiled the elder of the two girls. "Probably to make you think of spending your retirement in solemn contemplation."

Paddy grimaced gently at that.

28

"It's thoroughly ugly!" blurted out Mary, wanting to knock hell out of the staff for giving her husband such a revolting memento of his life's work.

"No, it's interesting," said the younger girl. "I think it might be meant to be Confucius."

They examined the object in silence until Paddy suddenly gave a dry titter. He gathered up the ornament, winked at the girls and left the room. Confused, they smilingly shrugged at each other and continued happily with their cooking.

Meanwhile, Paddy made for the lounge, where he placed the figure on a sturdy corner-table under the glow of a wall-light. Relaxing into his armchair he stretched his legs before the brightly-burning coals in the grate.

From his breast pocket he unfolded the two letters he had removed from the folder of the newly-appointed junior and threw them into the fire. He didn't want the lad's local government career to be blighted by the existence of references like that. Flames danced up to consume them.

Funny bunch, the staff, he mused, easing deeper into the comfort of the chair; funny to gain amusement by presenting him with such a hideous sculpture. He wondered how they would react when they discovered the present he had left them; how they would cope with his having appointed to their ranks the most hapless misfit fate could ever have shown the doors of a committee room.

The cosiness of the fire encouraged him into a contented snooze and soon into sleep.

Only the corner-bound figure, the bone idol, witnessed the ashes silently collapse as the flames died and a blackened fragment of paper floated slowly to the hearth where it lay crinkling, smoking and bearing in ghostly white ash the words: 'With reference to your enquiry regarding Mr Arnold Locock...'

Chapter One

It had been three years earlier when Arnold had first got a job, and even then, with all the advantages of having no work record to which a prospective employer might refer, it had come as something of a shock to his despairing parents.

"I've got a job!" announced Arnold.

"What as? A paper boy?" His father raised his eyes from a book. "I'll tell you what, I'll give you a job! You can get yourself down that garden and clear your dumps out of the netty! Lighting cigarettes in there'll cause a fire one of these days! I'm sick of the mess you leave!"

"And if you're in the mood for work you can cut the hedge!" his mother interjected.

"I'm telling you! I've got a job! At the metalworks! Full time!"

"You can't have got a job, Arnold – you're too young! You're still at school!" his mother said, pouring a cup of tea.

"Look!" insisted Arnold, "I've got a job at the metalworks and I start next week!"

"But aren't you supposed to stay on at school until you're sixteen these days?" his mother asked.

"No!" replied Arnold, ignoring the tea his mother pushed towards him. "You can leave when you're fifteen! And today's my fifteenth birthday!"

'Is it?' asked his father, glancing at the clock on the mantelpiece. "That's funny! I thought it was half past five!"

Arnold gave up. It would be a different story next week when he arrived home with his first wage-packet.

It was.

His mother, who thought that life should be set to music, wanted it framed, while his father, who thought that life set to music was for those who could afford it, wanted it banked, while Arnold, who didn't think anything, spent it on his way home from work.

It didn't occur to him that his parents might attribute some significance to his first wage. Very little did occur to him – his fifteen years had passed by without his ever having felt the compulsion to do, or be, or think anything.

He was a dreamer. He dreamed of greatness, fame and success, and was convinced that these were his destiny.

On the face of it, his conviction seemed somewhat premature. From a family in which depression and poverty were endemic, a street noted only for its staid contribution to the town's sense of mediocrity, and a neighbourhood completely undistinguished by the personal achievements of its inhabitants, he had never excelled at anything.

Kindly souls might have claimed that his background and surroundings were not conducive to excellence, but their kindliness would have been misplaced; Arnold had never noticed his background and surroundings. Had he done so his sense of superiority would have been boundless. Only much later in life would he recall them as a fashionable claim to working-class roots.

He had first gone to school at the age of five, only to be sent home for swearing at a teacher. Thereafter an alarming attitude of resigned pessimism attended his every contact with authority.

Yet, despite this, he absorbed some superficial knowledge during his ten years of formal education. In the same way that, despite a fictional sickness record second to none, he was never actually ill, and despite every effort of his parents and teachers (though never jointly), he contrived to avoid being at school whenever examinations were taking place. He had happily invented the funerals of no less than seventeen grandparents, and it became a matter of course for him to destroy end-of-term reports immediately on receiving them, by the simple expedient of tearing them up and dropping the pieces down a convenient drain.

As he reached adolescence, his teachers, who were mostly well-meaning if none too bright, tried to help him realise some potential they believed must lie dormant – a frustrating exercise.

The games teacher, for example, felt that a dose of physical exertion might counter Arnold's lassitude. So, against the voluble protests of its members, he was put into the school football team. He didn't like it any more than they did. He disliked sport. It encouraged competition – competition led to wars. Football attracted mob support, and from what Arnold had seen of the mob, its taste was decidedly questionable. His stay in the team was short, however, thanks to a hat-trick in his own goal – and the games teacher lost interest in him. But others took up the challenge. Some reasoned that as he was an only child he must have qualities of leadership. An interesting theory, but not one to gain in credibility at the hands of Arnold. Few of his school-day contemporaries will forget the concert where the chorus and band were given differing music parts and in the resultant cacophony the soloist, a talented if highly-strung young lady, threw herself hysterically from the stage to land in the grand piano; or the school play which began and ended with a series of flashing explosions from the footlights; or the school shop where all the goods were freely provided, yet Arnold contrived a financial loss.

The teachers tried hard. It was not as if Arnold was rude, objectionable or uncooperative. Quite the reverse: he was polite, well-spoken and obedient. But they couldn't make contact, and didn't know why.

Arnold knew why. It was obvious. The history teacher failed because he had been a conscientious objector during the war and Arnold knew that such people twisted history to suit their own cowardly viewpoint. The geography teacher failed because Arnold felt that as an alleged expert on foreign countries the man should have actually visited them all – book-learning was no substitute for experience. The mathematics teacher failed because she had never been to university – experience was no substitute for book-learning. The English teacher failed because she drove an

American car, the French teacher, predictably, because she was not French, and the headmaster because he was a noted Socialist and Arnold knew that headships in the county were given only to those of that political persuasion.

It need hardly be said that Arnold, living in an area of unrelieved Labour Party domination, saw himself as a Conservative. His father did, after all, own his own house and had once owned a fish-and-chip shop. And hadn't Labour made all the buses the same colour? Cause enough for Arnold to believe for the rest of his life that Socialism stood only for drab uniformity.

Uninfluenced by his teachers' attempts at what he would later call intellectual rape, he was even less influenced by other school-day activities. He didn't fight, play games, hang about street corners or brag about imagined sexual exploits. He hardly seemed interested in girls and never attended school dances. He'd once thought of joining a gang – 'The Quarry Hawkers' – but after hearing of an initiation ceremony decided against the idea.

It would have been reassuring if some religious or moral restraint prevented his involvement in these activities of adolescence but, despite every exposure, at the insistence of his parents, to Sunday school, church choir, boy scouts, piano lessons and the like, this was not the case.

No one had impressed him. No one had aroused his interest. No one had found in him the faintest glimmer of true enlightenment for all their efforts.

Without envy, pride, ambition, desire or purpose, Arnold Locock was inviolate.

As with most school-leavers in Mankley, the question of further education towards university never having been discussed, Arnold left with the only qualification he thought necessary for the future: the legal right to leave. And at the Youth Employment Bureau he accepted the first job offered – as a labourer at the metalworks.

Mankley Metal Industries Limited was not far from his home and his interview there was a masterpiece of brevity. An employer seeks two talents in a labourer and Arnold had them both – good health and the ability to hold a shovel.

It was fortunate that an ability to communicate was not equally essential; it would have posed problems, for Arnold was put to work with a squad of Italians who spoke little English; in fact, as Neapolitans, they hardly spoke Italian. But, as speech was well nigh impossible in the noise and dust of the foundry, it scarcely mattered. There wasn't a lot to be found in the shovelling of sand that required much comment.

It might well be thought, bearing in mind Arnold's apparently anti-social inclinations, that his job would have been entirely fulfilling but, surprisingly, after some time, he began to feel that life should have a little more to offer and, by dint of some well-spoken deception regarding his skill at arithmetic, secured for himself a position in the same factory as a wages clerk.

This, he thought, was a step in the right direction: no more noise, no more fleas, no more calluses on his hands, and no more factory hooter summoning him to work at eight o'clock in the morning – the office staff didn't start work until nine, and that, more than anything, suited Arnold.

His calculation of the workers' earnings, however, didn't suit the management. Exactitude had never been Arnold's most apparent characteristic, and he was surprised to find that the workers gave it such emphasis when examining their payslips. The ever-lengthening queue of complaining craftsmen and labourers on each successive pay day became obvious, and it was not long before Arnold found himself promoted out of harm's way to the position of cost clerk. At least, reasoned the management, that would avert the likelihood of a major strike.

For a time he was reasonably happy in his unexpected new post, but eventually tired of its limitations and began to peruse the 'Situations Vacant' column of the local newspaper.

The advertisement to catch his eye was straightforward enough:

Mankley Borough Council
invites applications for a

JUNIOR ACCOUNTS CLERK

to be responsible for books of
prime entry and to assist
generally in the department.

Written applications to Mr
Patrick Kean, Deputy Borough
Treasurer, Town Hall,
Mankley, stating details of
career to date and names and
addresses of two referees by 12
noon on 25th August.

Salary on General Division
£300-375 p.a.

"Dad!" said Arnold as he passed the paper across the table, "what do you think of that?"

His father studied it for a few minutes before replying.

"It's a job for life that, son!" he replied, his clear grey eyes aimed directly into the dull brown of Arnold's. "If you were to stick in at a job like that you could qualify for something."

"Yes," responded Arnold, eyes falling away from the steady gaze.

His father, as usual, had turned what had seemed like a good idea into something with the ring of hard work about it. All Arnold cared about was that the job offered a release from the one that now bored him and six quid a week into the bargain, and, from what he'd heard, nobody in the town hall exerted themselves much to get it.

He put the newspaper in his pocket. He'd discuss the job with his friends at the pub that night.

*

Arnold couldn't be described as a drinker any more than he could be described as anything else but, like many people in the North-East, he enjoyed his weekly pint or two.

He would never once have thought that pleasure could result from the consumption of good ale in the company of a few mates, but he had taken to the habit with enthusiasm. No Friday night at the local passed without Arnold's presence, or that of his friends.

Many who were aware of his existence would have been surprised to find he had friends. Perhaps it was his indifference and complacency that made him easy company. Or perhaps it was simply that the people he thought of as friends had nothing better to do than drink where he drank.

He had not, of course, simply taken it into his head one day to start drinking. He had been inspired to it by Midnight Masomi, Head Moulder at the metalworks, who'd suggested that Arnold should celebrate his eighteenth birthday by going to the pub.

Midnight was a good soul, a man of wisdom and kindliness, with the rare gift of knowing that he was happy. That was why he had always refused promotion. Contented with his job, he enjoyed the respect of his employers and the crude fondness of his men.

It seemed to matter to no one that he was black. His family had lived in Mankley for five generations and Midnight, six feet five inches tall, broad-shouldered and muscular, had never heard of racial intolerance. Perhaps that was why he had befriended Giuseppe Mescolare, a graduate of Turin University who had come to Mankley to gain practical experience in the iron and steel industry, under Midnight's guidance.

It was these two who had helped Arnold celebrate his birthday, and since then the diverse trio had drunk together every Friday. And others regularly joined them: Fenwick Fancourt, who had gone to school with Arnold, Marjorie and Joan from the metalworks' offices, and Ernie Moon, who'd attached himself to the little group from nowhere and not to anyone's particular liking.

It was Ernie who was speaking as Arnold arrived.

"I bet if you were off work you'd get dole money and if you were sick you'd get free medicine and that!"

"Yes," responded Giuseppe, "but I pay for it. Every week I pay."

"But we've paid into it for years," said Ernie, who'd never had a job in his life, "and you get just as much as we do. Don't you? Eh?"

"The English are very kind," smiled the little Italian as he tried to rub his hand against Marjorie's leg.

"Stop that!" she frowned. "Here's Arnold!"

Giuseppe didn't see why the arrival of Arnold should be reason to suppress his natural desire to fondle the personal parts of Marjorie but, nevertheless, he took his hand away.

It was a pity he chose Marjorie on whom to practise his Latin charm. Had he made similar advances to Joan he might have found a keener response. Joan had once visited Rome and she thought everything Italian was wonderful.

Taking advantage of the disruption caused by Arnold pushing his way to a seat she leaned forward towards the Italian.

"I think you have the most beautiful-sounding name," she said softly, "so melodious, just like opera."

Giuseppe smiled and returned Joan's torrid glance.

"I mean," she continued, "English names don't sound nice at all, do they?"

The Italian's eyes melted into hers. He was about to reply, but Midnight banged a pint of beer on to the table.

"Get that down you, Gweppsy," he said gruffly. "It'll put hairs on your chest!"

Midnight had never mastered the correct pronunciation of Giuseppe's name.

Joan ignored the interruption and kept her eyes on the Italian's.

"Do your names sound as melodious to you as they do to me? I mean, names like Ferruccio and Mario?"

"*Allora*!" said Giuseppe, sensing the promise of conquest. "I think that..."

"Tell her what your name means in Italian, Gweppsy!" urged Midnight.

The Italian went a shade pinker than dirty brown.

"Come on, Giuseppe, what does it mean?" Marjorie intervened, hoping to see the Italian deflated.

"I'll tell you what it means!" said Midnight. "It means Joe Shuffle!"

Marjorie sniggered, lit a cigarette and crossed her legs.

"Joe Shuffle!" Midnight repeated, laughing. "Now you can see why he's over here in England, can't you? All the girls in Italy know what a stupid name he's got! If I were called Everard Ramsbottom, I'd emigrate somewhere where the girls might think that my name sounded 'melodious, just like opera'!"

Midnight rolled his eyes at Joan, who tried to ignore him, and slapped his great, ebony hand on Giuseppe's back.

Meanwhile, Arnold was struggling to get the newspaper out of his jerkin pocket, but it had caught on the zip. After some manipulation, however, it came free.

"What do you think of this job?" he asked.

The laughter died as he passed the newspaper to Midnight.

"Have you been fired, Arnold?" asked Fenwick, who'd had some experience in the field.

"No, I'm just thinking of trying for something better, that's all."

"Where at?" asked Ernie.

"The town hall," Arnold replied.

At that, Midnight stopped searching the 'Situations Vacant' and found the advertisement to which Arnold had obviously been referring.

"If it's a council job, it'll be fixed," said Marjorie.

"Aye," Ernie supported her, "that's right. Which department?"

"The treasurer's," Arnold answered, feeling discouraged.

Marjorie frowned and uncrossed her legs, knocking the table slightly and jiggling the full beer mugs so that their contents spilled, wetting the table.

Midnight looked up from the newspaper which he now used to catch the few drips falling from the polished wood.

"It'll be a good job," he said, wrinkling his brow.

"That's what I thought," replied Arnold.

"For life, if you get it," the Negro added, "and I don't think it'll be fixed. Only the top jobs are fixed."

"I'll tell you what, though," said Joan as she moved beer mats around to dry the table, "if you do get the job, you'll have to look a damn sight tidier than you usually do!"

"All I'll have to do is get a suit." Arnold was defensive.

"The first thing you'll have to do is write the application," said Midnight.

"Yes," agreed Arnold, as he took the now sodden newspaper back from the outstretched black hand.

The conversation drifted to other subjects and Arnold soon forgot about the prospective new job. Three pints later it was ten o'clock. The little group of friends prepared to leave.

"G'night!" they chorused to the barman. "See you next Friday!"

"You won't," he responded sourly. "The pub'll be closed for alterations. It's changing hands."

Outside, this information gave cause for only brief discussion before Fenwick and Ernie left to buy fish and chips, and the girls, Giuseppe with an arm around each of them, went to catch a bus.

Opposite the pub, the town hall clock chimed the quarter-hour as Midnight and Arnold strolled along the dimly lit streets. It wasn't long before they found themselves outside Arnold's house.

"Listen," said Midnight, "if you like, I'll come in with you now and help you write the application. At least, then, I'll know you're doing something about it!"

Arnold hesitated; he was tired but he knew Midnight was right.

"Okay," he said, inserting the key into the front door and swinging it open.

With pen and paper in front of him, Midnight got down to the job.

"We'll have to make it formal," he said, "so we'll send a letter together with an attached curriculum vitae."

"Yes, of course," muttered Arnold, not wanting to admit that he didn't know what the big man was talking about; it sounded to Arnold like some rare, complicated disease.

Midnight smiled. He guessed that Arnold didn't know what 'curriculum vitae' meant.

"That's details of your life and experience," he intimated. "Who are you going to use as referees?"

"You and Ernie, I suppose," said Arnold, but only to avoid hurting Midnight's feelings.

"You can't use Ernie! He can hardly write! How about a teacher?"

Arnold was relieved. That was what he was going to do originally, but faced with the question he now had to think hard before coming up with the name of the only teacher in his school who'd had nothing to do with him.

"Don't forget to warn him," advised Midnight. "These things are important, you know!"

To Arnold the only thing that was important was that the town hall shouldn't seek references from the chief accountant of Mankley Metal Industries or the headmaster of his old school.

"It'll be okay, honest!" he said.

"Right! What's your present position?"

"Cost clerk."

"And before that you were a wages clerk, weren't you?"

"Yes. And before that I was a labourer."

"We're not telling them that!" Midnight was emphatic. "Those town hall wallahs might all be members of the Labour Party but, I can tell you, they don't want labourers anywhere near them. We won't say what your first job was. Let them think you just stayed on at school a bit longer than you did."

Midnight made a few notes.

"Have you ever studied anything?"

"No."

41

"Didn't you work with the Italian squad in the foundry?"

"Well, yes," said Arnold, hesitantly.

"So you must have picked up some of the language? Have you studied anything else?"

"I once went on a weekend course with the trade union. It was to somewhere near Carlisle, but I don't remember what it was all about. I only went because somebody asked me to and I'd never been to Carlisle before."

"Never mind. That'll help."

Arnold yawned; this was boring. But Midnight persevered.

"Now, what about hobbies and interests?"

"I haven't got any," Arnold lied. Actually he had many interests but, having been so often jeered about them by the futile society in which he was condemned to live, for day-to-day purposes he forgot he had any.

"Have you got a camera?"

"Yes. In fact, I've got a photo of me mam here somewhere." Arnold opened the bureau and fished out a scallop-edged portrait of a smiling face. "I took it."

Midnight looked at the snap appreciatively.

"A kind woman, your mam. Any sports? Swimming?"

"I can't swim."

"What about education?"

"I haven't had any. Unless you count school."

Midnight sighed as he went through his notes, writing out the details more carefully on a separate piece of paper.

"There y'are!" he announced when he had finished. "All you have to do is copy it out and post it off."

"Thanks very much, Midnight," said Arnold, looking at the pages and stifling another yawn.

Midnight stood up to go.

"I'll just say goodnight to your mam and dad and I'll be off," he said, making for the hall and shouting a cheery farewell to the lit room at the end of it.

"G'night Mr an' Mrs Locock! I'll have to run now or the wife'll kill me!"

"G'night, son." Arnold's father popped his head round the door frame, "I didn't know you were here! Look after yourself."

Arnold saw Midnight out then returned to the sitting room to copy what had been written. When he'd finished he read it carefully. He liked it. Especially the curriculu-what-not. It made him feel important to see his life set out so formally, though he was surprised to find that he'd been described as a fluent Italian speaker and student of trade unionism. And his one snap of his mam had given him the impressive interest of 'photography – with particular emphasis on portraiture'.

Undeterred, however, he addressed the envelope, folded the pages neatly into it, sealed the flap and, deciding to save the cost of a postage stamp, walked to the town hall to pop it through the letter box.

A week later he received an invitation to attend interview. He bought a suit. It wasn't new, but the salesgirl in the second-hand shop said it looked very smart on him. He resolved to keep it exclusively for his new job.

On the day of the interview he sat outside a committee room of the town hall together with three other candidates. Conversation was minimal.

Meanwhile, inside the committee room the members were assembled and the deputy borough treasurer cast his eye down the list of names in front of him.

Paddy Kean had long ago come to the conclusion that references received from persons quoted on applications were of little value. He always ignored these. Particularly today. He was looking for special qualities in the new junior.

It had taken only a few enquiries to discover where best they could be found. The written references from the headmaster of Mankley Central School and the chief accountant of Mankley Metal Industries gave all the confirmation needed. Christopher Oates Postlethwaite and the staff of the Treasurer's Department were going to find themselves with the most unsuitable junior accounts clerk in the history of local government.

Arnold, of course, did not know it as he sat shuffling his feet and trying to avoid eye contact with his fellow applicants but, as his friends in the pub had said, it was fixed – he'd got the job before entering the committee room.

And Postlethwaite did not know it either – he was still on holiday in the Lake District.

Chapter Two

Face-aching practice and the features of a melted wellie had always given Eugene something of an advantage in the primitive art of gurning, but it was his inventive skill which won him the championship every year, and his gimmick which caught the attention of the television cameras.

He took out his teeth, crossed his eyes, forced his lower lip over the tip of his nose and vehemently puffed out his cheeks. Purple of face, with veins pulsating, he writhed against the restricting horse-collar. A burst of applause encouraged his efforts, then it was over for another year.

All the competitors lined up at the front of the ramshackle stage, each contorting his face into a gruesome mask. It was a medieval scene.

Suddenly, powerful lights scattered the shadows and, as a few drunks collapsed sideways in surprise, the TV cameras moved forward for a close-up of the human gargoyles.

Eugene, the undoubted winner, did his usual party trick – closing one eye he stuck a clay pipe upside down in his mouth and croaked the chorus of 'Popeye the Sailorman'.

"Great stuff!" enthused Dodie Ochiltree, the TV presenter, as Eugene allowed his face to resume its normal, though no less revolting shape and, with much gum-sucking and expectoration, reinserted his teeth.

It was a transformation Ochiltree never tired of inflicting on his viewers, despite an annual deluge of complaining letters to the studio. All he knew was that the whole thing was ethnic, the encouragement of which was regional ITV's *raison d'être*.

Those few onlookers still unwarmed by the cosiness of alcoholic encapsulation shivered slightly in the evening chill. In order to stimulate circulation they clapped their hands together and stamped their feet. Interpreting this as an expression of approval, the judges came on stage to formally close the contest and thank the chairman.

Fortunately for the judges, their decision to declare Eugene the winner of the gurning championship was roughly in line with the collective opinion of those in the audience. Otherwise there might have been bloodshed.

Twice already during the course of the evening the onlookers had shown their ability to express disapproval of the judges' decisions.

In the Clay Pipe Smoking Contest, the audience, to a man, felt that Geordie should have won. Calmly, this rugged stalwart had kept his pipe smoking steadily for over four minutes, whereas Jonta, the adjudged winner, had collapsed in a lung-bursting, bronchitic heap after only three and a half.

Jubilant Geordie-supporters cheered as the chairman came forward to announce the official result.

"Geordie's the winner!" they yelled in ragged chorus.

"No 'e's bloody not!" the chairman yelled back, clutching the empty Woodbine packet on which the judges had inscribed their decision.

"G'arn!" "Balls!" "Styoopid boogar!" was the varied response.

"The winner," thundered the chairman, going crimson, "is Jonta!"

Clods of earth hurtled towards the stage as the chairman vanished to confer with the judges.

He returned to noisy abuse but held up his hand for order which, after a fashion, he got.

"The judges 'ave rooled that Jonta's the winner 'cos 'e used a smaller pipe than Geordie! An' the judges took into consideration that Jonta's a dyin' man, an' if 'e'd 'a' been fit 'e'd 'a' knocked spots off Geordie! An' any'ow!" the chairman screamed into the tannoy, "Geordie won last year!"

The crowd remained restive after this explanation but, in the main, conceded that the judges might have a point. So Jonta, proudly grasping his 'First Prize' rosette, and gasping agonisingly for breath, was bundled into a waiting ambulance and speedily returned to the terminal ward of the local hospital.

Geordie, meanwhile, hot with anger, smashed his clay pipe on the back of a nearby chair and stamped off. Nine seconds later the stage lighting faltered and died as he pissed on the fuse box.

This retaliatory act delayed the start of the Sentimental Song Contest and gave time for the mob to take advantage of the licensed refreshment that was available. This time they'd be better prepared for any suspect judicial decision.

Seamus won the song contest with an abbreviated rendering of 'Galway Bay'. No competitor actually succeeded in completing a song, but for brevity and mediocrity, Seamus was in a class of his own. Checking his flies, he staggered into view, took the microphone, and gave a resounding belch. Raucously, he then belted out, "IF YOU EVER GO ACROSS THE SEA TO IRELAND..." – and that was as far as he got. Terrified by his amplified efforts, dazzled by the lights, he muttered, "Oh, fuck it!" and, lurching into the sound equipment, reeled from the stage.

No sooner had the chairman announced that Seamus was the winner than all hell broke loose. Half-bricks, empty beer bottles, greasy chip papers, all accompanied the stream of invective to be directed at the luckless chairman.

He squared his chin for battle and bellowed, unrepentant, "The judges 'ave rooled that, as this is an international gatherin', we 'ad to be fair to competitors from overseas!" before being felled by a well-aimed shovel.

Seamus, the local dustman since his arrival in the village from County Tyrone twenty years earlier, never got his 'First Prize' rosette. He crawled away to the beer tent and stayed there until the licensees pulled it down around him the next morning.

*

Mr and Mrs Postlethwaite did not feel the chill of evening as they walked away from the field, their heavy tweeds and sensible shoes keeping out the cold and damp.

Postlethwaite felt cheated. What was the point of advertising the event as a Crab Fair if there were no crabs? It was the prospect of seafood that lured him to the village in the first place, and he had stayed so late only because it was free. Now, even that was a frustration – he couldn't demand his money back.

Nevertheless, he thought, the holiday had been reasonably pleasant. It had coincided with the last of the summer's good weather, so making it possible to enjoy hill-walking, sightseeing and fishing. All free and much to his taste.

Mrs Postlethwaite, on the other hand, had found it all rather a bore. As she trudged along, her husband a few paces ahead, she gladly anticipated getting home to Mankley; to the school where she taught music, the church choir, the Anglo-Soviet Friendship Society, the local RSPCA committee and her language studies.

As she got into the car and wrapped a rug around her legs, she shuddered at the recollection of the gurners lined up for the collective final grimace. Not the ideal memory to carry on a three-hour journey through mysterious countryside at night. She was pleased she had taken her sedatives.

She always took sedatives prior to a drive with her husband. Neck-wrenching jerks, sickening swerves and hair-raising emergency stops punctuated every trip. He habitually used second gear for pulling away, disengaged the clutch before braking, switched off the engine at the approach to every downhill slope, and maintained a speed of forty miles per hour irrespective of warning signs, other road users, or passenger comfort. His was a driving technique developed solely for maximum fuel economy.

Mrs Postlethwaite had once tried to reason with him. She suggested he take a course in advanced driving. His response was to give her an irrelevant lecture on home economics and point out that the carrying of a passenger added three per cent to fuel costs.

So sedation became the answer. It calmed her rising panic at the sight of every approaching bend, deadened the pain of bouncing her head off the windscreen, and diffused the sounds of

49

ugly curses from other motorists. Invariably Mrs Postlethwaite travelled with the vaguely happy countenance of the totally unaware.

But on the drive from Cumberland, her natural tiredness combined with the drugs to send her peacefully to sleep, as the car slewed and bucked its way across the fells towards Mankley and home.

Sunday morning found Postlethwaite anxious to get into his back garden. His wife did the front, but the back was his. Keeping it perfect was his one domestic interest. And it *was* perfect. Perfectly weedless, perfectly square and perfectly green. Within the surrounding walls and outhouses Postlethwaite had created a lawn – just that. No bushes. No flowers. No garden gnomes. Just grass: well-trimmed, uniform, pure, and costless.

It was the costlessness, of course, that had first fired his imagination. But, over the years, in striving for the definitive back lawn, it had become a thing of beauty to him; something to take pride in, to stand back and admire.

Nobody sat on it. He chased away any birds he saw near. The day he found an old sock lying there had him apoplectic to the police to insist on a special watch being kept on the back lane from which the offending footwear had obviously been thrown.

No such sacrilege had been committed, however, while he had been away. His lawn, apart from growing a little, was as he had left it. He carefully ran the mower over its close-cropped green blades, recreating the sharply-defined lines he so favoured – just like the cash columns of a ledger – then, with hands in pockets, he absorbed its perfection for a while before returning indoors to prepare his mind for the week ahead.

This meant some hours of joyful anticipation. Kean was gone, and the capable but unambitious David Smith had become deputy. Postlethwaite could foresee a future of ease and fulfilment. Now he could devote himself to pure administration and to becoming the treasurer he had always aimed to be: guide, advisor, theoretician; influential public official. He would write speeches and initiate systems – and he would develop a new image.

It had occurred to him of late that up to now he must have seemed something of a shadowy figure to his staff. He should pay them more attention. He'd like to be loved. Respected, of course, but loved as well. He'd bought a little book of jokes, intending to memorise one a week.

And he would adopt a more kindly, approachable facial expression. Practising before a mirror he found one he liked. It comprised of tilting his head slightly to the side, carefully twinkling his mirthless green eyes and talking with a twisted smile on his face.

The voice too required attention. Years in the North-East had modified Postlethwaite's Yorkshire accent. It now fell somewhere between the vaguely effeminate tones of a grammar-school-educated Novocastrian and the extrovert whine of a Lancashire trade unionist. Only when angry or surprised into parting with money did the glottal stops and dropped consonants of his youth emerge to cast doubt on his social desirability. But, he thought, a little attention to detail would soon correct matters.

The remoulding of his personal image so absorbed him he didn't notice the day slipping by. He'd even forgotten to follow his wife around the house to switch off lights behind her. This realisation brought him out of his reverie with a shock.

As he fussily plunged the house into dismal half-light after its masquerade as Blackpool Illuminations, Postlethwaite was brought back to earth. It was all very well to appear more expansive and approachable, but he must never forget that above all he was a creative local government accountant. And with that multi-contradictory terminological inexactitude firmly in mind, he went to work next day.

In his panelled office he sorted through the past week's mail. To his left he piled invoices, statements, receipts, cheques and letters of complaint or query. To his right council minutes and agendas, invitations to conferences and the *Financial Times*.

The pile on the left soon disappeared in the direction of David Smith, but the pile on the right occupied Postlethwaite for the remainder of the morning.

It was rare for his mail to contain anything unconnected with public finance, but today there was a wee note from Doreen, the wages clerk, inviting him and his wife to a wine and cheese lunch on the coming Saturday. It was an annual event, always attended by Postlethwaite and the staff, though Paddy Kean had consistently excused himself. 'Perhaps next year,' he would say, and Doreen would smile. 'I hope so,' she'd reply.

Not a sentiment shared by Postlethwaite, who traditionally accepted his own invitation only after ascertaining that Paddy would be absent.

The treasurer always enjoyed 'The Cheese Do', as everyone called it; not only because he had the staff to himself for a while, but because they were an audience before which he could show off. This was the time of year when he usually bought a new car and, he being the only car-owner in the department, the staff took some academic interest in his somewhat tasteless display.

Postlethwaite had occasionally pondered the reason why his ex-deputy had never appeared at Doreen's, but never so much as to actually enquire about it. He was happy to let the situation remain undisturbed. Paddy, of course, with his family commitments, had treated all weekends as sacrosanct and certainly had no interest in socialising with Postlethwaite.

By lunchtime the treasurer had completed his diary, so turned his mind to the minutes and agendas. There was nothing urgent, so he decided to visit the local car showroom. Before leaving, he opened the door to the outer office and glanced around. In response to an enquiring raised eyebrow from David Smith he nodded, nearly smiled and gave a little wave. He was happy. Kean was really gone.

And it was a good time of year to be buying a car, a time of depression in the motor industry.

*

Fenwick Fancourt, the Monk Garage's only salesman, had known little of industry in his short lifetime, but of depression he had had a bellyful. And the new job hadn't altered the trend –

after working in the showroom for over two months he had sold only one car.

Yet, he thought, as he saw the lanky figure of Christopher Oates Postlethwaite striding across the forecourt towards the office, this might be a lucky day.

G'morning!" Postlethwaite greeted the young man.

Fenwick dumped his cigarette, straightened his tie and offered his hand.

"Good morning sir, can I help you?"

Postlethwaite leaned forward in a confidential manner.

"Triumph Herald Convertible," he said, as if imparting a state secret. "Ordered for delivery Friday next."

Fancourt didn't know what Postlethwaite was talking about; it had been the previous salesman who'd taken the order. But it didn't matter; there were plenty of unsold Triumphs at the back of the garage.

"Ah, yes sir, very smart model, I'll see if it's ready. What was the colour again?"

"That's the ticket!" enthused Postlethwaite, rubbing his hands. "Two-tone black and white, actually."

"Newcastle supporter are we, sir?"

"Yes, yes, a fine city, a fine city..."

He laughed down at Fancourt and adopted his carefully rehearsed alternative facial expression.

"Here's a tissue," said the salesman.

"What?"

"Oh, sorry, I thought you were going to sneeze."

Fenwick left the office, wiped down the only suitably-coloured Triumph he could find and drove it into the showroom.

Postlethwaite inspected it almost paternally and pronounced himself satisfied. He and his wife would look quite swish arriving at Doreen's in that – positively continental.

"I'd like it delivered to my home early Friday evening," instructed the treasurer, "and you can collect my trade-in car then."

"Where do you live?" asked Fenwick.

53

Postlethwaite inscribed his name and address on the salesman's pad.

"Are you Mr Postlethwaite, the borough treasurer?"

"Yes, I am, actually" replied Postlethwaite smugly.

"That's interesting," commented the salesman. "There's a pal of mine going to start working for you."

"Really, in what capacity?"

"Eh?"

"What job is he coming to do?"

"Oh, I think he's starting as a clerk or something. Next Monday. He went to school with me, you know. He's called Arnold."

Of course, thought Postlethwaite, this must be the new junior that Kean had appointed. Here was an opportunity to boost his image and have the newcomer join the staff with a good impression of its chief already formed.

"Do you know this young man's surname?"

"Er, Locock."

"Well, give Mr Locock my personal congratulations on his appointment and tell him we all look forward to his joining us, will you?" Postlethwaite almost gushed.

"Aye, I will, thanks," said Fenwick. "Will you want the car fitted with mudflaps?

"Mudflaps?" Postlethwaite sounded suspicious.

Fenwick explained their function and the treasurer, still in a bid to enhance his image, agreed they would be essential to an open car. He went on to agree to have fog lamps, a radio, reversing-lights, white-wall tyres and a wood-rim steering-wheel. Fenwick couldn't believe his good fortune. Perhaps he was born to be a salesman after all.

And Postlethwaite left the showroom with the heady feelings of a man who had taken the first tentative steps on the road to a new life.

He took further steps on his return to the office. He joined the staff for their tea break. He was chatty and jovial. The staff hated it.

They were barely used to the idea of working in an atmosphere untainted by the baleful presence of Paddy Kean, so the unexpected and unwelcome entrance of the treasurer did nothing for them. Postlethwaite, however, simply took their dismal silence as shyness and, to break the ice, related one of the little jokes he had memorised. It was received with embarrassing disinterest.

Later in the week he tried to ingratiate himself by sending the staff a box of cakes. This gesture might have been more appreciated had it not been that, a few hours later, everyone was in agony with mysterious stomach pains.

Postlethwaite had entrusted Malcolm Birstin to purchase the cakes, but Mr Birstin went one better: he knew where he could get them for nothing. There were cakes and pies and all manner of foodstuffs in a corner of the Public Health Department. In fact, for months, Birstin had been helping himself to this hoard. He never thought to connect his almost permanent bellyache with this habit, nor did he realise that the heap of food in the Health Department had been collected from suspect manufacturers to await the attention of the public analyst. He simply attributed the drawing sensations in his gut to overwork, and guessed he must be heading for an ulcer.

But Postlethwaite was a realist, he kidded himself, and did not expect to be loved by everyone all at once. The important thing was that he was making contact, so increasingly he looked forward to the wine and cheese lunch.

On the Friday evening, just as arranged, Fancourt delivered the Triumph to Postlethwaite's house.

Mrs Postlethwaite was enchanted.

"It's absolutely delightful!" she cried with a brilliant smile as she admired the sleek lines and sporty appearance.

The little car shone, its brightwork glittered. It was fashionable, looked extravagant and, when the salesman lowered the hood and switched on the radio, it was magic.

Yet, pondered Mrs Postlethwaite, as she ran a finger round the wood-rim steering wheel, this was not typical of her Christopher –

like a few other characteristics to have shown themselves of late. That odd look he had adopted, as if he were going to sneeze, that strange nasal voice, and he had been calling her 'Dear' – all a bit peculiar, she thought, drumming her fingertips on the boot lid.

"Will I put the hood back up? asked Fenwick.

"No. Just leave it as it is," replied Postlethwaite dully.

Fancourt gave a sigh of relief. Already he'd caught his fingers in the struts when lowering it, and had learned earlier how difficult it was to raise – he'd required the assistance of two garage hands.

"Well, it's a bit stiff with being new, and it's tricky to get the clips attached to the top of the windscreen..."

"I'm capable of reading the handbook, young man!" snapped Postlethwaite, studying the invoice Fancourt had shoved into his hand. The extras had cost a fortune. "You'll find my old car in the back lane. Here are the keys."

"Okay," Fancourt shrugged.

Postlethwaite grunted and went into the house.

*

Saturday began with clear sunshine – perfect for an open car. Immediately after breakfast Postlethwaite eased it from the garage to park in the street where passers-by would see it. Even stationary it was exhilarating to sit in.

"Do you think it'll stay fine?" his wife called from the front garden where she was weeding.

"Of course it will, dear! Not a cloud in the sky that I can see!"

In that case, thought Mrs Postlethwaite, I'll wear the lilac silk dress and the floppy hat with real ostrich feathers. After all, she supposed, today was almost celebratory – the first Saturday in months when her husband hadn't brought home work from the office. That lazy old deputy had certainly ruined any hope of leisure at weekends. She had seen Paddy Kean only once or twice, pointed out to her by Christopher from their car, but she hated him.

A few minutes later, her hands cleaned of soil, she went to the bedroom to dress, and when finished she looked stunning.

Even Postlethwaite, tired of sitting in the car in the hope of admiration from the neighbours and having gone upstairs to change, had to admit to himself that he'd married an extraordinarily beautiful woman. He felt he ought to make some appropriate comment to this effect.

"Er... lovely dress, dear," he managed.

"Mm," replied his wife, adjusting her gigantic hat to a more seductive angle. "I meant to wear it at the mayor's garden party but..." She swung away from the mirror, picked up her handbag and left Postlethwaite wondering if he'd said what he'd meant to say.

Downstairs, after some consideration, she decided not to take her sedatives. It was only a short drive to Doreen's and she felt she had a duty to be awake for the event. But she'd keep the bottle handy for the journey home. Her husband's driving became even more eccentric when he'd had a glass or two of wine.

"Time to go, dear!" she heard him call from the hall.

"Incidentally, Christopher, who's the mayor this year?" she asked as she joined him.

"Er, Mrs Slattery, I believe," muttered Postlethwaite, who took little interest in changes of political power.

"You're joking!"

"No, dear," he said blandly.

"She's an animal!" said Mrs Postlethwaite.

He didn't know about that, but it was true that, for reasons he'd never fully understood, this year's mayor had been seen little in public and, strangely, there had been no mention of a mayoress, traditionally the sister or sister-in-law of a female mayor. Still, he thought, it had kept civic functions to a minimum, so reducing costs to the borough.

They set off in grand style. It was Postlethwaite's first taste of open-air motoring and he liked it. He liked the purpose of the journey, the sunshine and breeze on his face and, more than anything, the fact that his first week at work without the spirit-crushing aura of Paddy Kean permeating his department was over, and he'd received no hint that he should not, now and for ever, run the finances of the borough in an extravaganza of leisurely orderliness.

Just as the golden sunshine now brightening up the countryside gave no hint that behind the little car there was building up a formidable array of very black clouds. The hint came only as Postlethwaite looked up to see if something wet might be falling from the overhanging trees – then he saw the swirling nigrescence of the sky.

Too late, however. The heavens opened, thunder deafened, and within seconds the track became a quagmire.

Mrs Postlethwaite, frantically but in vain, sought protection for her hat as her husband pulled to the side and brought the car to a halt. He leapt out, his feet slithering in the mud, and leaned over to release the hood from behind the rear seats. Despite his straining and cursing, however, the wet canvas remained obstinately in place.

Just then, camouflaged by the downpour and with hardly a sound as it approached, an imposing silver Jaguar saloon sloshed by, showering Postlethwaite with sludge and shocking him head first into the back of the Triumph.

"Get his number! Get his number!" he screamed at his wife as he extricated himself from the footwell.

"Whose number?" came a muffled, enquiring response. Mrs Postlethwaite's vast hat, now a dripping mass of felt and feathers, had sagged, completely enveloping her face.

"That road hog! That damned fool! That..." Postlethwaite spluttered inanities. Petulantly he thumped his fist into the side of the car. The hood popped up, the rain ceased, and a rainbow began to form with the returning sun.

A normal man would have driven home for his wife to change and then returned with some apology for a late arrival; but not Postlethwaite. He simply knocked the hood back into its place and drove on, determined to overtake the Jaguar and remonstrate with its driver.

A minute or so later, the Postlethwaites sped bumpily towards the cottage. At its door the silver Jaguar was coming to rest.

From it emerged a tall, cool, elegant, exquisitely-dressed young lady who arranged herself by its side. The treasurer's staff gathered round – they hadn't seen anything like this since visiting the dentists and thumbing the pages of *Vogue*.

Postlethwaite, gathering speed, neared the little group. His wife, silent and unseeing under her hat appeared indifferent, but instinctively searched for her pills.

The driver of the large saloon now appeared and began to greet people.

Postlethwaite, going white, stamped on the brake.

It would have been all right if the driveway hadn't been curved, or if its shingly surface hadn't been greased with fallen leaves. It would have been all right if Postlethwaite's bonny new car had not been so responsive to sudden action. As it was, however, he didn't have a chance. With brakes locked on, the car flew out of control, its back end arcing wildly to smash into the solid stone gatepost of the cottage. A few of the throng, startled by the noise, glanced over at the mud-splattered convertible with its mysterious, hooded passenger.

Postlethwaite buried his head in his wood-rim steering wheel and tried to die.

His wife, disturbed from immobility by having walloped herself on the windscreen as the car shot sideways, lifted the sodden brim of her hat to see what was happening. It took a split second to take in the scene. With a bizarre, squeaky giggle she let the hat slop down and emptied the bottle of sedatives down her throat.

She wasn't noticed. The eyes of the staff were on the Jaguar, the girl and her driver.

It was hardly surprising: the car was impressive, the girl stunning – and this was the first time at Doreen's 'Cheese Do' that Paddy Kean had turned up.

Chapter Three

For Arnold Locock, the only advantage weekends had over weekdays in the relief of boredom was that they gave opportunity to stay in bed for longer in the mornings. In fact, he judged the quality of a weekend purely by how much of it he could avoid by sleeping.

Given freedom from the related activities of eating, drinking and relieving himself, he might well have contrived to spend the whole of every weekend between the sheets, but inevitably a desire to satisfy either his stomach or his bladder – usually the latter – would prove compelling enough to persuade him to rise.

And once out of bed he was not given to returning to it. Not, it must be said, because of a puritanical or otherwise masochistic streak in his nature, but only because, in the Locock household, it was necessary to dress to visit the lavatory. It was eighty feet away from the house at the bottom of a walled garden, overlooked by adjoining houses and the upper storey of the Catholic school for girls.

He had, of course, experimented with alternatives. For a while he had kept a bucket in his wardrobe. But the stink had become unbearable – even worse than his socks – and he had once knocked it over when full, provoking a memorable response from his parents in the kitchen below, who found its contents, arriving by way of a crack in the ceiling, an unwelcome addition to the breakfast table. He had tried peeing out of the window. For fun, he used to aim at the dog in the garden next door. That was stopped following a visit to his father by the prim headmistress of the girls' school whose charges, she claimed, had been seriously corrupted by the sight of Arnold's disgusting habit.

The visit at least provided Arnold's father with an answer to why the ivy growing beneath his son's window was a different colour to the rest.

The bathroom, next to Arnold's room and containing a washbasin and bath might have proved usable, but the basin was too high for him to pee in comfort and using the bath made too much noise to go unnoticed in other parts of the house.

It might be thought that he could have dressed, made a visit to the lavatory, then undressed and returned to bed. But that would assume a lack of vigilance on the part of his mother who, once aware that her son had stumbled from his bed, would rush upstairs, clear out his dirty clothes, strip the bed down to the mattress and open the window to the limit of its sash cord, thus making the room uninhabitable for one of Arnold's comfort-loving disposition.

The Lococks had never given thought to the idea of an inside lavatory. To Arnold's parents, brought up within the confines of a Northumbrian pit village and its over-the-back-lane earth-closets, the idea of a flushing cistern remained something of a novelty, and to have such a contraption inside the house smacked of ostentation, to say nothing of the noise and stench that would waft through every room.

And Arnold did not disagree. When younger, he had once spent a week at his aunt's in Newcastle, only to return home full of complaints about the questionable hygiene of a household where 'the netty was right next to the bedroom!' – a point of view not uncommon among a certain social class in the North-East of England. It was considered not only more healthy to have the netty a good distance from the house, but it was also thought to improve the overall quality of life.

Life, after all, held precious few pleasures for the pitman or ironworker. At home there would be a brood of unruly offspring and a resultant nagging, overworked wife; at work, reluctant subservience to foreman and management.

There was only one place to be alone and composed – the netty. There, in the darkness, a man could be a man, with all his dreams of glory. He could sigh, groan, hockle, spit, sing or pray in complete privacy.

In fact, singing in the netty was usually the only way to indicate to others that it was occupied. Few netty doors were lockable. And the soaring strains of some popular ballad were effective cover for the less tuneful, though equally satisfying noises the security of solitude encouraged. There is no better way to aid the movement of one's bowels than to belt forth in song.

Indeed, it could be said that the modern fashion for prissy little indoor privies has done much to inhibit the North-East's traditions of male choral singing and made the audition a necessary preliminary to joining a choir.

Not so in the days of pit villages with their long rows of stone-built terraced houses and, across the back lanes, the evenly spaced netties where, between which, late at nights after the pubs had closed, would lurk local choirmasters on the listen for new talent.

Not only could these working-class impresarios judge the tonal quality of a voice heard echoing over the middens, but they could accurately gauge its potential range. The more regularly constipated a defecating songster might be, the more likely he would have developed a high voice. And, though the practice was always denied, it was not uncommon for male voice choir masters, on the eve of competitive festivals, to tamper with the natural processes of their choristers' bowel movements by taking to one side a struggling tenor and suggesting the odd sprinkling of cement on his leek pudding, 'just to bring the voice up a bit!'

So the netty gave much to vocal harmony. It also contributed to spiritual harmony. With your trousers round your ankles, having exhausted your repertoire of bowel-encouraging songs, there is little else to do than have a chat to God.

Not so easy, of course, for those of the Roman faith or for Anglicans – you can't kneel and defecate at the same time; not without the risk of distraction.

But Methodists were laughing. They didn't kneel to pray.

A Methodist could sit there – head in hand in the pose of 'The Thinker' – and pray with an easy conscience, and the firm belief that what he was doing was in the fundamental spirit of Christian behaviour. In Matthew 6:5 are we not told that our Lord Jesus Himself instructed: "When thou prayest, lock thyself in thy closet and shut the door"?

A Methodist in a hurry, of course, would sing hymns – thereby at once satisfying both his bowels and his conscience. The spectacular growth of Methodism, therefore, and its tradition of joyful hymn-singing also had much to do with the outside netty.

So, wherever bowel-clogging dust is common, wherever pits and ironworkers are found, wherever the netty once dominated the private lives of the workers, there will also be found male voice choirs and Methodism.

To this day, when listening to a North-East male voice choir assaulting the final triumphant chords of 'Crossing the Bar', melodiously intoning 'Speed your Journey' or urging to tears with 'Soon Ah Will Be Done', there will be sensed greater depths of feeling than can be inspired merely by careful rehearsal and love of music. There will be sensed the expression of a race-memory: of needle-sharp Northumbrian winds laying siege to an outside netty in the grip of winter, and a lone pitman with his trousers round his ankles competing in song whilst straining against the constipatory coal-dust in his innards.

And to this day, during a Methodist service of worship in such an area, by keeping watch during the prayers, there will be seen in the chapel members of the congregation, in the pose of 'The Thinker', silently communing with God. The outside netty may be fading into folklore, but the lavatorial crouch lives on.

Regrettably, Arnold Locock's netty was not the place for such devotions. In fact, Arnold was beginning to think it better to have an indoor toilet. Particularly on a Saturday morning after a night on the beer when the struggle to get into his clothes became a frantic race against the spasms of his bladder, or the cat would trip him as he hopped cross-legged down the stairs, or his mother would impede his clamped-bum rush through the kitchen, or, on arrival, he would find his father using the netty for something other than its proper purpose.

Actually, on Saturday mornings his father used it for almost everything. This was his day of the week for messing about in the garden. He certainly wouldn't be caught in the house where his wife, demonish house-proud, would be cleaning and washing and catching up on all that her weekday job prevented at any other time. So, in his cap, wellies, and a disreputable pair of wartime fireman's trousers, he would work outside. And, lacking a shed, he had discovered a wide range of uses for the netty. Its height allowed the storage of ladders and long-handled garden implements, its wood-clad inner walls were sufficiently sturdy to support boxes full of nails, screws, spanners and files, and its distance from the house made it safe for the hoarding of flammable, toxic and explosive liquids.

Arnold's father had lots of these – all noxious. There was his home-made fertiliser of crushed cod's heads and stale beer, a pungent chemical insecticide, a large tin of varnish, a gas canister, and, in containers of various types, there was paint, creosote, fly-repellent and anti-freeze: all essential to his compulsions and all frequently in use, especially his cleaning-mixture – consisting mainly of petrol – which he used for scouring the engine of his old car which usually lay in bits near the back door.

Arnold's father was never more content than when sloshing about with stinking liquids. And whatever was surplus to his requirements was chucked down the netty.

It says much for the durability of vitreous enamel that the Lococks had a lavatory pan left to use, though there were times, particularly in summer, when the atmosphere within and surrounding the little timber and brick-built cubicle made it less than inviting. Add the natural odours of urine, excrement and exhaled cigarette smoke and the undesirability of having it inside the house becomes clear.

But, on the first Saturday of Arnold's release from the metalworks, the Saturday before he was due to start at the town hall, his emergence to the wakened world was not accompanied by a bursting bladder. Not having spent the preceding evening at the pub – due to its temporary closure – his liquid intake had been minimal. His bladder therefore had held out, but his bowels ached for relief.

His mother had finished her housework, the cat was asleep in front of the fire, and the lavatory, when he reached it, was not occupied by his father.

Locock Senior was, in fact, busy pouring petrol mixture from a tin bath on to the gearbox of the car. He hardly noticed his son trudge past to ensconce himself in the netty.

Thoughtfully, Arnold lowered his behind on to the black-painted wooden seat and tried to make himself comfortable among the tools and tins. Automatically, he looked up to check that the knotted string hanging from the ceiling was properly laden with squares of newspaper, then lit his first cigarette of the day.

As the tobacco smoke curled slowly upwards to disappear through the triangular ventilation hole in the wall, he heard a distant clap of thunder, then the sound of heavy rain beating on the ground outside – quite unexpected on what seemed to be a bright day.

The sudden downpour, the same that at that moment was ruining life for Postlethwaite, was about to do something for Arnold. The netty door was yanked open to reveal his father prepared to hurl the bathful of cleaning mixture towards the space his son's behind was occupying.

"Just a minute! Just a minute!" protested Arnold, panic stricken.

"Oh! Are you in there?" his father asked, rhetorically as always. "Well hurry up! Its pouring out here! And put that cigarette out! This stuff's flammable! Why the hell do you always smoke in the lavvy? You make a right bloody mess! And I've told you before about the fire risk!"

Arnold ignored the outburst. He was used to it.

The rain was torrential.

Hastily his father put the tin bath on the ground.

"When you've finished, pour that down the lav and don't forget to pull the chain!" he shouted. Then he ran towards the house, his wellies slapping on the concrete path.

When Arnold had done, he pulled the rusty chain, fastened his trousers and trod his cigarette end on to the stone floor.

Typically, of course, he forgot the bathful of cleaning mixture until he tripped over it.

Muttering, he picked it up, poured it into the lavatory bowl, and again pulled the chain. But there was no second gurgling rush of water from the overhead tank. The cistern was old, the pipes furred up. It took a while to refill. He would return later to flush it all away.

Back in the house, his mother and father were preparing to go out.

"Are you coming with us to your grandfather's?" his mother asked.

"No!" replied Arnold, without hesitation.

It was not so much his grandparents to whom he objected. It was the horde of aunts, uncles and cousins that gathered there clan-like at weekends. He found their family chat uninteresting and comments on the activities of their offspring depressing. He was sick of hearing of how Anita had got eight O levels, or how James was progressing in his attempts to become a boilermaker, or how Thomas was doing at college. He was sick too, of the ability of his relatives to remind him of childhood indiscretions, which always made his ears burn with embarrassment. In fact, he thought his family was altogether too familiar and took advantage of their blood connection to be ruder than necessary.

"All right," said his mother, who understood something of Arnold's sensitivity, "we'll see you when we get back. We'll be on the last bus."

Arnold slumped into a chair and reached for a newspaper. His mother bent down and kissed his brow.

"At least it's stopped raining now," she said, "so you'll be able to go out."

"Yes," replied Arnold, "I'll go to the library."

His parents left and Arnold, finding nothing of interest in the newspaper, drifted off to sleep. When he awoke, about an hour later, he drowsily searched the house to collect together the library books he was due to return. They were on top of the piano. For a few minutes he sat at the keyboard and played the music in front of him, the middle section of Chopin's 'Marche Funèbre' – it suited his mood. The afternoon was bright and warm. As he walked through the park he saw old men playing bowls and youngsters cavorting mischievously on the swings and roundabouts. He wondered if the new library assistant would be on duty today. She was slim, fine-boned, pale, with an aristocratic nose and, of particular interest to Arnold, she wore spectacles. That, by his guesswork, meant she was unlikely to have a boyfriend and was probably intelligent. So, of late, he had taken to borrowing books on as wide a range of subjects available in the limited selection to be found in Mankley's civic library. He hoped that in time he would hit on something in which the girl might express a passionate interest as she wielded her date stamp. But up to now, despite his having waded through everything from *Manx for Beginners* to *The Care and Maintenance of a Modern Bee Farm*, she had remained as passionate-interest-proof as a week-old soufflé.

As usual, he was ignored as he handed over his books. He wandered around for a while trying to look haunted by mystery, then selected a volume entitled *A History of the Theatres Royal in Newcastle upon Tyne* and another about Samoan musical instruments, after which he looked for something to read. Taking a Dennis Wheatley and a PG Wodehouse, he returned to the counter. The girl, still as dead-pan as a post office counter clerk, took as much notice of him when he left as she had when he'd arrived. It was as if he'd been cast in a play as an off-stage mute.

Back at home he banked up the fire, put a selection of operatic records on the radiogram and settled down to the Dennis Wheatley. The cat stretched lazily at his feet, he lost himself in the world of the French Revolution and the exploits of a host of characters whose names he couldn't pronounce.

When the front doorbell rang he didn't want to respond; but when it rang again he did – but only to stop it ringing. He opened the door to Ernie Moon who wondered if Arnold 'fancied gannin' t' th' pitchas'. Arnold, in fact, did not fancy 'gannin' t' th' pitchas' at all but he was too polite to say so, especially as Ernie had gone to the trouble of calling at the house. So off he went to

The Regal where he sat through *The Purple Heart*, an American war movie, wishing he was at home with the cat.

*

"Eeh! You should have seen it, Mary!" Paddy slapped the arm of the chair. "I just drove past and over the bugger went! By hell, it was funny!"

He wiped away tears from his twinkling eyes. It had been a last-minute decision to go to Doreen's, but it had been worth it, despite his natural nervousness. And it had been touch and go with the car – the garage had been late delivering it. Yet, in the end, all had been well and, what with Postlethwaite's open car and the unexpected downpour, Paddy had got a bonus.

"You'll be off to the Club, I suppose," smiled Mary.

"Aye," he replied, getting up from his chair, "I'll enjoy a drink the night."

"Off you go, then – and don't be late back. We've a lot to do tomorrow, and... Paddy," she put a hand gently to the side of his face and looked at him steadily, "I'm glad today made you laugh."

Paddy took her hand and kissed it.

"Mary, love," he said seriously, "if I do nothing else for the rest of me days, the memory of that bugger Postlethwaite doin' a dicky-dance in the mud'll send me to me grave happy!"

Well, thought Mary, she had at last seen that stern face of his free of care and the eyes without a look of fading hope, for Paddy had never really believed his day would come.

After he left, Mary wandered the rooms of the house. This would be her last opportunity. Tomorrow, just as they had begun to plan it twelve years before, she and Paddy would be moving to another home and a different life. The girls would miss their familiar surroundings when they came to visit but, like Mary, they would forget neither the days they had spent here, nor the security and joy they had shared.

Mary caught sight of the photographs of Anne and Margaret, taken as each had graduated from university. She thought back to the circumstances of their births, and shuddered.

69

The years had flown by. It seemed only yesterday when they had first come to this house; when Mary, then so ignorant of all things decent, had glimpsed a kinder future. She recalled the early days of her marriage; how Paddy had struggled to overcome his shyness with the children, how he had fussily planned their weekends so that each was different and exciting. As if every hour spent with his family had been specially given him by God, he had left Mary and the girls no time for reflection, only for fulfilment. Like a spring tide flooding shingled sands, the memories came easily – one in particular, which Mary would never share.

It was of soon after she'd married: a summer's day on a long beach. Paddy in his stuffy suit, striding along, ill at ease with the children and unaccustomed to play, his face set stiff and stern against the wind. Mary had felt unequal to intruding on his thoughts. Casually, she had amused the barefoot girls by spinning stones across the waves. But little Margaret had run after Paddy and tugged at his jacket.

"Please, Mr Kean," she had pleaded as Paddy frowned down in embarrassment at her earnest wee face, "can we call you Daddy, now that we live with you?"

And Paddy, after a pause, knelt in the sand before her and stroked her hair.

"Have you ever wanted to be a lady?" he asked gently.

Mary could recall no more than that vision and those words, but from that day on, Paddy had devoted himself wholly to their welfare and happiness. It had been a wonderful marriage.

'And now', thought Mary as she blinked away a rare tear, 'it's going to pay off for you, Paddy Kean! With knobs on!'

*

Paddy manoeuvred the Jaguar into the car park behind the club. Still feeling jovial, he went inside. He was looking forward to a chat and a pint of ale. And there would be a bit of committee work to do – it was almost time for the annual Leek Show.

He had been a member of the committee virtually since first joining the club some five years before. His talent for organisation was well known to other members, many of whom were on the fringes of local politics. A few were Mankley Borough aldermen and councillors, and some felt a nagging unease at Paddy's treatment at the town hall. They were also aware that over the years he'd had time to observe their activities in some detail. If that had not been the case it is doubtful if Paddy would have been allowed to join the club in the first place. But councillors and their like were essential to his plans and, in Mankley Labour Club, now that he had retired, there were some who would do almost anything for Paddy. The recipient of his hearty backslap was one of these.

"Evenin', Archie!" said Paddy. "Can I get you one?"

"Eh? Oh! Aye, thanks. A pint'll be very welcome, very welcome!"

"Have a short. I'm after some information."

"Oh, in that case, I'll have a whisky, a whisky!"

Alderman Archibald Carrigan, Leader of Mankley Borough Council and retired solicitor, had a habit of repeating words when excited, which was just about always.

"Do you want water with it?" asked Paddy.

The pillar of Mankley's political life shook his jowls in horror.

"Eh? No! Water has some wonderful qualities," he replied, "you can sail ships on it, sail ships on it! It's good stuff for flushing out drains! I've heard that some people die for want of it! But not me! Not me! I'll have my whisky neat, if you don't mind!"

Paddy brought the drinks and joined Archie at the table.

"Have you any news for me?" Paddy asked.

"I have, I have," responded Archie, leaning back in his chair and frowning at the table. "They won't let you have it!"

"What?"

"Chairman says it's obscene!"

"Well, I'm going to appeal!" said Paddy.

"You haven't got time, got time. Not if you want to open a week on Monday!"

Archie downed his whisky, banged his glass on the table and looked steadily into Paddy's eyes as if about to impart significant information.

"I'll have another, I'll have another," he said.

Paddy, clearly disappointed, went to get it.

"Y'see, the trouble is, *the trouble is*," said Archie emphatically when Paddy returned with the drink, "you'd have got away with it with the old chairman. Old Ned would have liked your name for it. But this new fellow – no bloody help at all. He's ambitious y'see. Wants to be an MP. Goes everywhere with his mother, *his mother*. Nothing queer about him, mind. Used to have a girlfriend, actually, a girlfriend. Took her home one day to meet his family and his father buggered off and married the lass! Feels he owes his mother a lot now, one way and another. Goes everywhere with her. He'll get into Parliament all right. They've got nothing on him. Forty-five, balding, takes his mother out – bound to get on. Tall, too. Tories like that. Smacks of public school and being good at sport. They'll give him a safe seat. He'll get on all right. But he won't let you call your pub The Windy Cow!"

Paddy looked miserable. Archie took a swig of whisky before continuing.

"It's okay about the neon sign!" he said. "No trouble there. Got planning permission last week. Nice fellow in the planning office. Knew his brother well, very well. Alcoholic he was. Always drank neat vodka. Funny habit, drinking neat vodka. Tasteless bloody stuff. Anyhow, there was no trouble in the planning office."

Paddy muttered a few words of thanks, but he was far from happy. He couldn't imagine what to call the pub now. Not much point in having neon lights if the name wasn't right.

Archie pushed a sheet of paper across the table and winked.

"What's this?" asked Paddy.

"Read it, read it!" chortled Archie, obviously very pleased about something.

Paddy cast his eyes down the typewritten sheet and his face immediately brightened.

"By hell, Archie!" he almost shouted. "I'll walk it!"

"Aye," smiled the rotund alderman. "Nowt but the best, nowt but the best! You did well at the interview. You'll walk it!" and he banged his glass down on the table. "I'll have another!"

*

Ernie enjoyed the film. When it had finished, he talked enthusiastically about it.

"Smashin', wasn't it?" he kept saying.

And he and Arnold went for a drink. Quite a few drinks. Too many really.

When the pub closed, they bought fish and chips, and Arnold, regretting the idea even as he mouthed the words, invited Ernie home for a cup of tea. Ernie agreed.

"Better than eatin' the chips in the street, eh, Arnold? 'Cos all the vinegar runs on to your fingers, doesn't it, Arnold, eh? And up to your elbow, eh? Sticks you to your shirt!"

Arnold made a pot of tea and buttered some bread. He laid the table and was careful, for some reason, to select proper fish knives and forks.

"Smashin' to have a big house like this, eh, Arnold?" remarked Ernie, looking around him. "Not like the council house we live in. It's rotten, that."

Ernie prattled on comparing the qualities of private and council housing until Arnold virtually ceased to listen. Arnold, in fact, wished that Ernie would push off, but after they'd finished their fish and chips Ernie produced four bottles of beer from his coat pockets.

"I saw Fenwick yesterday," he said. "He told me about you gettin' the town hall job. Midnight told him. So I thought we'd celebrate, like."

Arnold's spirits sank.

"I'm going to have to meet my mam and dad off the last bus from Newcastle."

"Aye? Why, it's only eleven. We've got an hour yet, haven't we, Arnold, eh? Time for a bottle each."

73

Ernie put two of the bottles back in his coat pockets while Arnold got glasses.

"There's nowt better than goin' t' th' flicks an' havin' fish an' chips and a pint afterwards, is there, Arnold?"

Arnold nodded.

"Do you live far from here?" he asked.

"Oh, aye. But I'm not goin' home th' night. I'm goin' down The Clock to meet Sally."

"Who's Sally?"

"You know. That big barmaid. Her husband's back to sea the night so I'm sleeping with her. Get me leg over, eh?" Ernie leered as he pulled from his pocket a packet of contraceptives. "I've got me stocks in an' all. Use all these by morning!"

Arnold was disgusted. It didn't occur to him that Ernie might be exaggerating his relationship with the barmaid. Nor did he imagine that Ernie had been carrying the same packet of contraceptives around for months in the hope that he might one day find an opportunity to use one for its proper purpose.

Arnold had often wondered what it would be like to make love. It seemed to him that it must be one of the great private beauties of a man's life.

"Beer doesn't half make you want to shit, doesn't it Arnold, eh? Where's the lavvy?"

"The what?" asked Arnold, brought back to earth and irritated by Ernie's crudeness.

"The lavvy? The netty?"

"Oh. It's down the garden."

"Eh?"

"Down the garden; I'll give you a torch."

"Is there not one in the house?"

"No. You'd better put your coat on. It'll be cold down there."

"Aye."

Arnold gave Ernie a torch, showed him to the back door and indicated where the lavatory was.

"Fancy havin' an outside netty with a big house like this," muttered Ernie, amazed, as he wandered down the long garden into the night.

Arnold returned to the room to clear away the dishes and chip papers. His parents wouldn't be long in arriving home.

Ernie fumbled with the sneck of the netty door, got it open, lowered his trousers, flicked his coat behind him and straddled the pan. It was quiet, a night for contemplation. He'd enjoyed the night with Arnold. Made a change from his usual Saturday night. Smashing house Arnold had. Comfy chairs. Posh really. Ernie's dream of the high life was a pork pie and a randy woman, but with a house like this the possibilities were endless. From now on he'd keep well in with Arnold. Good thing to have a friend who lived like this.

He pulled his cigarettes from his pocket, slowly selected one and put it to his lips. Through the space at the top of the door he could see stars shining in a clear sky. He struck a match. It was so calm the sound was distinct, and in the darkness, for a moment, the glow created strange shadows. Drawing smoke deep into his lungs he eased up slightly from the netty seat and into the bowl beneath his backside he popped the still flaming match. He listened for the hiss of it being extinguished.

In the house, Arnold was in equally pensive mood as he stacked dishes by the kitchen sink. He too could see stars as he looked through the window into the garden. And he could see the cat settled on the netty roof in preparation for its nightly hosting of the street's feline population.

It was the cat that was uppermost in Arnold's suddenly scrambled mind as he remembered the unflushed petrol and, when he saw the faint glow of light filtering through the top of the netty door, he guessed immediately what Ernie was doing. 'God,' he prayed, 'don't let Ernie put his match in the bowl.'

But it was too late.

Ernie never heard the sound of the match being extinguished. And the cat lost all interest in its forthcoming liaisons. After a pause, during which the first lazy flame in the bowl spread to Ernie's shirt-tail and more rapidly to the squares of newspaper

75

hanging on the string, the netty exploded in multi-coloured sheets of roaring flame. Silhouetted against them Arnold had a momentary vision of Ernie apparently flying, his trousers flapping behind, his coat ablaze; then darkness and a heavy silence.

It was broken by two muffled bumps as Arnold tore down the garden. One was the cat returning to earth, all claws, teeth and confusion; the other a full bottle of beer, obviously once inside Ernie's coat. But Arnold was more concerned with what might be coming down that had once been inside Ernie as he dodged falling buckets, cans and tools.

Ernie had landed only a few feet from the netty but was already almost buried by broken bricks and roofing tiles. He began to groan, but a half-fermented cod's head silenced him.

"Just a minute!" Arnold shouted. "I'll get an ambulance!"

The Lococks didn't have a telephone, but a neighbour did. Arnold ran through the house to the front street where, by an amazing stroke of luck, he saw an ambulance. He waved it down to stop outside the house.

He was relieved when one of the two ambulance men explained that, while badly hurt, Ernie would probably live. "Though what's left of him isn't much use," he added grimly as he rolled Ernie onto a stretcher. "What happened exactly?"

Arnold told them. The men laughed. Arnold was shocked – it did not seem right to laugh at such misfortune. But, on the way from the garden to the ambulance the situation struck the ambulance men as funnier by the second. Guffawing hysterically, they dropped the stretcher twice.

*

Paddy Kean heard the explosion as he drove home from the club. A few minutes later he saw the ambulance speed by with its headlights blazing. But he had no reason to think anything of it. He had problems of his own – like what to call the pub.

He discussed it with Mary over a cocoa. But she couldn't help. She was secretly pleased that Paddy had been stopped from calling the pub The Windy Cow. She'd never liked the idea even though she understood her husband's somewhat droll reasons for choosing it.

"Perhaps we'll think of something clever after a good night's sleep," she suggested.

"I would sleep better if we could think of something now," grumbled Paddy.

"Well, I, my love, am going to bed. I've worked my fingers to the bone today, and tomorrow we've no time to be idle!"

Mary cleared away their cups and removed them to the kitchen. As she washed up there came an unintelligible yelp from Paddy. He rushed up the hall.

"You've cracked it!" he laughed delightedly, his arms encircling her waist.

*

When the ambulance had gone, Arnold looked at his watch. His parents would be home any minute. He hurried back to the garden and, with the aid of an extension light and a shovel, began to tidy up. Hastily, he gathered together tins and tools and replaced them inside the doorless, roofless netty. Anything he found which had not been there before he threw over the back wall into the shrubs surrounding the girls' school, particularly Ernie's bottles of beer – which, miraculously, had stayed in one piece – and his packet of contraceptives.

There was something else Arnold found which was obviously Ernie's – but he doubted if it would ever work again, even if medical science ever discovered a way to sew it back on; so that too disappeared over the wall.

At any other school such acquisitions would have proved invaluable to the biology teacher, but not at Mankley's Catholic school for girls. It didn't have a biology teacher.

The bottles of beer, however, and the contraceptives were welcomed by the pupils like pennies from Heaven – leading to some interesting confessionals for the young Irish priest who had recently joined the parish.

Arnold finished the garden just as his parents returned.
They had enjoyed their day out.
Arnold said nothing about the netty.
Perhaps it would look all right in tomorrow's daylight.

Chapter Four

The first member of the Locock household to see Sunday's daylight was Arnold's father.

The second, predictably, was Arnold.

"What's the matter?" he protested as he was pulled from bed by his left foot. "What time is it?"

"It's seven o'clock!" replied Locock Senior in a voice that betrayed intense emotional restraint.

"In the morning?" asked Arnold unbelievingly.

"Yes. Mornings do actually exist at weekends for normal people!"

"But, it's daylight!"

"Aye, it's bloody daylight!" yelled Arnold's father, restraint breaking down as he hurled Arnold's clothes towards him. "It's daylight in the park! It's daylight in the street! It's daylight in the garden! And it's daylight in the bloody netty – thanks to you!"

Downstairs, to where Arnold was propelled at speed by collar and crotch, he tried to explain what had happened the night before, but his father stopped his flow with upraised hand.

"No explanations! You'll need cement, nails, wood, a hammer, some sand, and a hell of a lot of muscle! Now, get cracking!"

Arnold had a strong impression that to argue would provoke more violence.

He spent the day repairing the netty, interrupted only by the return of various of his father's implements arriving airborne with curses from adjoining back gardens.

*

80

At the Kean household, activity was just as obvious, though less unwilling. No one who'd known Paddy as deputy borough treasurer would have recognised him as he fussed from front door to furniture van and back, checking his lists, joking with the girls, smiling and gesticulating.

*

Christopher Oates Postlethwaite was active too, in his own way.

He was thinking.

First of all, the car; that would have to be repaired. Then, his marriage; repairs, even reparations, might be necessary there. The relationship somehow lacked togetherness – a fact blatantly exposed by his wife's behaviour at yesterday's 'Cheese Do'. He had hoped to make some attempt to be sociable after crashing the car, but she'd simply sat under her hat and gone to sleep. And later, at home, there'd been no apology – she'd just yawned and gone to bed. She was still there now. Still in her damned hat. She hadn't spoken once.

But more than anything, Postlethwaite was thinking about his damaged pride and the setback to his new image. Repairs there were vital.

All day Sunday he thought, uninterrupted until the early evening when his wife appeared, savaged by ennui and dressed for church. For a moment Postlethwaite hoped she would ask him to accompany her. But no. Apart from acknowledging his presence with a withering stare, she left the house in silence.

Postlethwaite was very unhappy.

*

So was Harry Moon. Though not quite in the same way. Harry had cause. Harry, in fact, might have questioned the right of the likes of Postlethwaite ever to be unhappy.

He aimed his boot at the gas meter and, for the third time, it clanged loudly.

"Bastards!" he bellowed.

"Aye," said his wife, Florrie, "see where the bugger gets his beer money from now, I told our Nora."

She drew on the cigarette which always dangled from her lips as she leaned against the door frame watching, her eyes screwed up against the smoke.

Clang!

Again Harry's boot clashed against the meter. Red-eyed and shaking with rage, he knelt down to look at it more closely.

"'Aye, that'll upset him,' I said," his wife taunted.

He cursed.

What he couldn't work out was how this funny-looking new gas meter had been installed without his knowing. He tried to think back over the preceding week. It was hard. The drink fuzzed his memory. One day had been much as another. The pub, the fight in the back lane, money in his hand for a cartload of lead, the boys pulling him away from attacking the barman.

"Frank!" he yelled.

"He's out," drawled Florrie.

"Somebody else, then!"

"They're all out!"

"Ernie!"

"He didn't come home. Neither did Anthony or Fred."

Harry looked up pleadingly.

"You've got a few bob, haven't you?"

"Not a penny! Not for you to get drunk on!"

"Howway, just five bob?"

Florrie shook her head and retreated into the cramped kitchen where three of the younger ones were shouting and fighting as they played mammies and daddies.

"Bed, you lot!" screamed Florrie through their din.

And they dutifully tripped upstairs to one of the four bedrooms the thirteen-strong Moon family had been allocated by authority as sufficient for their needs.

Authority ruled the Moons. It hadn't been so bad in the old street, for all its lack of hot water, gardens or open spaces. People looked after each other then. They had to. But Authority had pulled down the houses and the Moons were given this one, among strangers. Authority had decreed their social level. Everybody knew that Railway Street was the last staging post of the socially unacceptable. All the 'problem' families were put there, in a ghetto sandwiched between the railway sidings and the chemical works.

Actually, the Moons had not been a 'problem' family – it was just that there were a lot of them. Too many for Authority to equate with respectability. It had upset Florrie and Harry to move. After all, they weren't Irish or Catholic. At least they had that to feel proud about.

Harry had soon lost his job for consistent bad timekeeping – buses came nowhere near Railway Street – so Authority in time was proved right. The Moons became as unrespectable as everyone else there. And where the church and good neighbourliness fell short, Authority stepped in.

It painted their houses the same colour as the others. It imposed on them heating they couldn't afford. It wrote letters about the state of their garden and it made them complete questionnaires to assist them to become statistics. And Authority took pride in it all.

Florrie had coped better than Harry. She had used Authority. She had learned the tricks. Authority to her was no more than a large dim-witted animal that could be controlled. She'd played its silly games, filled in its forms, and answered its myriad questions. And when threatened, she'd played daft and inadequate, acting the role Authority understood was hers. By such means her large family was brought up, and she'd raised some big, healthy boys to manhood. Strong lads all – strong enough to smash furniture! And when they did, Authority gave Florrie chits to buy more!

Most of the boys were men now. They lacked Florrie's gift of coping. They fought back. Authority took away their dignity, their right to be men. They gave Authority an occasional kick in the teeth. Vainly, however, for Authority got its own back. Every so often it would throw one of them into prison, or call one up for National Service. A godsend for Florrie. It was only with the help of the courts and the army that she had had an occasional breathing space. Now, in fact, with conscription being ended, she was worried. She could only hope that some of them would marry and live elsewhere.

"So how do you get the money into it?" asked Harry, innocent-like – by learning that he might discover how to get it out.

"I told Nora you'd ask that."

Harry grunted and made for his box of tools.

"'You don't have to put money in it,' I said. 'They send you a bill every three months!'"

"What?" yelped Harry, going rigid.

"Aye!" his wife laughed horribly. "'That'll learn him,' I said!"

"Shut up!"

"'Natural gas, is it?' she asked. 'That's what they call it,' I said."

"Shut up!" Harry repeated, this time fetching Florrie a clout with the back of his hand. These imaginary conversations with her sister Nora irritated him. Nora hadn't spoken to the Moons for years, not since she'd become a councillor.

Florrie looked at him brazenly.

"Everybody's got them! The whole street! There's nothing you can do about it!"

"We'll see about that!"

Harry disappeared back into the hall, a hacksaw in his hand. Florrie sighed sadly as she heard him sawing through the newly-installed pipes.

This had all happened before with the Electricity Board. He'd always been breaking into their meter for beer money. It wasn't long before they put in a quarterly one. And Harry ripped it out in a violent rage and dumped it on the counter of the local showroom with a stream of drunken abuse. That didn't achieve much. Just set fire to the stairs and earned them weeks without lights. Harry's three months' imprisonment was hardly a fair compensation. God knows what would happen this time.

Triumphant, he returned to the kitchen, the sawn-off meter in his hands.

"You're mad!" said Florrie, stirring the floor with her foot.

"The bastards'll get it back the morrow!" muttered her husband, putting the meter on the table, the sawn-off pipes sticking out from its sides like a couple of spouts.

Florrie glanced at it, then went into the hall to inspect the damage. Hearing the hiss of escaping gas she turned off the main tap. She sniffed. No smell with this new natural gas. The men had been right. She noticed something distinctive about the pipes sticking through the floorboards. The inlet and outlet pipes were of the same diameter.

"Harry!"

"What?"

"Come here!" she shouted. "And bring that meter thing with you!"

"I'm not putting it back!" he argued as he came through the door.

"Just bring it here!" ordered Florrie, now on her knees, eyes hard in concentration.

He brought it, in the hope of five bob, and fitted it back into position. After a moment Florrie lifted it to her lips and blew through one of the pipes. Then, turning it round, she blew through the other. A kind of smile crumpled her biscuity face.

"Have you got any rubber tubing?"

"Aye," said Harry, mystified. "But I'm not putting it back!"

"Bring some here."

Harry, scratching his head, went to get it. A row broke out upstairs.

"Mam!" came a voice.

"What?"

"She's in my bed!"

"Get to sleep!"

"She's in my bed, Mam!"

"No, I'm not, Mam!" came another voice.

Florrie dropped the meter and flew up the stairs. Slaps, cries and tears were followed by silence.

When she came down Harry was standing stupidly in the hall, rubber tubing in his hands. Florrie took it from him and fitted it on to the pipes, this way and that, then used two lengths to reconnect the meter. She turned on the main tap.

"Go and put the cooker on," she said, looking up at Harry.

He went to do that and Florrie, fascinated, watched the little pointer spin round its dial.

"Put it off now!" she called, disconnecting the tubing and turning the meter to face the wall, then reconnecting it. For a minute she paused, frowned, then went to her handbag for a mirror.

"Put it on again!" she shouted.

Harry did as he was bid.

With an expression of extreme satisfaction, Florrie again watched the dial, now reflected in the mirror which she held against the inside back wall of the cupboard. This time the pointer was going round backwards. She called her husband.

"See that!" she said when he came to stand behind her.

"Aye. So what?"

"So no more gas bills, you stupid sod!"

"Eh? How, like?"

Florrie demonstrated by showing him that if the pointer went backwards when she reversed the meter, the counters would register less gas used. After three demonstrations, it dawned on Harry. He laughed. This was a kick in the arse for Authority. Better than taking a pickaxe to a telephone box.

"But we'll never have to let it register less than the previous reading," Florrie warned, "or they'll find us out. Because then, they'd owe us money!"

After the pubs had closed, the lads drifted in. Florrie told them all about it. They thought it was funny. Some of the lads had drink with them. They shared it out. Everybody had some. When it was finished Florrie got some more from behind the cupboard. The Moons got roaring drunk. They sang noisily. The bairns upstairs cried. A neighbour told the Police.

Harry answered the door.

"Keep the noise down!" the policemen said.

And Harry, laughing, said, "Aye!" and, because he was happy, he didn't hit them.

Nobody missed Ernie.

"They're up to something," said one upright, uniformed guardian of the law.

"Keep an eye on the twats," muttered his buddy.

"Aye," was the profound reply.

And they strode out of the ghetto, their eyes flitting nervously from side to side.

Chocolate, the Moons' enormous two-tone brown mongrel, watched them go and, snarling softly to himself, loped slyly back to the house. He'd got their scent.

It was a pity his doggy sensitivities weren't so acutely partial to the olfactory appeal of natural gas, for when Harry Moon had kicked the gas meter a hairline crack had formed in the supply pipe. Not where it was visible above the composition floor, but in a joint connecting it to the mains beneath and from which a minute but constant flow of gas began to seep into the sealed space under the Moon's house.

Chapter Five

Monday morning found the treasurer defiant. He had concluded that his best course was to ignore the events of the wine and cheese party, stick rigidly to his original plans, continue to develop his new image and cultivate good relations with his staff. Saturday may well have been a setback, but it wasn't the end of the world. Paddy Kean had had his moment of glory, and it was over.

After all, reasoned Postlethwaite as he drove to work in his bashed-in car, he was the man the staff would be seeing every day from now on. They'd probably never set eyes on Kean again. Postlethwaite doubted, in fact, if anyone would even remember the old deputy's name in a couple of weeks.

Cheered by this thought, he parked the Triumph on the forecourt of the Monk Garage and walked from there to the town hall. He was late in arriving, but not as late as Arnold Locock.

The new junior accounts clerk had been late before leaving the house – he guessed that nobody would complain on his first day – and then lost himself twice within the town hall. By the time he found the treasurer's office Postlethwaite had already begun to sort the mail.

Arnold, of course, was expecting to find himself working for Paddy Kean. It was Paddy who had interviewed him and signed his letter of appointment. The subtle distinction between borough treasurer and deputy borough treasurer was lost on the new junior.

Had the pub across the road not been closed for alterations he might, of course, have been told by Fenwick Fancourt of the treasurer's identity and probably given a description, but Arnold and his friends hadn't had a drink together for over three weeks, not since the night he'd written his application. They'd always met at the same pub and nobody had thought to suggest an alternative. Pub loyalty is a powerful emotion.

So is a sense of territorial rights. And Postlethwaite felt strongly that these had been infringed when, without the preamble of a polite knock, his office door was thrown open and a shapeless youth grasping a three-page letter in one callused hand and an ash-laden cigarette in the other, shambled into the office.

Postlethwaite raised an enquiring eyebrow. Arnold flicked his cigarette towards the hearth and sat down. After staring at Postlethwaite for a couple of seconds, he spoke dully.

"Hello, I'm supposed to meet Mr Kean."

Postlethwaite's mouth gave a convulsive twitch at the sound of the name but he kept his voice normal.

"May I enquire who you are?"

"Oh, I start work here this morning," replied Arnold, waving the letter vaguely in the direction of the treasurer. "This letter says I should meet the treasurer in his office."

"Well," said Postlethwaite, seizing the opportunity, "you've met him!"

Arnold stopped waving the letter and looked thoughtful.

"I know I have," he said slowly, as if speaking to a person of drastically subnormal intelligence. "I met him at the interview."

"You've met him now!" Postlethwaite's eye glinted. "I'm the borough treasurer."

Arnold looked puzzled.

"You weren't at the interview," he pointed out.

"No. But let me assure you. My name is Christopher Postlethwaite and I am the treasurer of Mankley. My ex-deputy, to whom you have referred, is now retired!"

Arnold thumbed through the pages of the letter and a show of understanding slowly passed over his face.

"This must be your name printed at the top then!" he exclaimed.

"It is!" stressed Postlethwaite, losing grip on his new image and sneering. "You haven't made a very good start, have you, Mr Locock?"

The treasurer then launched into a critical assessment of Arnold's progress so far. Consisting mainly of clichés and long words, to Arnold it was boring; but he gave a good impression of concentration. So good that Postlethwaite was disarmed. He ended the harangue on a quieter note and moved from behind his desk towards the young man, intending to terminate their meeting on a note of goodwill.

"So we can start, as it were, from scratch," he smiled, oozing magnanimity, "as if, at this moment, we were meeting for the first time ..."

He offered his hand.

But Arnold, who had actually stopped listening quite a few sentences earlier, misunderstood the gesture, and, as there was no ashtray within reach, dropped his fag end into the treasurer's open palm.

*

At lunchtime, just as in the week before, Postlethwaite set out for the garage, but it was a changed Fenwick Fancourt who grudgingly attended him.

In the first place, Fancourt had achieved his sale so Postlethwaite no longer excited challenge; in the second, Fancourt's manager had brought to the salesman's attention an extensive list of defects found in Postlethwaite's trade-in car on which the salesman had allowed the full list price and, in the third, the sales director of the company had that morning telephoned with a three-month ultimatum of dismissal if the sales figures didn't very soon build up to something approaching average.

Fenwick, with head in hands, was mulling over the situation as Postlethwaite arrived.

"G'morning!" Postlethwaite greeted him breezily.

"It's afternoon," replied Fenwick, flatly.

"About the car, the Triumph, seems to be something wrong with the gears."

"Better see the mechanic then," muttered the salesman.

91

"It's still under guarantee, you know! You should deal with it really!" the treasurer whined.

Fenwick sighed. He got no commission on repairs. Grumbling under his breath, he pushed past Postlethwaite, went to the forecourt and checked the car's gear change. It was crisp and precise.

"Nothing wrong with that!" he muttered as he got out of the driving seat. "I suppose you were going to try and claim under the guarantee for bashing in your back end. Thought you'd blame it on faulty gears. It's dishonest, that!"

Postlethwaite was mortified. That, of course, had been his intention. It had seemed quite a clever idea. But for him, the borough treasurer, to be accused of dishonesty by a car salesman, especially one who was friendly with his new junior, was horrifying.

"No, no, no, no!" he stuttered. "Not at all, not at all!"

"Look," said Fancourt, calmly. "Don't get worked up about it. I'm not going to call the police or anything. Everyone tries it with Triumphs – it's with the gear positions being so close together." The car salesman curled his lip. "Don't know why a fellow in your position buys a cheap little car like this, anyhow. They can't take the bumps. Not like the car I sold last month. Jaguar it was. Beautiful!" Fenwick drooled at the memory. "Coincidence really, it was a bloke from the town hall who bought it. Must have a good job to afford a car like that. Now... what was his name...?"

Fenwick frowned and drummed his fingers on the battered boot lid of the Triumph. Postlethwaite tried to change the subject but Fenwick ignored him.

"You'd probably know him," he persevered. "Little fellow, smartly dressed, silver hair... I've got it! Kean! That's what his name was. Paddy Kean! Do you know him?"

Postlethwaite shook his head as he backed away. He muttered about an urgent appointment, then disappeared.

Fenwick put his hands in his pockets, gave the back wheel of the Triumph a hefty kick and, whistling merrily, returned to his office.

He'd upset somebody. That cheered him up.

*

By visiting the garage the treasurer missed an interesting spectacle. Opposite the town hall a group of workmen had arrived at the pub, removed the 'SOLD' notice and unscrewed the old name sign.

A silver Jaguar drew up and an ornament was removed from its boot. There was some discussion and then a trolley, on which there rested a marble plinth, was pulled from the pub doorway.

Into a shaped depression on the upper surface of the plinth the men poured steaming glue on which they carefully positioned the ornament.

The Jaguar pulled away and the trolley was returned to the pub.

There was only one witness from the Treasurer's Department to observe this – David Smith – who watched through the office window with great interest and strangely mixed feelings of excitement and embarrassment.

*

Postlethwaite's head was bowed low as he entered his office. To suggest he was on the brink of insanity would probably be an exaggeration, but mention of Paddy's name twice so early in the day had jolted his equilibrium.

There was a nervous twitch at the side of his mouth as, on impulse, he sprang from his desk to open the door to the outer office a fraction and peer through with one eye, as if expecting to see Kean sphinxing it with his pencil; but only the tidy and efficient David Smith stared back in bewilderment. The treasurer gave a queer little smile and closed the door softly. The reassuring sight of Smith restored an aspect of normality. He turned his mind to some notes he'd made about certain changes he intended. They were to do with the layout of the outer office.

After a while, he called for his new deputy.

"I've been looking at the positioning of the office furniture," Postlethwaite said smoothly, handing a rough-drawn plan to Smith.

"Yes, Borough Treasurer?"

"I've drawn up a plan. As you will see, it makes everything more convenient for the staff. More efficient!" – he tapped Smith on the shoulder – "Ergonomic!"

"I'm sure the staff will appreciate that," said the loyal Smith, lying through his teeth. Ergonomic (whatever that meant) or not, he knew damn well that the staff would loathe any changes to the office. The desks hadn't been moved for sixty years.

Only Birstin and Locock were willing to help rearrange the office. The others refused point-blank and milled around rebelliously while the work was carried out. The treasurer's popularity – already of the 'un' variety – reached a new low. Later in the afternoon, when he came to inspect the alterations, the atmosphere was heavy with disapproval.

But Postlethwaite was not to be discouraged. The rearrangement of the office was part of his new order. No amount of sullen disagreement would deter him. He intended to change everything that reminded him of past days. He would lay the ghost.

A little later, Smith knocked gently on the treasurer's door.

"Come in!" called Postlethwaite, guiltily stuffing the *Financial Times* into his desk drawer.

"Only a small problem, Borough Treasurer. Sorry to trouble you with it."

"Problem? That's what I'm here for, Mr Smith!"

"It's about the new layout. Apparently, the tea lady can't get her trolley between the desks."

"Can't she?"

"So it appears."

This was a possibility unforeseen by Postlethwaite. He scratched his head, pursed his lips, grunted, fiddled with his tie, stood up, raised an eyebrow at Smith, sat down, coughed, and, after what looked like considerable thought, walked over to the window.

Smith, in the face of what might well be some sort of professional instruction, wasn't sure what to do, so limited his activities to shifting his weight from foot to foot, as he hoped would be proper for a deputy.

"Do you think I ought to see her?" Postlethwaite suddenly enquired.

"I'm not sure. It might help," said Smith, though, for the life of him, he couldn't see how. The only way to put the situation right was to move two of the desks back to their original positions.

"You'd better bring her in then."

"Into your office?"

"Yes. I'll see her in here. You can sit in the armchair. We'll both hear what she has to say," said Postlethwaite. "You can take notes."

"Certainly, Borough Treasurer. I'll get her."

A minute later, an attractive but flustered woman of about forty stood before the treasurer's desk, dishcloth over her arm and regulation catering department overall adorning her rounded but appealing figure.

Postlethwaite was at his most accommodating.

"Bit of a problem, I understand?" he asked as Smith settled himself in the armchair behind the woman, his notepad on his knee.

"Well, I can't get my trolley into the office, if that's what you call a problem!" the woman replied, staring with interest at the treasurer.

"In that case, I'll have to see what can be done to assist you," smiled Postlethwaite. "We must have the staff refreshed by your efforts. I will see to it personally that tomorrow there is adequate access for your chariot of victuals."

The tea lady sniffed.

"Is that all?" she asked, unimpressed by Postlethwaite's picturesque vocabulary.

"Er... yes... for now," replied the treasurer, realising with some surprise that it was.

"Can I go and get on, then?" she asked, waiting for Smith to stand up and open the door. Smith, however, was too busy trying to spell 'victuals'.

"Yes, yes, of course, Mrs... er, I'm sorry, I'm afraid I don't know your name," stuttered Postlethwaite vaguely.

The woman stared him straight in the eye.

"You wouldn't. I just started this morning. The name's Mary," she said, "Mary Kean. My husband used to work here!"

*

"I didn't think he would look like that!"

"Like what?" muttered Paddy.

"You know, normal-looking. He didn't look as evil as he is. Funny, he didn't say anything when I told him who I was – just went a weird grey colour and started to bang his desk drawers in and out. The other man..."

"Smith," said Paddy.

"... showed me out. He seemed a bit embarrassed about something."

"I'll bet he was! You don't have to do the job, you know."

"Rubbish!" said Mary, lightly flicking her duster at Paddy. "I'll enjoy it. It's good for me."

She went behind the bar counter to wipe glasses and bottles. She had no intention of giving up her part-time job at the town hall. It was a way to keep in touch with anything that might affect Paddy's future. All sorts of information came the way of tea ladies. Besides, it had taken six months of being pleasant to various councillors to get the job in the first place, a chore for which Mary intended to get a full return.

"Where do you want this thing putting?" shouted a perspiring workman from the other end of the bar counter as he struggled with a heavy marble column.

Paddy went to help move it near the entrance, to the position he had chosen. It was stood upright and screwed firmly to its base in the floor.

"What's it for?" asked the workman.

"It's to stand that on."

The man looked disapprovingly at the ornament still resting on the trolley.

"We'll need a block and tackle to get that thing up there!" he grumbled as he went off in search of his mates.

Paddy looked around. The place was a mess. He hated disorder. So much to be done, and only a week to go.

There was a sharp rat-a-tat on the door and Archie Carrigan squeezed his stomach past the ornament-laden trolley.

"Bloody hell! Bloody hell! What in God's name's that?" he asked, staggering backwards and pointing his walking stick at Paddy's hideous retirement present.

Paddy's face relaxed at the alderman's typically bluff arrival and he called to Mary, who was still behind the counter, "A large whisky, love! Without water!"

"Thank you, thank you," said Archie, pulling up a wooden crate and sitting on it. "Most welcome." He gave a solemn grunt, then suddenly announced, "I've swung it for you, lad!"

"Good," the novice landlord replied. "That's one worry less."

"Aye," continued Archie, "I had a chat to him, a chat to him. Reasonable enough fellow really; he thought your new name for the pub a great improvement, a great improvement. So, informally, of course, you can consider it fixed."

"I'm grateful to you."

"Aye," responded Archie, draining his glass.

"I think Paddy's worried that we won't be ready in time for the opening on Monday," said Mary, hoping that Archie would give reassurance.

He didn't let her down.

"Looks just about ready now, I'd say," he observed, looking around. "Anyhow, my lad, you'd better be ready because I've got some news for you! I've managed to persuade the mayor to come. And most of the council members. The buggers'll go anywhere for a free drink!"

He looked over at Mary as he said this and placed his empty glass on the counter. With a wry smile she refilled it and Archie nodded his appreciation.

"And I've got the vicar coming. Best play safe, play safe. And, best of all – now, are you listening? – best of all, I've spoken to the manager of the theatre. Do you know him? Interesting man, one way and another. Calls himself Jacob S Cracker – likes to see his name around the place. Compensates the poor sod for not being the world's greatest actor. He always wanted to be an actor, an actor. Not much hope for him, though, what with his stutter and his lisp, to say nothing of his drinking habits. He can hardly stand most of the time. Anyhow, I thought I'd do you some good. And he's agreed, he's agreed! We're having the cast of next week's play come to the pub next Monday. And Gloria Lessingdale – Gloria Lessingdale, mind you! – has undertaken to officially open it for you! Now, there's a scoop, there's a scoop! So we can get the press along! Television as well! Bit of publicity! Eh? Eh? Can't do your pub any harm! Nowt like it! Must say, though, it's a funny name you've chosen, a funny name. I mean," Archie lowered his voice, "why do you want to call it The Bone Idol?"

Paddy and Mary exchanged glances and smiled knowingly at each other.

"Too long a story for a Monday night, Archie," said Paddy.

*

Arnold had never experienced anything like it. He'd always heard that people in the town hall didn't do much in the way of work, but this was unbelievable.

It had taken only five minutes for Smith to explain the duties of the junior accounts clerk and Arnold, hardly the type to encourage work for himself, had waited to be told more in due course. But he wasn't told any more. By the Wednesday afternoon he realised that what he'd been told was it. It was hardly a job at all.

Having come from private industry, where employees were more or less expected to earn their wages, the attitudes in local government baffled him. Most people he'd worked with in the past had been damned glad to be in work and had done everything possible to stay that way. But not here. This was a fantasy world. You couldn't get sacked.

He calculated he'd be able to do what his new job entailed in about two hours a week. It worried him. He sought advice.

"Excuse me, Mr Smith," he said, "is there anything more I'm expected to do apart from what you told me on Monday?"

"No," replied Smith brightly, "there's the Swing-Bridge Tolls Book, the Notifiable Diseases Book, the Ground Rents Register, the Petty Cash, and the Sundry Debtors – that's it!"

He paused to smile reassuringly at Arnold, then went on.

"Every fifth week, of course, you'll be expected to work a Saturday morning as part of the rota."

"Does it pay overtime?" asked Arnold, with interest.

"Oh, no! But you get a morning off the week following. We never claim overtime if we can get time off in lieu – unless someone is sick or on holiday; then, in order to protect the person who's off, we have a duty to charge overtime."

"I see," said Arnold, thoughtfully.

Smith opened the top drawer of his desk and extracted a green-backed booklet.

"Here," he said, "read this – it'll answer a lot of questions for you."

Arnold took the booklet and returned to his seat. Idly, he flicked through the pages until he came to a clause headed 'Special Leave'. He read it carefully, then turned to the front cover: 'SCHEME of Salaries and Conditions of Service for Administrative, Clerical and Technical Staffs'.

He would study this.

It struck him as a document of considerable potential.

*

Postlethwaite felt very alone. Still his wife hadn't spoken.

She'd looked after the house, cooked, cleaned, gone to work, dealt with correspondence, everything as normal – but she wouldn't speak.

And every night since Saturday she'd gone to bed in nothing but her hat. Postlethwaite couldn't decide what it was that disturbed him most: the regular sight of his wife's naked body or the feathers in the hat which tickled his nose if he turned over in bed.

He wondered if she was hinting at something; like the time years ago when she'd taken to serving up food still in its tin or packet, just because, in response to her request to go out for a meal, he'd said that food is intrinsically the same no matter how it is served or prepared.

That was clear enough, even obvious, but what she could mean by prancing stark naked from dressing table to bed, with her head encased in felt and feathers, was too subtle for Postlethwaite.

Anyhow, he thought, his wife was always doing weird things. He sometimes wondered more about her sanity than her subtlety.

At least, at the town hall these days, nothing much was subtle. Not that it brought the treasurer any joy. Unsubtlety was an art form with Mary Kean, for instance. She was about as subtle as a claw hammer, bashing her way around the place with her tea trolley like a demented earth-mother dispensing noisy goodwill to all and sundry. Her popularity sickened Postlethwaite, but fortunately she never had need to visit his office. He didn't indulge in tea breaks; except when he had visitors and could charge the cost to the council's hospitality account.

And it was the thought of hospitality that gave him an idea.

Since the alterations to the layout of the office the staff had become silently antagonistic (except Arnold, who was totally unsusceptible to atmosphere, and David, who knew which side his bread was buttered on); indeed the mood was so bitter that Postlethwaite had given consideration to changing the office back to its original state, but that was against the principles of his new order. Another route to improving relationships would have to be found.

Hospitality might be the answer. He'd buy them something. Perhaps his wife was hinting for him to buy her something. Maybe he could kill two birds with one stone: invite the staff out to dinner and bring his wife as well.

He telephoned a few restaurants for quotations. Amazed and unbelieving at their replies, he dismissed that idea. Yet, he felt he was on the right track. He needed to get everyone together in an informal setting.

He went to his office window – a habit when in deep thought – and through it saw a prominent notice on the building across the street: 'OPENING MONDAY', it advertised.

Curious, he called Arnold.

"What's that over the road?" he asked.

"A pub," said Arnold suspiciously.

"Mmm. I'd like you to go over there and see what it's like. See if it's suitable for entertaining, what kind of food they serve up. See if you can get a price list."

"Righto!" replied Arnold, glad of an opportunity to get out of the office for a while.

"Of course, I don't expect you to sample its wares," joked the treasurer.

"What?" enquired Arnold.

"It's all right," sighed Postlethwaite, ushering the junior to the door, "off you go."

Off Arnold went.

As he crossed the street, a workman came out of the pub doorway.

"Hello!" said Arnold.

"Oh, hello," grunted the workman.

"I've come to find out what this new pub's like."

"It's smashing! All new!"

"Are they going to serve food?"

"I think so. Pub lunches and that. They've got a kitchen."

"It opens Monday, doesn't it?"

"Aye. They're going to sell everything at pre-war prices on Monday. You should come!" enthused the workman.

"I will," said Arnold keenly. "What time does it open?"

"About twelve."

"I'll come over in my lunch hour, then."

Arnold was pleased to learn that the pub was reopening. He had missed his Friday-night drinks and the company of his friends. He wondered if they could come next Monday lunchtime.

He looked at his watch. He'd been out for only a few minutes, so reckoned there was time to call on Midnight and Fenwick. It was not as if Arnold had a lot of work to do in the office. So he visited first the metalworks, then the Monk Garage.

He was surprised, back at the town hall an hour later, that the treasurer took such a dim view of how long he had taken. Arnold didn't like to point out that, as he had nothing to do anyway, there was little difference between his being in the office or out of it.

But Postlethwaite was pleased with the one piece of information that appealed to his sense of proper economy. Pre-war prices were not to be sneezed at. He now knew what he was going to do. He telephoned the garage and asked to speak to its manager. It didn't get him anywhere. The car was still going to take three weeks to repair.

"I need it for Monday!" said Postlethwaite firmly.

"And you can have it!" replied the manager. "But it'll still be bashed in at the back!".

The treasurer rang off angrily, then dialled the garage's head office to speak to the sales director. He explained his problem and, almost conversationally, mentioned that the council would shortly be advertising for a supplier of vehicles to the Engineer's Department. The sales manager responded, equally conversationally, by promising that Postlethwaite's car would be delivered to him completely repaired, at no charge, Monday next.

*

On Thursday, staff were surprised to find on each of their desks a formal invitation to join the treasurer and his wife for drinks and lunch at the new pub across the road at twelve the following Monday.

They discussed the invitation quietly among themselves.

None of them would go, they decided, but they wouldn't tell the treasurer their decision until the Monday morning, so to cause him the most inconvenience, and teach him not to alter their desks around.

Malcolm Birstin was in something of a quandary. The allure of free food and drink was a mighty strong temptation, but he wasn't brave enough to be the only one in the office to accept the invitation.

*

During the course of that week, David Smith had seen a number of vehicles of one sort or another stop opposite the new pub, but on Friday he saw the one he had been waiting for: The Shine-On Neon Lighting Company. His sense of excitement was intense as the man from the van chalked an outline on an enormous name board. Sweat broke out on Smith's brow as he watched the fitting-up of the biggest neon sign in the town.

He sat down. For the first time in his career, he knew something nobody else in the office knew. The weight of responsibility terrified him. He clenched his hands between his legs. He was bursting to say something but, torn between loyalty to his chief and partisanship with the staff, he simply sat clenching his hands.

"What's the matter with you?" muttered Stan Scrimshire, looking gruffly over his spectacles at the tortured deputy. "Got a hernia or something?"

It was no good. Smith was not a man of iron-willed self-control.

"Have you seen over the road?" he asked, breathlessly.

Stan looked up.

"No, I haven't," he replied loudly.

"Sh! Keep your voice down!" Smith whispered, burying his head in a pile of papers.

"What do you say?" shouted Stan, who was slightly deaf.

His voice carried as far as Doreen's desk. She came over.

"What are you two whispering about?" she asked.

David groaned inwardly. It was too late now.

"It's the pub across the road," he said. "I think Mr Kean must be its manager or something. Look!"

Doreen stood on tiptoe, stretched up and peered through the window. Then she slapped a hand across her mouth to stifle an hysterical squeak.

"It could be coincidence!" she said, wide-eyed.

"It's not!" declared David. "I saw him carrying in that bloody awful ornament we bought him. It must have been Monday when he did that!"

"God! How embarrassing!" said Doreen seriously. "But I'll tell you what!" she continued more brightly, "I for one, will definitely be accepting the chief's invitation to lunch next Monday – I wouldn't miss it now for all the tea in China!"

And, once the word got about the office, everyone agreed conspiratorially to do the same as Doreen. Oh, yes! They'd all go now.

Of course, Malcolm Birstin, who was out of the office auditing the town's public conveniences, knew nothing of this turn of events. He had frequently been out of late. Since Paddy's retirement two weeks ago and the simultaneous promotion of David Smith, Birstin had at last found time to do some auditing.

And he had devised for himself a clear brief: cash control and cost cutting! He believed the latter to be an automatic consequence of the former, so his method was simple: he went through the expense vouchers, extracted anything that didn't have a receipt attached, then descended unceremoniously on whoever had had the cash.

He had plenty of scope. Most officers of the council with direct responsibility for a section received fixed expenses of one sort or another. It was a way of saving paperwork and, as most council employees were of known integrity, there was little risk in so expedient a system. It accorded the officers concerned a measure of trust and, as the various fixed amounts were rarely increased – and then only by the most detailed of applications – a measure of thrift was imposed.

But such a system did not accord with Birstin's ideas. No scope there for the principle of cash control as he understood it. Or for the career accountant.

His first victim was Emlyn Cruddle, the town officer, whose duties included driving the council's Daimler limousine.

Now Cruddle, whatever else he was, was honest. And his expenses, a fixed amount of three pounds per week – which he had drawn from petty cash for the past fifteen years – were paid him in lieu of petrol, oil and repairs.

Fifteen years ago this amount was more than adequate, even generous, but prices had risen, and it was only by Cruddle's ingenuity and mechanical know-how that the stately old car was kept on the road. Cruddle didn't mind. The car was his responsibility. He took pride in its condition. In fact, he looked after it as if it were his own.

"What are these for?" the auditor demanded to know, waving a fistful of vouchers under Cruddle's sizeable nose.

"What do you think?" was the prompt defensive response.

"I don't think anything… yet!" threatened Birstin.

"Fuck off!" said Cruddle, a rising inflexion in his voice and a rising heavy-duty mole wrench in his hand. "Or I'll wrap this round your neck!"

Birstin fled. The town officer gave a tight little grin. He wasn't worried. He'd always kept a careful account of his expenses. But he wasn't going to tell Birstin that. Cruddle was answerable to the town clerk, not some ill-mannered minion of the treasurer.

But, later in the day, after Birstin had spoken to Postlethwaite, and Postlethwaite had spoken to the town clerk's idiot assistant, and a few points had been made between them about maintaining properly authenticated accounts, the auditor, armed with an impressive letter of authority, returned to the fray.

And Cruddle's heavy-duty mole wrench didn't help.

He lost his weekly allowance, and with it the little touch of trust and respect it implied. Instead, he was given a pad of order forms, a logbook and a rubber stamp. No more would he simply draw his three pounds each week, bank it, then buy whatever he required for the car from his own pocket. Everything now was to be channelled through the Treasurer's Department.

So Birstin got cost control. He had struck a blow for the advancement of his profession.

Cruddle would have liked to strike a few blows, but decided to bide his time.

A similar episode occurred a few days later at the council morgue where the keeper found himself encumbered with a new Birstin-inspired stock control system. Something of an extravagance, he thought, looking at the bloated body dragged that morning from the river.

And again, at the animal shelter, the Swing-Bridge tollbooth – where tolls had in fact been abolished in 1936 – and the crematorium: the responsible officers found themselves with paperwork never previously thought necessary.

With the public conveniences, however, it was different. The inspector in charge had a system already so cluttered with paper there was nothing Birstin could introduce.

But here his training came to the rescue.

Obviously, with all that paperwork, the inspector must be hiding something. So Birstin decided to carry out a full audit. He would do a physical cash count at every public convenience just ahead of the inspector on his weekly rounds, then compare his totals with those on the official returns.

On the pretext of examining the possibility of securing for the inspector a car allowance, he soon discovered the route this officer regularly took, and organised his cash count accordingly.

He headed his audit notes: 'Physical Cash Count' – he liked using the word 'Physical', it made him feel he was doing something manly.

So, on Friday, while the staff were discussing the exciting prospect of a further confrontation between Postlethwaite and Kean, Birstin was counting pennies from the doors of Proglund Street public lavatory.

He wasn't missed by the others. Least of all by Postlethwaite, who sauntered into the office. The treasurer was too uplifted, flattered and overwhelmed by the staff's sudden mood of goodwill. Of course, thought Postlethwaite, his policies were paying off. Firmness coupled with generosity could never fail. Why, the staff even laughed at one of his little jokes. Almost hysterical they were. He would relate that one to his wife when he got home. It might encourage her to speak to him.

But when he got home, there was no wife to tell it to. She had gone to her mother's for the weekend. She'd left a note. Postlethwaite took heart from this. At least, now she was communicating.

He drew wide the curtains to make use of the last rays of light filtering weakly through the clouds, and mindlessly sat in a chair.

It was too late in the year for mowing the lawn. Perhaps, tomorrow, he'd look for some weeds.

He wondered what he would do on Sunday.

*

At the back of the hospital, Chocolate lay low, muzzle rested on paws, listening, sniffing.

This had become his regular beat on Fridays. Sometimes he was lucky. At the front of the building he had checked that the big car had gone then, like a wraith, had padded to the back.

His timing was perfect. Out came two porters.

"Is that bloody dog around?"

"Can't see it!"

"Got away with a gangrenous foot last week!"

"Probably poisoned the bugger!"

Chocolate instinctively lowered his belly to the damp grass. This was the tricky bit. He lifted his scarred nose and sniffed, deep and long.

The breeze changed. He lost the scent. But, to his delight, another odour assailed his senses. It was Jess from the post office.

Chocolate savoured the airborne message – she'd be due in three days. He had missed her last time round: two days solid waiting on the pavement, turned his back for a second to chase a passing cyclist, out comes Jess and, quick as a flash, that cross-eyed terrier was in there.

These idle thoughts were banished as the breeze reverted to its former flow. Chocolate cocked his ears – or, more correctly, one ear; the other lay flat: ripped strips of mangled fur.

The coast was clear. In a bound he was up, snarling and slavering, to smash over the plastic dustbin, bounce off its rubber lid, and sink his fangs into whatever the day's offering might be.

But today, literally, he bit off more than he could chew. This was bigger than your average bone.

He tugged and heaved, spreading his forelegs, savagely jerking his head to and fro. The departing porters looked around, shouted and ran forward. Chocolate's lips writhed and a bloodcurdling warning rose from his chest. The men hesitated. Chocolate's prize came free. For a second he dropped it, gave a threatening charge towards the men, then trotted back, snatched it up and loped off across the lawn.

The porters watched him go.

"Are you going after him?"

"Like hell! I've got a wife and kids! You go!"

"Not bloody likely! If the patients see us chasing that thing with an amputated leg in its fangs it'll set the buggers back for months!"

Chocolate made good speed but his jaw ached, and the limb kept bending at the knee, kicking his flank as he ran.

He stopped to rest. Again the breeze brought a message. His tail wagged. He sensed clinking bottles. Not just any clinking bottles. These were clinking bottles in a string bag rubbing against a dirty green, lightweight raincoat worn by a slightly inebriated Florrie.

The dog took a better grip on the leg and again set off. He soon caught sight of his mistress weaving along the pavement and overtook her at the shops, just before she entered the ghetto. Circling her once, the leg knocking against disgusted passers-by, he got ten yards ahead, dropped his tiring load, sat on his haunches and proudly barked before leaping at her face and licking it.

"Eeh! Hello, Chocolate, me bairn!" cried Florrie. Then, seeing the leg, she screamed, "What the hell's that?"

Chocolate cowered at the change of tone, and ran to place a protective paw on the limb.

"Away with you!" yelled Florrie. "Get out of it! Get that bloody thing out of here! My God! What'll people think!"

Chocolate knew when she was serious. Grabbing his hard-won leg he disappeared with a bound into the line of back gardens that ran behind the houses.

*

"Hey! Look at that!" exclaimed Harry next morning as he looked through the kitchen window. "There's a foot sticking out of the soil!"

Florrie didn't hesitate. With a curse she booted the sleeping Chocolate out of the back door and belted down the garden path.

Taking a spade, she hacked at the stony earth around the half-buried leg. Then, looking faint, she stopped and her eyes glazed over. Howling, she ran back to the kitchen and pulled at Harry's arm.

"Come and look!" she wailed. "I should've known that dog was tryin' to tell us somethin'! Dumb animals indeed! They know more than us when the chips are down! Touched by God they are!"

She ranted on, pulling the reluctant Harry down the path to the source of her hysteria. Chocolate kept his distance.

"See?" Florrie nudged her husband with her elbow. "See that scar?"

Harry studied the extruding limb for a moment, then took the spade and unearthed the whole leg.

"Aye!" he said. "It's Ernie's! I wondered why the bugger didn't bring his pay home!"

"But where's the rest of him?" Florrie cried, bursting into an uncharacteristic flood of tears.

She found out later in the day.

As soon as Chocolate had seen Harry unearth the leg, he had loped away to the playground to terrorise the children. But this amusement had its limitations: the kids were getting used to him, they didn't panic anymore.

Feeling lonesome he returned home. Once in the back garden he came to a stiff-legged halt. Where his bone had been there was now only a dug-over mound of clay and stones.

He sniffed the air. Reassured, he lay down.

It was not too long before Florrie came out to throw an empty whisky bottle into the bin. As she lifted the lid, a beckoning aroma of dug-up leg wafted over to Chocolate. He stirred, saw Florrie, and with a desperate urge to tell her something, tried to look winning. Not easy for a dog with his features.

"Aye..." she crooned, "you know more than you can tell us, don't you, me bairn?" – and her cigarette ash fell on his nose, making him sneeze.

"Trying to talk, are you?" asked Florrie, bending down to him.

Chocolate gave her a half-hearted lick and rolled over on his back, a pleading expression in his brown eyes.

Florrie didn't respond.

The dog got to his feet, cocked his head on one side, stamped his paws playfully on the ground, ran round in an eccentric circle, and sat down again, giving a yelp.

"I know," moaned Florrie, "you're tryin' to tell us where our Ernie is."

Chocolate was doing nothing of the sort. He was trying to tell the old bag he was starving and wanted his leg out of the bin.

But Florrie just chuntered on drunkenly.

'Sod this,' thought Chocolate, 'I'm off to the hospital to see if I can get another one.' Suiting action to thought, he trotted to the corner of the house.

Florrie's eyes followed him.

Giving her a last chance to open the bin, Chocolate paused, looked back at her and whined.

"Are you goin' to take us to him, then?" gasped his mistress, busily attempting to fasten her pinny.

Chocolate watched.

'That's it,' he thought, giving up hope, and off he trotted along the street. The drunken Florrie wobbled after him. He saw her over his shoulder as he turned a corner. Increasing his pace, he ran past the shops to the footway leading to the hospital grounds.

"Wait for me!" called Florrie behind him, coughing and spluttering.

Chocolate heard her cry and, spurred on by it to escape, he veered on to the hospital lawn, fair racing towards the back entrance where the porters usually dumped their titbits.

Florrie, undaunted, flew after him, her pinny loose and flapping round her neck, one stocking gathering at her ankle, spindly legs in tartan slippers splashing through muddy puddles.

By the time she reached the back entrance Chocolate had come to the conclusion that he was out of luck. He sniffed around the doors for a while, then sat on his haunches.

Florrie, knackered and looking like something that had been dragged from a midden, sat down beside him.

"Is this where he is, then? Is our Ernie here?"

Just then the door behind her swung open and a porter backed through, pulling a trolley filled high with rubbish. Chocolate prepared to beat a retreat but felt unable to leave his mistress – a confusion of interests which produced an involuntary growl.

The porter spun round in shock and, seeing the canine Quasimodo, made a dive for the doors. Once safely behind them he made straight for the administration block. Five minutes later he returned with a pale, bespectacled young man clutching a damp handkerchief to his nose. They stood at a side window overlooking the back entrance where Florrie sat leaning against the wall, apparently sleeping, while Chocolate stretched up on hind legs to examine the contents of the rubbish trolley.

"Well? What do you expect me to do about it?" sniffed the administrator. "Just get rid of them!"

The porter had half-expected that response.

Nervously, he eased open one of the doors about an inch and shouted through the crack, "Hey, you!"

At the sound of the voice Chocolate stopped rummaging, dropped to his feet and gave a little whine. If he was nice to this man he might get another leg. He put his head on one side and cocked his sole controllable ear.

Encouraged by this, the porter came outside. The dog sat down expectantly.

"Hey!" the porter again shouted.

"I'm not deaf!" responded Florrie, who hadn't been sleeping at all, merely getting back her breath.

"Is that your dog?"

Florrie struggled to her feet.

"Aye, it is! A bloody fine dog an' all!" She hiccoughed and fell forward slightly, but saved herself by grabbing at the lapels of the porter's overall.

He stepped backwards, more under the onslaught of Florrie's breath than anything else.

"Well, you want to keep it under control," he said, trying not to inhale. "He pinched a leg from here yesterday!"

"He did!" said Florrie, regaining her balance. "And he brought it home where it belongs! That was my son's leg, y'know," she added tearfully. Then, looking up at the porter, she gave an anguished cry, "Where's the rest of him, mister?"

The porter, not unkindly, told Florrie to wait and went back into the hospital.

"I think I've solved your identity crisis," he announced to the administrator.

"What?"

"The lad who was brought in last weekend by that stupid-looking ambulance crew. His mother's outside. Apparently that dog that pinched the leg yesterday took it home and it turned out to be her son's..."

"For God's sake, shut up, man!" protested the administrator, his sodden handkerchief pressed to his nose. Why the staff should always be going on about sawn-off legs and blood and entrails he couldn't imagine. None of that had anything to do with administration. "You can bring her into the office."

The porter returned to Florrie and took her arm.

112

"Howway in, pet. We'll see if we can find your lad."

Chocolate, now back to grubbing about in the trolley, hadn't taken much notice of the porter's return. He was obviously part of the scenery round here. But when part of the scenery suddenly extended an arm to touch Florrie it was a different scenario. With a savagery that was awe-inspiring, he turned, baring his fangs, caught his dewclaw on the top of the trolley, overturned it on top of himself and, momentarily distracted by half a kipper, disappeared under twelve hundredweight of refuse.

"Aye," said Florrie as the porter yanked her rapidly through the doors, "very possessive is our Chocolate. One wrong move and he'd have your throat out!"

The porter, shaking, didn't doubt it.

The administrator overcame his revulsion at Florrie's appearance, established her name and that of her son, and derived some small satisfaction from knowing that, at least, his forms were now properly completed.

"... if it hadn't been for our Chocolate dragging that leg all the way home, we'd never have known. And he buried it in the garden to keep it safe. And Harry saw the foot stickin' out of the soil..."

A doctor arrived to revive the retching, sickly administrator and to lead Florrie along to the ward where Ernie lay. He was in a bad way and had been in a state of drug-induced unconsciousness since he had arrived – but he would recover.

*

"It's no good, Harry! I'll have to go to the police!"

"You'll not!"

"I'm tellin' you! Somebody blew him up! It's a crime to blow people up!"

"You're not goin' to the police! You can't trust them bastards! Me and the lads'll sort it out! We'll find out who did it!"

Desperately frustrated, Florrie got very drunk on Saturday night, and topped herself up on Sunday. And, on Monday morning, she had sunk half a bottle of sherry before breakfast.

Chapter Six

Mary rolled over and breathed softly into Paddy's ear.

"Somebody's knocking at the door," she whispered sleepily.

Paddy stirred, clenched his face and stuck a foot from under the blankets to feel the air.

"Come on, love," Mary breathed into his ear again, "wake up! It's eight o'clock!"

She switched on the bedside light.

Eight o'clock. That shocked Paddy out of bed. Throwing on his dressing gown, he stumbled downstairs and through the pub to the front door which was now being noisily kicked.

Withdrawing the heavy bolts he swung it open.

He should have guessed.

There, in the rain, stood Emlyn Cruddle. Paddy now knew why the doorbell hadn't been rung – the town officer wasn't tall enough to reach the bell push. And, in any case, Cruddle never unnecessarily took his hands out of his pockets.

Apart from his diminutive stature, Cruddle possessed other interesting physical characteristics: his head, for example, was completely flat – a shape well suited to his official peaked cap. And his body, disproportionately long for his height, was almost perfectly cylindrical. In fact, with his hands plunged deep in the pockets of his ankle-length mackintosh – a seemingly permanent article of clothing – he looked from three sides like nothing more than a drab, grey pillar box – an impression enhanced by his habit of appearing suddenly, always without notice and invariably without welcome, whenever required, without being observed in motion, as if sprouted from diseased seed into stunted growth by virtue of a duty to be done. And the square, lipless mouth, with its blackened teeth, could have passed muster easily as a receptacle designed for the receipt of Her Majesty's mail. Only the beak-like nose and vacant wall-eyes that surmounted it deterred the more observant from actually ramming their pools coupons down his throat.

"Hello, Emlyn," sighed Paddy, struggling to fasten a bow in the cord of his dressing gown. "I didn't expect you until later this morning."

Cruddle looked up at Paddy. Not that the landlord could tell. The town officer may well have got Paddy clearly in focus but, for all the world, his right eye was aimed at the top of the door frame while his left doggedly followed the progress of Big John, the Laughing Postman, now striding towards the pub.

"I've come to check the arrangements," croaked Cruddle, impatiently flapping his mackintosh. "Got to check that everything's all right for the mayor."

"Well," said Paddy, staring straight at the bridge of Cruddle's nose in the hope that he was looking the man in the eye, "you'd better give me an hour or two to get things sorted out. Come back at..."

It was too late.

The town officer was past the landlord and into the pub before he could be stopped, determined to avoid a doorstep confrontation with Big John.

It was this servant of the Crown to first express the view that Cruddle looked like a pillar box. And the postman lost no opportunity to revitalise his stroke of original wit. Even now, seeing Cruddle at Paddy's doorway, John quickened his stride, pulled a bunch of keys from a pocket of his uniform and noisily waved them in mock threat to open Cruddle up, "To see if there's anything in there for me bag!" he shouted as the town officer disappeared.

As he took a bundle of letters from John's hand Paddy could hardly help grinning.

He shouldn't have grinned; the big postman needed no encouragement.

"There y'are, Mr Kean! Take me keys! There'll be a little door just where his belly button should be! Ha! Ha!" He leaned helplessly on Paddy's shoulder, shaking his head. "No wonder we get letters goin' astray! Bloody mobile pillar box you've got in there! Hee! Hee! Stuffed full of letters he is! Won't stand still long enough for us to get them out of him! Ha! Ha! Ha! Always gettin' complaints we are!"

Big John laughed until tears came to his eyes, his chins wobbling like patted jelly.

Heaven knows why. He had nothing to laugh about.

His incessant hilarity had been a contributory factor in his father's suicide, his parrot's lack of feathers and his wife being killed by a tram – her ears so stuffed with cotton wool that she didn't hear it coming.

Big John still laughed. Only on the rarest of occasions would he stop, wipe away a tear and look doleful; then he'd be off again, in kinks at the absurdity of stopping in the first place.

But no one ever told him a joke. Anything really funny might do him a mischief.

Being a postman, he was okay. People got him only in small doses.

"I see you've moved, Mr Kean," he said. "Living above the pub, are you?"

"Been here a week," replied Paddy. "Saves getting the bus to work."

"Ha! Ha! Ha!" bellowed John. "Bet you're tipplin' all day long, are you? Ha! Ha!"

Typically, the laughter died away.

"Aye, well... see you the morrow," and off he went.

Paddy returned to the bar where Cruddle was busy measuring the room.

"Have to have a top table," the town officer muttered.

"I've only planned a buffet lunch!" protested Paddy.

"Got to have a top table. Mayor won't come if she's got to stand to eat. It's her varicose veins. Ould cow!"

"Will it have to be set?"

"Course it'll have to be set! Here!" Cruddle thrust into Paddy's hand the official council measuring rod. "You can measure out the place settings with that. But I want it back, mind you. It's the only one we've got."

The town officer, with eyes constantly and independently circumnavigating the room, manhandled furniture from one place to another.

Paddy left him to it and, after telephoning the caterers with new instructions, went upstairs to bathe, shave and dress.

*

It was a quarter to eight when Mrs Postlethwaite arrived home, her weekend bag slung casually over her shoulder.

"Hello! Christopher!" she called as she entered the house. "I'm back!"

Upstairs in the bathroom her husband promptly cut himself with the worn-out Rolls Razor he had been given as a birthday present when he'd first started shaving. His wife had spoken. Obviously the weekend away had done some good, he thought, as he dabbed his bleeding face with a towel.

"Hello, dear," he replied. "Did you have a good weekend?"

"Wonderful, thank you. I'll have a coffee with you before I go to school."

A few minutes later the Postlethwaites took on the mantle of normality.

They attempted a chat over coffee.

Only twice was there awkwardness. Once when Postlethwaite made to remove a brown-paper parcel from the table where his wife had placed it.

"Don't touch that!" she screamed, her eyes immediately showing the hot signs of withdrawal that had dominated the preceding week; and again when Postlethwaite casually remarked that at lunchtime he had arranged to take the staff for a drink and a bite to eat.

"A newly opened public house. Going to sell drink at pre-war prices. Publicity, of course, but I think it proper for the borough treasurer to support new expressions of confidence in the town's future..."

Mrs Postlethwaite raised her eyebrows contemptuously, silencing her husband – then radically changed the subject.

Still, thought Postlethwaite as he set off for the bus stop, it seemed his marriage was not the complete failure he had begun to imagine.

He wouldn't have been so confident had he witnessed the scene on his back lawn less than two minutes after he left the house.

In the middle of his well-kept patch of green Mrs Postlethwaite arranged a circle of bricks. In it she set paper, twigs and her brown-paper parcel. Then, with difficulty in the rain, she struck a match and applied it to her little bonfire.

Cross-legged on the damp grass she sat as if in prayer and watched the parcelled-up hat smoulder and burn, the stench of smoking felt and feathers rising slowly heavenward like an offering to a primitive god.

*

Finished at The Bone Idol, Cruddle scuttled across the road to his apartment behind the town hall. In motion he resembled more a drab, grey penguin than a drab, grey pillar box.

Little legs can move at remarkable speed on the level, but the steep iron stairs leading to his flat slowed him down. He was panting as he opened the door.

It was a peculiar building, almost as peculiar as its occupier. Once the upper floor of the council's stables, it now straddled a ladies' public convenience and a garage for the Daimler. But it was home to Cruddle, and to his cats: sleek, well fed and numerous.

As he closed the door behind him they emerged, mewing coyly, from all ends of the apartment. He fed them boiled fish from a pan which stood permanently on the stove.

The place was garret-like, imbued with an air of debauched poverty. Take away the cats and it could have served as a set for the first act of *La Bohème*. Even an easel was there, casually angled against the attic-type window, but no budding masterpiece rested on its pegs; only a few carefully preserved photographs pasted to a board. And Cruddle's mackintosh, which he hung on a hook at the back of the door, was no *vecchia zimarra* so beloved of Colline; its capacious pockets had never nurtured the secrets of poets and philosophers – simply fish for the cats.

But Cruddle was not without an occasional whim for the observance and appreciation of beauty. In the floorboards in a corner of his room there was a knothole through which he had a view of the toilets below. He could actually see into two cubicles at once, and, as soon as he had fed the cats, it was the work of a second to fold back the carpet, extend himself on the floor and glue one eye to the boards.

He was lucky to have a head so shaped as to fit flush against the skirting board. Without it he wouldn't have been able to see through the hole.

Nature always compensates.

*

In a bizarre way, Nature had compensated Malcolm Birstin. His regular greedy consumption of the condemned stock of the Public Health Department had built up in him an outstanding microbic intolerance to fresh food.

A weekend of home cooking produced roaring diarrhoea – an affliction which caused discomfort but at least encouraged a sense of urgency when going from place to place. It always ensured his early arrival at work on Monday mornings.

And this Monday he was particularly early, the better to get his note turning down the treasurer's invitation to lunch on to the chief's desk without a confrontation. It was bad enough having to reject an offer he wanted to accept without the possibility of having to provide justification for it.

Birstin was fortunate, for the treasurer, first delayed by conversation with his wife, then by his ignorance of the local bus timetable, was nowhere near his office as Birstin hurriedly placed the note on the in-tray. And the auditor, in his haste to avoid detection, failed to notice the pile of acceptances from other members of staff which had lain there since Saturday.

So, still in ignorance of the staff's change of mind, he gathered up his audit notes and set off to check the cash in the last six of Mankley's public conveniences.

Considering the state of his innards, he was relieved that, for the remainder of the morning, he would not be far from a toilet. He was dwelling on that comfort as he left the town hall – just as Postlethwaite arrived.

"G'morning, Malcolm!" breezed the treasurer. "Off on your rounds again?"

"Oh," stuttered Birstin, dropping his notes in embarrassment, "yes. Should be finished by the end of the morning."

"Good, good. That's the ticket. We'll see you later, then?"

"Well, actually," muttered the auditor, awkwardly picking up his notes to avoid eye contact with Postlethwaite, "I've left a message about that on your desk."

He pulled up his coat collar to his ears and shot down the side of the town hall, straight to the ladies' lavatories.

The attendant, as usual at this time of day, was away for her tea break. But Birstin wasn't going to let that delay him. This was the first call on his day's list, and auditors have orderly minds – besides, he didn't want the inspector in charge of public conveniences to arrive and become aware that an audit was in progress. It would be a pity if the whole exercise were to be jeopardised for the want of a little care and discretion.

Very attentively he listened for sounds of occupance from the half-dozen cubicles in front of him. Hearing none, he pulled a key from his pocket, swiftly opened the brass box on the first door, checked the cash and noted the total on his worksheet.

At the second door, however, he made a mistake. He did not see the semi-circular 'ENGAGED' sign; he was unable to – it had been worn away with years of twirling, and as he inserted the key a shrill voice froze him to the spot.

"Just a minute!" it cried. "I won't be long!"

Birstin didn't dare answer.

He didn't have time.

The echo of that voice had hardly died on the green tiles before he heard the simultaneous flush of the cistern and the sharp crack of the door-bolt being withdrawn.

The kindly smile on the face of the gigantic, well-dressed lady who swung back the door turned into a revolted snarl of rage as she lashed out with her handbag.

"Filthy pervert!" she screeched at the top of her voice, beating Birstin across the head.

"I'm not!" he protested as he hit the floor. "I'm an auditor!"

"Is that what you call it?" the woman screamed hysterically.

"I've been doing it all last week! You can look at my notes!"

Horrified by the admission the woman again swung her bag, but this time she lost her footing and, with even more deafening screams, crashed down on top of Birstin.

He went silent instantly.

He had fainted.

Upstairs, Emlyn Cruddle, one eye still glued to the knot-hole, could hardly contain the ecstatic fit of joy that overcame him as he reached for the telephone and dialled the local police station.

*

Happily, the treasurer flicked through the little notes accepting his invitation to lunch, then turned his attention to his in-tray. A frown creased his brow as he read Birstin's curt refusal.

Postlethwaite called for Smith.

"Good morning, Borough Treasurer," greeted the deputy dutifully as he took the usual armful of mail.

"G'morning, David," grunted Postlethwaite, "I see young Birstin doesn't like us any more!"

Smith waited for the treasurer to continue – he was becoming accustomed to being a captive audience for the chief's new turns of phrase.

"He's not coming to our little get-together at lunchtime!" The treasurer sounded pained.

Smith gulped. He had forgotten to tell the auditor about the staff's change of heart.

"Perhaps," he suggested, in a moment of unprecedented quick thinking, "he feels committed to working his lunch hour in order to complete his audit."

The treasurer was unconvinced, but he smiled at Smith.

"Ask Mr Birstin to have a word with me when he returns to the office, will you?" he asked softly.

Smith, concerned that Birstin might now inform Postlethwaite of the staff's original mood regarding the forthcoming lunch break, retreated without a murmur.

*

"Didn't give his name, Sergeant," said PC Griffiths, putting down the telephone.

"Never mind about that! Let's get over there! Get the car!" urged Sergeant Horace Goodenough, whose demonic hatred of all things sexually-motivated was known throughout the area. "And I want four of you with me!"

"Four, sir?"

"Yes, four!" the Sergeant bawled, practising a swing with his truncheon.

*

As Birstin came round from his faint he tried to think of how to reason with the lady still pinning him down, but even if he'd thought of anything he'd never have got enough breath into his body to say it. Her weight was unbelievable.

Through a whining in his ears he became aware, however, that they were no longer alone.

"They should be castrated!" came the voice of a woman who had been attracted to the lavatories by the screams.

"Eeh! It's terrible!" said another. "Right on your doorstep an' all! Will you manage to hold him while I get the police?"

"I think so," replied the large lady.

Birstin, almost asphyxiated, was in no doubt.

But as the newcomer, filled with the excitement of the moment, made a dramatic dash to the street, Sergeant Goodenough and four rough-looking constables, equally excited, made a dramatic dash into the lavatories.

And the newcomer, first knocked to the ground by the truncheon-wielding sergeant, then trampled on by four pairs of size elevens, lost all interest in dramatic dashes, to the street or anywhere else.

Birstin's world now took on all the qualities of a very bad dream. His initial relief at the arrival of the forces of law, order and justice, coinciding with an ability to breath again as the large lady was pulled from his chest, were replaced by a cringing fear for his life as Goodenough's truncheon hurtled towards his temple and four heavily-shod feet swung at his crotch.

He didn't hear the words of justification for such action. He passed out again.

"Resisting arrest," panted the sergeant, trying to get a better swing with his right arm.

Birstin was still unconscious when he was dumped in a cell.

*

It was with a measure of reluctance that Paddy saw Mary off to work. He would have valued her companionship this morning.

He checked the time. It was nine thirty. Archie should be arriving soon, and Anne and Margaret to acquaint themselves with the bar before acting as barmaids for the day. Paddy was grateful for their willingness to help – they were good girls – and Mary herself would be back before twelve.

He scanned the room, looking for clues to something undone. There were none.

He checked the angle of the spotlight that shone on the columned ornament, the place names on the formally set table and the volume setting on the amplifier – his would be the first pub in Mankley to have background music.

Everything was satisfactory, yet, with that sense of uncertainty which always afflicts the conscientious, he continued to fret.

But a knock on the front door and Archie Carrigan's subsequent arrival dispelled the landlord's mood of apprehension.

"I'll bet you were worried, bet you were worried," chuntered Archie, pouring himself a large whisky and downing it in one.

"I must confess, I am a bit worried about it all," admitted Paddy, shuddering at the thought of all that whisky falling into an early-morning stomach.

"Nothing to worry about!" encouraged Archie. "The mayor arrives at half past ten, the theatre people at eleven, councillors and guests shortly after that; we'll have the official opening at noon – I've written the speeches, you know, the speeches – then you open to the public. Couldn't be easier, couldn't be easier! Nothing for you to worry about. I'll see to the press and television. Oh, and incidentally, you'll have to have a top table. Had a word with that town officer bloke – funny fellow that one – said he'd arrange it with you."

"Yes," interrupted Paddy, "he's already seen to it."

"Mayor can't stand for too long. It's her legs, her legs."

"Will I have to arrange anything else specifically for her?"

"A spittoon would come in handy," laughed Archie. "She's a coarse ould cow!"

"A what?" cried Paddy. "I don't think I've got one!"

"Only joking, only joking. Stop worrying!"

Archie patted Paddy's shoulder.

"You've no problems, no problems at all."

"I hope you're right."

"I am. Can I use your phone? I want to call the theatre."

"Aye, here it is," said Paddy, sliding the phone along the counter to Archie as he waved to the girls who were now arriving, "help yourself."

Archie poured himself another whisky.

"Aye," he said, dialling a number from a scrap of paper he pulled from his pocket.

If Archie had known more about the theatrical profession he would have delayed making the call. It was only quarter to ten; the crack of dawn to the manager and licensee of Mankley's

'Royal Gaiety' theatre.

*

And it was the crack of dawn to the occupants of 46B, Gorbals Glen Heights – Mankley's one block of council flats, some thousand yards from The Bone Idol, where councillor Mrs Nora Slattery, Mayor of the Borough, heaved her bulbous old body up the bed and scrabbled her hand around the bedside table for her spectacles, her Woodbines, and her teeth.

Clutching these, and clad only in her night attire of well-stretched brassière with winceyette bloomers, she was a less than scintillating sight as she waddled into the kitchen to fill the kettle. Staring blearily through the curtained window at the rain outside and sucking in her cheeks with a squelch, she stretched, yawned, scratched her belly with her teeth, and lit a cigarette.

A hacking cough of excruciating harshness racked her body, leaving her faint but relieved. Now she could put in her teeth. That cough, arriving unexpectedly, had been known to send them the length of the council chamber.

And now she could phone Cruddle. But when she did there was no answer; at least, not immediately. This made Mrs Slattery angry.

Here she was, having overslept and not an hour away from her first official engagement since becoming mayor and the one person who could help her wouldn't answer his telephone. Well, she thought, she would leave it ringing till he did. It was pissing down outside and, as Mankley's First Lady, she had no intention of walking to the town hall; not when there was a chauffeur-driven Daimler lying around doing nothing. And that po-faced ould git, the town clerk, with his sanctimonious shite about misuse of council funds, could jump in the river.

"You must never forget that it's public money," he had admonished her following the outcry after she'd spent her year's entertaining allowance in her first month of office.

Well, sod that, she thought, furiously rapping her knuckles on the table while she waited for Cruddle to respond. She hadn't become a councillor to worry about 'public money', nor mayor just to get a conscience about the perks.

In fact, Mrs Slattery had not particularly sought mayoral office. It was simply her turn. The Labour Group's policy was straightforward – every serving councillor got a turn at being mayor.

It was a policy, however, which in its formulation hadn't allowed for the likelihood of a Nora Slattery ever being elected to council. It was only since the war, with every councillor being of the same party, that public apathy towards municipal elections had given scope to her type. 'Stick a Labour ticket on a camel and they'd vote it into office,' said the cynics. Though, in fairness to the public, after the capitalist-inspired depression of the thirties, which left Mankley and many towns like it with six years of almost total unemployment, no one was likely to vote Tory. Labour was the only respectable alternative.

And in fairness to the Labour members, every effort had been made to prevent Nora from becoming mayor – the prospect of her sister Florrie as mayoress a further discouragement. It was just that excuses had worn thin and to pass Nora over once again might have become obvious – and possibly dangerous. Even the Noras of this world have their political allies. The best that could be done, and that by a most intricate series of political moves, was to give her a year of office in which as little as possible was likely to happen, so to minimise public exposure of the council's most embarrassing, though actually most truly representative member, and extract from her an undertaking that she would not insist on her sister becoming mayoress.

So, in 1960, completely against the national trend of expansion, everything in Mankley stopped. No buildings completed, no new ones begun; representation at national shindigs was curtailed, civic hospitality slashed. The council Daimler hadn't been used ceremonially since Mrs Slattery had taken office. There had been nowhere for the mayor to go. And there was no mayoress. Not that Nora cared – she had always considered her sister beneath her.

But Archie Carrigan, who, in the next year or so would require considerable political support, sensed in the volatile though inactive mayor a degree of frustration, the relief of which might earn him a lot of gratitude. So, at last, she was to be given a public airing, and her first ride in the council's limousine.

Emlyn had been polishing it.   That was why he hadn't answered the telephone. Only when he realised that it wasn't going to stop ringing did he climb the stairs to his flat to pick up the receiver.

"Town Officer," he panted.

"Oh, hello, Emlyn, pet," gushed Mrs. Slattery familiarly. "Are you goin' to be a sweetheart and collect us from home this morning?"

"Town Clerk says I can only run you from the town hall," Cruddle replied. "It's the rule!"

"Aye, I know that, hinny, but just this once?" she wheedled. "Just for me?"

"I can't!" Cruddle insisted. "I've got this logbook to fill in. The auditor checks it. He's always on me back. I can't get the bugger off!"

"Aye?" snarled the mayor. "Well that's what *you* can do! You bugger off!"

Full of hell, she slammed down the phone, pushed her spectacles to the top of her nose, pulled up her bloomers – snapping the elastic against the flaccid white folds of her stomach – drew hard on her Woodbine and flung herself into the bedroom.

With face suffused with anger, and pendulous breasts threatening to avalanche out of the vast brassière, she leaned over the double bed and in one strenuous movement tore off the covers.

"Gerrup, yer scruffy little bastard!" she screamed in a flurry of fag ash and spittle, the effort sending her reeling round the room coughing in breathless agony.

Jimmy Slattery rubbed his sunken eyes and awoke to the wonder of a new morning.

*

"Hello, sir? It's an alderman, sir, an Alderman Carrigan, sir. Says he's rang three times, sir!" The plaintive wail of the stage door keeper came through the intercom.

"Put him through," ordered Jacob S Cracker in his plummiest theatre-manager voice.

"He seems very annoyed, sir. It's about a reception."

"Yes, yes. Put him through."

"He's got your ex-directory number, sir. Says he rang the stage door in desperation, sir!"

"Yes. Fine. Just put him through, will you!"

"Righto, sir!"

Click.

Cracker picked up one of his three telephones, then spoke.

"Good mor..."

"Is that Cracker?" barked Archie.

"Yes."

"Right! Now listen here, Cracker! I've been ringing your office for the last twenty minutes..."

There was no hint of the bluff, genial, father-of-the-council figure Archie usually portrayed. Cracker was left in no doubt that here was a man full of anxieties.

And Archie Carrigan was uncharacteristically succinct as to what they were. Like why was Cracker not in the theatre at nine forty five to answer the phone as arranged? And had Miss Lessingdale been properly informed about the reception? And what about transport? And why did Cracker not write a letter of confirmation?

But, by the time he put down the phone the alderman was reassured.

Jacob S Cracker, polished merchant of dreams, plausible entrepreneur, gifted frontman for fantasy, had calmed the troubled breast. And all without stutter or lisp – afflictions to manifest themselves only when he was drunk. So, in the pub, Archie Carrigan, still red-faced but no longer anxious, turned his thoughts to other matters.

Not so the theatre manager. Now off the telephone and alone with his conscience, Jacob S Cracker, senile piss-artist, inept conman and devotee of the easy life, thought of nothing else for a full ten minutes. Time enough to recall a vague memory of agreeing to something with someone in some pub somewhere, and time enough to recall doing bugger all about it.

Still, ever the optimist and a firm believer that Rome was built in an overnight fit-up, he buzzed the intercom.

"Yes, sir?" bleated the stage door keeper.

"Ask the company manager to come up!"

"Mr Federman, sir?"

"Yes, yes, if that's his name."

"Yes, sir. He's on stage at this moment, sir!"

"I want him up here, now!"

"Righto, sir!"

Click.

Cracker searched the top of his desk for that week's cast list. Finding it, he was relieved that it detailed only five characters.

Next, he searched the desk, his pockets, his diary and the waste-paper bin for a clue – anything – that might enlighten him further about Carrigan's telephone conversation. All Cracker had gathered was that 'they' were expecting 'Miss Lessingdale and the cast' at 'the new pub', that no transport had been laid on, that it was sometime in the morning and that Carrigan had 'written the speech, written the speech'. Not much to go on.

He pressed the intercom buzzer again, this time to contact his highly efficient press relations officer.

"Cancel the press call!" he instructed when she answered.

"Don't have to!" she replied. "It cancelled itself! All the press boys are going to the opening of a new pub!"

"Which pub? What time? What's it all about?" Cracker almost slavered with excitement.

"Don't know. Find out. Buzz you back."

Click.

Cracker got the feeling that today was not destined to be a typical sherry-at-eleven, glance-at-the-mail, lunch-with-the-star, crash-out-till-six, struggle-into-dinner-jacket, 'Good-Evening-and-welcome!' 'Fascinating-play!' pissed-with-the-press, 'Did-you-enjoy-it?' reception-for-the-artistes, pissed-with-the press type of Monday.

His thoughts were interrupted when into the office flounced the company manager clutching a clipboard and a glitter-gilded plastic tulip.

"Oh! 'Ello!" smirked the apparition as it swept its hair back and extended a wilting hand. "Gosh! What a lot of stairs!"

Cracker hid a smile behind his hand. At least this was reassuringly typical. Every new load of tat to be inflicted on the touring circuit seemed to carry with it an ever more outrageously camp company manager.

And this one was a peach.

"I must say, your stage crew's ever so good," it went on, "really super! Course, you won't have gone civic yet."

It sat down and flung a leg over the other.

"So, what d'you want, then?" it asked.

"Well, Mr Federman, I...?"

"Jules," it simpered.

"Er... yes. We... er... have a small problem."

"Don't we all?" smiled Jules, hitching himself round a little.

"And I hope you'll be able to help..."

"Mmm?"

"Well, there's a do this morning somewhere in town – I don't know all the details yet – the cast has been invited. All five of you."

"Four!" snapped Jules. "I play 'The Body' and 'The Butler'! Talk about doin' things on the cheap! It's sickening! I mean, it's all experience and that but they expect too much! I designed the lighting as well, y'know! That's the trouble when your willing!" He eased himself languidly to his feet. "Anyhow, I'll go back downstairs and try to phone them," and he floated off.

Buzz.

It was the press relations officer.

"Pub's called The Bone Idol. Fellow called Carrigan involved. High Street, opposite the town hall. Press boys assembling at eleven. Anything else?"

"No." Cracker was delighted. "That's fine!"

"With press call now cancelled, I've telephoned each of the cast and told them not to bother coming to theatre at lunchtime. All right?"

"No!" cried the theatre manager. "Get back to them! They must all be at the stage door for eleven!"

"Will do!"

Click.

Cracker groaned. He didn't want to be involved in this. It always depressed him to mix with people outside the profession. He found their little lives, little opinions, little conversations all distastefully pukey. And he didn't like entertainers and entertainable brought together without the safe divide of orchestra pit and proscenium arch. Normally he left this sort of banality to his assistant – a bright young man – but there was some memory of something, some vague threat. He didn't ponder; it just occurred to him, by whatever instinct for survival theatre mangers have in place of native cunning, that it would be wise to co-operate with Alderman Archie Carrigan.

The door was suddenly flung open, interrupting these sombre thoughts, and Jules, panting and seemingly upset, pranced in after another run up the stairs.

"Listen!" he whimpered. "What's goin' on? I've just rang round only to find that your girl's been on to them to cancel everything!"

Cracker explained, and Jules, dischuffed but still willing, once again rushed off to phone his cast.

Buzz

"Yes?"

"Right! I've contacted them," announced the press relations officer. "They'll all be at the stage door at eleven!"

Click.

Five minutes passed.

Bang!

The office door crashed open. It was Jules again, thoroughly exhausted.

"Listen!" he gasped pathetically. "I've just about had enough of this! I've been up and down those stairs so many times I don't know which way to turn! I've just rung them all again and your girl's beaten me to it again! What's the point of getting two people to do a job? Nobody knows what they're doing now! I mean, I've got a play to get on, you know!"

At that moment the press relations officer, Big Brassy Brigid, marched through the open door, conical, cast-iron breasts jutting forcibly forward.

"Oh, my God!" squeaked Jules, leaping aside. "It's King Kong!"

Brigid ignored the little queer and addressed herself to Cracker.

"All fixed. Taxi organised. You and I will go with them. Keep an eye on things."

"Just one taxi?" asked Jules. "You'll need two!"

"Why?" Brigid enquired. "There are only four of you!"

"Six!" contradicted Jules. "If you want to avoid trouble."

"How six?"

"Because, love," patronised Jules, "if Miss Lessingdale is coming, so is her tatty old poodle – and you can guess who's had to look after that on this tour! – and so is the man she's got in tow! Sickening it is. Can't keep her hands off him!"

"So that's six," said Brigid matter of factly.

"Eight!" corrected Cracker, pouring everyone a sherry. "If you count us."

"Eight!"

Brigid reached for the telephone to order an additional taxi.

*

"The bastard was caught in the act!" yelled Sergeant Goodenough.

"But the lady now accepts that she made a mistake! And I've checked out Birstin with the town hall. The papers he was carrying prove his story to be accurate. He was on official business."

Goodenough thwacked his baton on the desk.

"It's not your bloody job to get people off!"

He should never have allowed Constable Shawe-Iskay to interview the woman in the first place. Bloody college-trained, do-gooder cops had no place in the apprehending of criminals.

"It's your job to get the buggers locked up!"

"Well, the lady won't testify against him. We haven't got a case."

"Perverted filth, that's what he is, upsetting decent respectable people." Goodenough took a deep breath. "Charge him with resisting arrest!"

"There's something else you should know," Shawe-Iskay sighed – he was weary of trying to protect the sergeant from his own rashness. "His father is a Justice of the Peace."

Goodenough looked up, a new expression about him.

"Why don't you charge the woman with assault then?" he asked. "Why didn't you think of that with all your college training at public expense?"

The sergeant impatiently dismissed the young constable, went to the interview room where the large lady was sitting, gave her a warning about using unnecessary violence, then visited the cell where Birstin was struggling towards full consciousness.

"Ha! Ha! Ha!" the sergeant rumbled. "Bet you thought we were arresting you!"

He helped the prisoner to his feet. Birstin was surprised to find he could stand. His last memory, of four boots bent on emasculation, had left him with an impression of a limited physical future. In fact, the four boots had simply kicked each other; the auditor had been left undamaged. But there was a hell of a bump on his forehead. Her felt it gingerly as the sergeant assisted him down the passage, still talking.

"But we've given her a firm warning. She won't be so quick to attack anyone again. Oh, no! Thanks to you Mr Birstin, sir, that's one violent lady less for us to worry about. But we'll keep an eye on her. Don't you worry."

"This bump on my head," Birstin began weakly.

"Fell against the door," interrupted Goodenough from force of habit.

"I don't remember..."

"Of course you don't. Never mind. Off you go. Back to your auditing!"

Birstin found his audit notes shoved in his hand, shoelaces, watch and tie stuffed in his pocket, and a rather pretty policewoman escorting him to the door. Everyone seemed to be smiling, as if they were grateful for something. Confused, he smiled back. He had always had faith in the police despite the nasty things his father was always saying about them. It was reassuring to be a first-hand witness to their polite professionalism.

*

Councillor Mrs Nora Slattery wasn't betraying much polite professionalism. Nor was little Jimmy. Nor was the lift in the flats. It wasn't working.

"Call yourself a councillor!" exploded little Jim, kicking the lift door. "Can't even get the bloody lift fixed!"

Arguing loudly, they descended the stairs, Nora puffing and panting and favouring her legs by resting one hand on the banister and the other on Jimmy's shoulder.

Reaching the pavement, she leaned against one of the two decorative gas lamps specially erected outside the entrance to the flats to distinguish the building as the abode of the borough's mayor – a charming, if outdated custom of the town and one, this year, which had cost its citizens dear.

The area in which Nora lived was not the place for gold leaf detail on wrought-iron scrolling, and the neighbourhood's younger population had been quick to adapt the lamps to a more sympathetic shape and colour. By now they merged well with the overall street decor of multi-coloured paint splashes and carved initials.

"It's no good," groaned Nora. "I'll have to have me slippers. Go and get them, Jimmy, I'll never make it in these."

Little Jimmy protested but a warning glance from his wife stifled his incipient rebellion and sent him scurrying back up to the flat.

The rain seemed in for the day. Buses and cars splashed through puddles on the road sending up spray to soak the unwary. And loose paving stones belched out muddy water when depressed by hurrying feet.

Swollen, slipper-clad, slow moving feet had the same effect, and with every sodden footstep Mrs Slattery looked and felt less and less like the town's First Lady as she made her way to the town hall, the undersized Jimmy taking most of her weight on his arm.

Yet they were an awe-inspiring sight to Malcolm Birstin as he was propelled out of the police station. His feelings of faintness and confusion did not blind him to what questions might be asked if he were seen. Especially by the mayor, whose reputation for discretion was less than exemplary.

Hiding his face by pulling his jacket over his head – a reasonable precaution on a wet day – he ran to the town hall as fast as his legs could carry him.

Mrs Slattery, however, normally eagle-eyed in search of gossip fodder, had alternative preoccupations. A fit of coughing, brought on by screaming abuse at a passing splashing motorist had sent her teeth spinning into the traffic.

*

Postlethwaite had slipped up. He knew it as soon as he began to estimate the cost of the lunch: if everyone was coming to the pub, and Birstin was gadding about auditing lavatories, there would be no one to staff the office. He wondered if it could be done on a rota basis, but lacked the nerve to suggest the idea to the staff. After some thought he decided to get Locock to do it. He was the junior.

That sorted out, Postlethwaite realised that he had slipped up in another respect. He hadn't properly invited his wife. And he'd specially arranged for the car to be repaired for that morning so that he could collect her from work.

Tutting quietly to himself he looked up the school in the telephone directory and dialled.

"Grange Road School!" came the voice of the operator.

"Ah! G'morning! I'd like to speak to Mrs Postlethwaite."

"Moment!"

Click. Rattle. Buzz. Click.

"Hello?"

"Yes?"

"I'm afraid she's in class. Can she ring you back?"

"No!" shouted Postlethwaite. "I want to speak to her now! This moment!"

The operator responded to this hoity-toity attitude by blowing a whistle down the mouthpiece and disconnecting him.

Postlethwaite dropped the receiver in surprise, clapping a hand over his ear.

But he quickly redialled.

"Grange Road School!"

"I telephoned a minute ago to speak to Mrs Postlethwaite."

"Oh, yes. We were cut off."

"Will you get her."

"Sorry, she's still teaching."

"Well, send for her."

"Life or death?"

"No. But very important," Postlethwaite insisted.

"Sorry. Can't interrupt a lesson. It's the rule. I can pass a message if you want."

"Certainly not! I'm not having some slip of a girl carrying a private message between me and my wife! Get her to the phone at once or I'll report you to your superior!"

Another blast from the operator's trusty Acme Thunderer soon put a stop to that line of chat.

Postlethwaite dropped the receiver as if it were red hot, this time almost deafened. When his phone rang a few minutes later he heard it only distantly, through a high-pitched singing in his ears.

"Yes?" he shouted.

It was his wife.

"Stop shouting! Have you been telephoning me?"

"Oh, yes, dear. Sorry to trouble you at work."

"It's no trouble. I'm on my break."

"Oh, good! It's about the little drink I'm giving the staff at lunchtime. I do think it proper that you should be there."

"No. You can manage without me."

"No, I can't, the staff are expecting you!" He paused. "I *want* you there with me!"

"Oh," she responded in a small voice, "I see. Well. Yes. Of course I'll come, if you really want me to."

"Fine. I'll pick you up from school."

"No! Not the car!" Her voice rose by a diminished seventh, the Wagnerian connection wasted on the treasurer but threatening enough anyway.

"All right, dear," Postlethwaite backed down – it would save petrol anyhow. "I'll meet you off the bus at twelve."

"Thank you," she said, more Butterfly than Brünnhilde.

"See you at lunchtime, then," he muttered.

"Yes," she replied with a little sigh, as if waiting for him to say more.

"I'll look forward to it," he said, for want of anything better.

"Mutual," she breathed.

"Okay."

"Goodbye, then," she whispered.

Postlethwaite made to replace the receiver.

"Christopher!" Mrs Postlethwaite hollered.

"Yes, dear?"

"I'm not wearing a hat!"

The phone went dead.

*

Malcolm Birstin flew through the town hall foyer into the office where he sat down, wet and hot. His stomach felt terrible and he was still unsure that he had avoided the mayor's attention.

Ignoring everyone he began to reorganise his audit notes which had been dislodged from his clipboard during the scuffle in the lavatory. He was anxious to be out on his rounds again.

A shadow fell over him. Looking up he saw David Smith and Stan Scrimshire towering above his desk.

"Quiet word with you, son," said Stan. "The chief wants to see you about turning down his invitation to lunch."

Birstin gulped.

"Now, when you get in there," continued Stan, "don't you breathe a word about why the staff changed their minds and decided to go after all..."

"What do you mean? Are you all going now?" Birstin was indignant.

"Yes, actually," said Smith nervously, and went on to explain.

"So you just take your medicine, lad," added Stan once David had finished, "not a word about anything. Understand?"

Birstin understood all right. He was being done out of a free lunch. But maybe, he thought to himself, he could invent some story that left him unexpectedly available at lunchtime after all. Sudden change of circumstances, perhaps...

A couple of minutes later, an appropriate fiction in mind, he entered the treasurer's office, smiling confidently.

Sad really.

Postlethwaite was delighted, of course, that Malcolm was now uncommitted during the lunch hour.

But it didn't get the auditor the offer of lunch.

"Good! Splendid!" the treasurer said, slapping a hand on the desk-top. "You can look after the office."

*

It was ten thirty. The mayor, in her chambers adjacent to the town clerk's office, was reading slowly through the speech Archie had written for her. Her slippers were steaming gently on the radiator, and her teeth, the top set now in two pieces after a confrontation with a lorry, had been taken away by Cruddle for emergency repairs.

Archie stood stolidly, his back to the fire. The show of composure, however, disguised an inward terror of what might yet go wrong at the opening of the pub.

141

At last, a triumphant Cruddle returned with the mayor's teeth in his hand.

"Fixed them!" he croaked. "It's not a professional job but it'll have to do for now."

The mayor took them from him, wiped them on the sleeve of her robes and stuck them in her mouth.

"God Almighty!" she exclaimed. "They taste like cat's piss!"

"It's the glue," said Cruddle. "The taste'll wear off." Though, in fact, he had his doubts. His cats got everywhere these days. "The car's ready when you are."

"Right!" responded the mayor, clicking her teeth experimentally and adjusting her chain of office. "Jimmy! Come on!"

Jimmy roused himself from the comfort of a leather armchair and took her arm. Cruddle, resplendent in his chauffeur's uniform – and without his mackintosh – led the way, while Archie brought up the rear.

The Daimler was parked directly outside the town hall. To deliver the mayor to the pub, all Cruddle had to do was a three-point turn. It took twelve seconds.

"Is that it?" cried Nora, in the tones of one who'd lost her virginity to a premature ejaculation.

"Yep!" said Cruddle.

"What a bloody disgrace! It's not worth having a great big thing like this if that's all you can do with it! I'll be raising it at the next council meeting!"

The door of the pub swung open and a beaming, if hesitant, Paddy Kean properly stepped forward to greet the town's First Lady.

"Eeh! It's Mr Kean!" she cried in acknowledgement. "How are you, pet?"

For Paddy, what Nora's familiarity lacked in style and sense of occasion was more than compensated for by its obvious sincerity. It was just the touch of ordinariness he needed to help him over the moment. The tension had been steadily increasing over the past few weeks and, from the minute the mayor crossed the threshold, there could be no going back. Ahead lay a life in which there would be little place for natural shyness.

These thoughts were not far from the landlord's mind as he paid court to the mayor. It did not matter to him that the incumbent was Nora Slattery; it was the civic position that drew his respect. Nora thought he was lovely.

Paddy proudly introduced his stepdaughters. Nora thought they were lovely too. And the pub, that was lovely. And the dry sherry she was given, that was 'really lovely – but, mind, it goes straight to me arms!' Flattered for once in her life, Nora was at ease.

So was little Jimmy. Hugging a pint of beer, he found a quiet corner near the entrance and relaxed into a chair under the eye of the bone idol. He was used to being ignored.

But not Archie Carrigan.

"Did you hear what I said?" he nagged as he followed Cruddle past little Jimmy and through the front door.

"Yes, I did!"

"Why didn't you answer then?"

"'Cos you were tellin' me what to do. I just obey orders, me. Orders don't need answers. I don't know why you don't just hire a horse and cart to shift the ould bag around in!"

"That's enough of your cheek! She's the Mayor of the Borough!" snapped Archie. "See that you're here prompt twelve to pick her up, d'you hear?"

"Aye," muttered Cruddle, wandering over the pavement to move the Daimler back across the road to the town hall.

Archie remained in the pub doorway to await the theatricals. Despite the mayor's apparent docility he was apprehensive. He had seen Nora in action before. All he could do was pray her mood did not turn ugly. Even contented and happy she could cause problems. The alderman went clammy at the recollection of the opening of the Civic Art Gallery some years before when Nora, as Chairman of the Culture Committee, made response to the Prime Minister's inaugural speech.

"Well, I've never been able to draw meself, like. Not proper!" she'd begun, and, reacting to the consequent polite laughter, snatched off her spectacles and yelled aggressively, "Well, I haven't! What the hell are you lot laughin' about?", immediately stomping away, leaving the remainder of the civic party to face out the embarrassment.

At least, Archie comforted himself as he peered through the rain at the town hall clock, by writing the speech himself, he'd cut her chances of saying the wrong thing today. He was glad of that, but not so glad at the way the time was passing. It was after eleven. Waiting until ten minutes past and anxious once more, he returned to the bar to telephone the theatre.

No sooner had he left the doorway than two taxis drew up.

Jules Federman was about as anxious as Archie. His concern was how to keep the cast sober for the opening night – especially Miss Lessingdale, whose penchant for the bottle was almost as compelling as her lust for big, strong, and usually thick bedmates. When she'd been younger she had tolerated producers, theatre managers, directors and the like seducing her. But they had all been so preoccupied with their jobs, families or ideals, they were rarely fulfilling in bed. Once they'd satisfied their short-lived desires, they wanted to talk or read. Gloria had never been one for talking in bed – unless it was about another leading role – or reading. Better a buck than a book was her motto. So, ever since she'd been able to afford it, a buck was what she'd had. No brains, no desires other than what she paid him to have – just strong, healthy and active.

Carefully made-up, dressed in well-selected clothes, with her hair done by experts, by the skin of her root-filled teeth she was attractive enough still to turn heads and, thanks to a years-ago contract in Hollywood, there were sufficient of her old films about for the public to associate her with stardom. She regarded the last few years of ever-less-prestigious provincial tours only as a prelude to a comeback. The West End would beckon, Hollywood call, and Gloria Lessingdale would be back where she believed she belonged – in the starry dreamtinsel of universal acclaim.

But, sadly, the directors who had put her there once had found younger starlets to bed – and nobody had told her she couldn't act.

But she could drink. And that was what worried Jules.

"Just a min loves," he warbled over his shoulder from the front seat of the first taxi, "I'll have a little recce!"

Cradling Gloria's poodle he stepped on to the pavement, just as Jacob emerged from the taxi behind. Both wondering why there was nobody to meet them – and Jacob guiltily fearing he'd come to the wrong pub – they went in to look around.

"I mean! It's sickening, isn't it?" complained Jules loudly. "You'd think somebody'd be here to meet us!"

Little Jimmy heard the remark but it was none of his business so he concentrated on his second pint.

Anne, however, saw the two enter and approached them.

"I'm awfully sorry," she said, unaware of their identities, "we're not open yet. And I'm afraid you can't bring in the dog, sir. We're serving food, you see."

"Oh, God!" screamed Jules, stamping his foot. "I can't stand this! It's always the same – anywhere north of Palmers Green!"

Hearing the outburst, Archie looked over. Relieved at seeing Cracker, he smiled and raised his hand in welcome, then put down the phone, leaving a volubly frustrated stage door keeper at the other end of the line. Archie shook Cracker's hand, Cracker introduced Jules, the dog was patted and told it could stay, and Anne, blushing prettily, heaved a sigh, glad that Archie had taken charge.

*

Outside, Gloria Lessingdale gazed pensively through the cab window. Men in peaked caps and women in headscarves, some with umbrellas but most without, lumbered miserably along the street.

The overcast sky made it difficult to distinguish where the slate roofs ended and the threatening grey clouds began. The bright-painted riverside cranes, poised in the distance like ghostly birds of prey, gave little variety to the monotonous skyline, and the forlorn distant drone of ships' foghorns contributed only a melancholy contrast to the eternally uncoordinated splashing of the rain. It was all very depressing, thought the actress; how could

145

people live in a place like this? Not a bit like Godalming, where she shared a house with a mortgage like a lead duvet.

But, being a professional, and knowing that a free drink was at hand, she hid her feelings as Jacob and Archie appeared to escort her from the taxi to the pub. Jules, not wanting to get wet, hovered at the entrance, still cradling the poodle.

As Gloria passed she took the dog and gave it a little kiss on the nose. "Sweet, adorable little wooffin," she crooned, "aren't you, Winston, dahling?" and she fluttered her false eyelashes at Archie.

Once inside the pub she carefully struck an appealing pose, Winston held cutely against her face, until she realised that no star-struck crowd was there to be impressed. So she chucked the dog back to Jules and indifferently allowed Archie to lead her to where the mayor and Paddy were conversing.

The press had been delayed because in the shelter of the foyer of the town hall they were being talked at by Big Brassy Brigid. She had arranged it that way. To her the main event of the day was the play, not the opening of some pub. Unlike her boss, she saw her brief clearly; local politics and the survival of Jacob S Cracker as theatre manager were no part of it. So, having dispensed her publicity pack and ensured that the press boys understood it, she returned to the second taxi which, after ushering out the two remaining actors, she used to return to the theatre.

Meanwhile, in the first taxi, Gloria's man of the moment whom everyone had forgotten, was sound asleep. The cabby didn't mind – the meter was still running.

The Bone Idol gradually filled. The press wandered in, a few council members, the vicar; and the television crew began to set lights and microphones.

At an appropriate moment Paddy went behind the bar to switch on the background music, leaving the mayor talking to Gloria.

"... and I was really impressed with that one you were in about the dyin' opera singer. Eeh! I cried at that one – especially the bit where your mother's standin' at the side of the stage and you start coughin' up blood..."

Gloria smiled, inclining her head; a much-practised and rather engaging idiosyncrasy combining modesty and gratitude. Her eyes, however, coldly searched for escape, while the mayor continued: "... and do you act full-time, like, or have you got a proper job an' all?"

Gloria was saved from coping with this. Her helpless, silent appeal was caught by Jacob and he hurried to ease the star's discomfort. With suitable phrase and gesture, he spirited her away to join the press at the end of the bar counter.

Jules and the actors, Bill and Karen, stood together bored. Anything they had to say to each other had all been said before – everywhere from Richmond to Aberdeen, Bournemouth to Glasgow, Brighton to York, Cardiff to Norwich and, after six zigzag weeks on the 'B' circuit, the civics and the almost-closeds. It hadn't been a well-planned tour.

Still, they consoled themselves, only seven more weeks of the faded and dead and it would be over. Then into pantomime and, with luck, another tour before summer show, Butlin's or the dole.

"It's a dog's life," said Bill, philosophically tapping out his pipe in the ashtray.

"Prefer cats meself," replied Jules, disconsolately looking down at Winston and throwing a piece of cheese, which the poodle caught deftly in mid-air with all the style of a circus dog.

"You should live in Iceland," said Karen. "No dogs there!"

"Fat lot of good that would be," pouted the company manager. "No theatres either!"

"Be a bit different though, I suppose," mused Bill. "Different food and that. Walrus steaks. Polar bear meat."

'That's Greenland," Karen informed him. "Eskimos eat polar bears. They kill them by bending a sharpened stick through a piece of frozen meat, then when the bear gulps it down it unfreezes and the stick springs out straight, stabbing the animal to death from the inside."

"Oooh!" squeaked Jules. "I'll stick to me ulcers!"

Idly he tried to bend a plastic cocktail stick through a piece of cheese while Winston looked on in doggy curiosity.

"Don't know why anybody wants to eat meat anyhow," Karen went on, "it's immoral to kill animals when we can live better off plants and herbs."

Winston yawned and settled its head on its paws.

"I grew some herbs once," muttered Jules, frowning as he broke his third cocktail stick.

"Did you?" ask Karen naively.

"Yes, from a packet of mixed seeds I bought at Harrods."

"I'll bet they tasted good, being so fresh."

"Actually, I was a bit disappointed." Jules sounded sad. "Turned out I had all Rosemary and no Basil."

The actors became aware that something was happening.

"What's going on?" queried Jules as Paddy rattled down the bar shutters and whisked away the cheese and pile of broken cocktail sticks.

"Don't get worried," smiled the landlord. "I'll open up again after the speeches."

"Turgid speeches as well," commented Jules, groaning and gathering up Winston from the floor.

Mary slipped behind the bar counter.

"Glad you've made it," whispered Paddy, giving her a light kiss on the forehead.

"Is everything organised?" she asked.

"Yes. Archie and the girls have seen to everything. They're just about to start the speeches."

Sure enough, Archie was ushering people to their seats. As Paddy and Mary watched, they realised just how astute the alderman had been. There was hardly an aspect of the town's business or social life unrepresented.

"You'd better prepare yourself for a surprise." Mary nudged Paddy's arm.

"Why?"

"I heard it whispered at work this morning that Postlethwaite has invited the staff to join him here at lunchtime."

"What? exclaimed Paddy. "He hasn't!"

"He has!" said Mary with an impish grin.

"Bloody hell!"

*

The mayor seemed distressed as she took her seat.

"Is something upsetting you?" asked Gloria.

"Me speech. I can't find it," the mayor replied, flustered.

"Oh, I'm sure you'll think of something to say," encouraged the star.

Archie rattled a spoon in a cup and cleared his throat.

"Ladies and Gentlemen! Pray silence for Councillor Mrs Nora Slattery, Mayor of the Borough of Mankley!"

There was scattered applause and a scuffling of feet as Nora rose, fingering her chain of office as if it were rosary beads.

Dodie Ochiltree signalled the cameras and lights to action, a few flashguns popped and the press prepared to take notes.

"Well!" Nora stared about her brazenly. "I think this pub's the best thing for the North-East since Stephenson's 'Rocket'..."

*

In the town hall Postlethwaite put his pen in his pocket, donned his overcoat and called for Smith.

"I want you to take this," he said, handing his new deputy a five-pound note, "and arrange the ordering of food and drink. I have to meet my good lady. We won't be long in joining you."

"Yes, Borough Treasurer, thank you."

"And I think, for today, we can be a little less formal, David." The treasurer gave his twisted smile. "Call me Mr Postlethwaite."

"Yes. Of course, Borough Treasurer," David stuttered before returning to the outer office.

Within a few minutes he and the staff were ready to tidy up in preparation for setting off but, rather than waste time on arrival at the pub, David sensibly took note of the drinks everyone wanted before they left.

Sympathetic courtesy prevented anyone distracting Malcolm Birstin from his paperwork but Stan and David each had a kindly word with him, promising to bring back a bottle.

By then Postlethwaite had left his office by the door that led direct to the town hall foyer and walked the hundred yards or so up the High Street to the bus stop. He sheltered there from the rain by standing in a shop doorway. Two sizeable ladies, similarly motivated, stood in front of him. That way he was kept warm and dry, and saw nothing of the events soon to occur on the width of cobbled road that separated the town hall from The Bone Idol.

*

"... and it's the best thing for Mankley since the opening of the sewage works!"

'Oh, Lord,' prayed Archie, 'please give her laryngitis.'

"... it's a credit to the town! It makes the Clock Hotel look like a doss-house!"

Mankley's only hotelier, whom Archie had thought it diplomatic to invite, suddenly took an interest in his feet. The vicar's complacent smile froze on his face like a death-mask.

"... look around you!" bawled Nora exultantly.

"She's got the bit between her teeth now," whispered a councillor.

"By hell, she has," replied another.

"Better turn off the background music." Mary nudged Paddy.

"Oh, aye," he headed for the amplifier.

"... that lovely statue!" Nora swung her arm dramatically in the direction of the spotlit, columned ornament, the heavy sleeve of her robes scattering a three-tiered cake-stand full of squashy cream cakes among those guests sitting nearest her.

The television cameras caught this, then panned the room, following her theatrical gesture to fix on the bone idol, beneath which little Jimmy now leaned, pint in hand and ash-laden fag dangling from his lips.

Ochiltree experienced exquisite excitement. All he'd expected from today's jaunt was yet another boring old actress to provide memory-lane fill-in material for his nightly local newsround; but this was priceless. It was television. It was ethnic.

"... all this posh music!"

Nora's hand flew aloft, just as Paddy switched off the sound, and bits of cake shot from her sleeve to fall like giant, claggy snowflakes over the manager of Lloyds Bank.

"... them lovely carpets!"

Archie, dying a million agonising deaths, desperately scribbled on a piece of paper.

"... the wallpaper and that!"

She stumbled on while everyone shuffled in their seats with lowered eyes. At the bar Jules was heard to repeat over and over again, "I don't believe this! I just don't believe it!"

"... but, mind you, I'm no expert on pubs! I haven't been in as many as my husband Jimmy! Oh, no! He's the one that should be makin' this speech, not me!"

'By God, you're right,' thought Archie, as he surreptitiously backed his chair from the table and prepared to squeeze along to deliver his hastily written note to Nora.

Gloria Lessingdale, being in full view of everyone, maintained a glassy-eyed stare throughout.

"... oh, aye! Our Jimmy's the real expert! He's been in every pub in Mankley! More than once an' all!"

Nora laughed, then noticed the oppressively embarrassed silence. Anyone else would have feigned death or insanity. Not Nora. She opted for humour – to lighten everyone's spirits.

"Aye!" she laughed again, coarsely, "there's many a night he's come home to me swimmin' in it! Couldn't bloo..., couldn't stand sometimes! And when he's had a skinful, he far..., I mean, he gets a bit carried away, like... like a brass band he is sometimes!"

The cameras pointed at her relentlessly. She saw faces, hard and cold. The vicar's fixed smile reminded her of the fleshless jaw of a corpse. She couldn't see his eyes for reflections in the lenses of his spectacles. Soft, pink, well-fed, privileged faces surrounded her.

Frustration built up.

She stopped laughing.

'Well, it's not as if we've had the money for stylish livin', is it? Not like you lot! You haven't had to beg food for your bairns, have you?"

Archie reached her side and gently pulled her arm. She shook him off irritably, covering his suit with cream cake.

"... you talk about the Irish potato famine! That was luxury compared with what your class did to us! Remember the depression?"

Archie somehow succeeded in distracting her.

"What?" she yelled at him.

"Just read this," he whispered, handing her his piece of paper and immediately withdrawing to preclude further argument, and to less obviously flick bits of cake from his lapels.

Still standing, Nora perused the note. In the stillness, her face paled to blotchy purple. She caught sight of Paddy and Mary behind the bar. They looked uncomfortable. They were nice, thought Nora; Paddy was lovely, a gentleman. For him, she calmed down, took a deep breath and gave another of her coarse laughs.

"But I'm not here today to put right your wrongs! I'm here..." she read carefully from Archie's note, "to welcome Miss Gloria Lessingdale to Mankley and thank her for agreein' to open this public house, the first new pub in the town since the war!"

She sat down abruptly, to the sound of a couple of coughs.

After a pause, Gloria rose, favoured the company with her famous ravishing smile and, with charming meaningless phrases, declared The Bone Idol open.

There were cheers – mainly of relief – and the festive pop of champagne corks.

Gloria sat down.

The mayor leaned against her.

"You did very well, pet," she said, patting the star's knee patronisingly.

*

At the Monk Garage, Fenwick Fancourt didn't see why he should have to deliver Postlethwaite's repaired car to the town hall.

"It should have been delivered before eleven o'clock!" said the sales director over the telephone.

"What about my lunch?" asked Fenwick.

"What about selling some bloody cars?" responded the sales director.

So Fenwick, not wanting to precipitate a crisis, and recalling his promise to meet Arnold for a drink, set off. He didn't raise the hood. At the speed he drove the rain would flow over the windscreen, leaving him dry. Even if not, he'd rather get wet than catch his fingers in the frame.

*

Outside the town hall Cruddle got into the Daimler. It was time to return to The Bone Idol to collect the mayor.

He started the engine, glanced around, and seeing only a bus approaching some distance away began his three-point turn. It wasn't often that Cruddle misjudged a road space, but he did today. By only an inch or two, the taxi, still parked outside the pub, prevented his getting the long limousine quite flush with the kerb.

Impatiently, he glared at the back of the taxi and pressed the Daimler's imperious klaxon.

Fenwick overtook the bus, drove on for a hundred yards or so, then smartly veered across the street to park in front of the town hall from where the Daimler had just pulled away. He saw the large car being manipulated to park behind the taxi but was out of the Triumph and into the town hall to meet Arnold before Cruddle had sounded the horn.

Inside the taxi, Gloria's 'friend' awoke with a start at the sound. He knocked on the dividing screen to attract the driver's attention.

"Where did the others go?"

"Into the pub."

There was another honk from Cruddle. The taxi driver turned away from his passenger, opened the window and yelled abuse at the large black car behind – by which time Gloria's man was out of the cab and heading across the pavement.

The cabby, impressed by Cruddle's ability to exchange repartee with as much crude gusto as himself, turned back to his passenger to find himself looking at an empty seat.

Cruddle angrily got out of the Daimler and went to the side of the taxi to remonstrate. He got there, however, just as the taxi driver, with eyes fixed snake-like on his ex-passenger's back disappearing into the pub, swung open his door to follow. And Cruddle, with his top-heavy body and little legs, was knocked into the middle of the road.

The bus driver peered through his misted-up windscreen with an expression of pained surprise.

His eyes throbbed from a long morning's drive in poor visibility, his head pounded from the clacking and whining of the windscreen wiper, his left leg was roasted by heat from the engine, while his right froze in the draught from the cab door. His arms ached from heaving the heavy, notched steering wheel, his fingers were cut by the release-grip of the handbrake, and his piles vibrated like sandpaper in a vice with every movement of the bus. He was in no mood for quick decisions.

As he chugged along the High Street he had already seen the taxi ahead on the left, and the Daimler swing across to come behind it. Anticipating that the Daimler wouldn't succeed at first shot, he had adjusted his position on the road to compensate. Even when the Triumph shot past the bus to park on the right, he saw the whole situation as nothing more than a standard of road behaviour typical of the private motorist, worthy of only an inward groan.

But the sudden arrival of Cruddle in the middle of the road, the only bit left for the bus to use, put a new complexion on the scene.

Driver 108/Rumley of the Trans-Mankley Traction Company now had three alternatives: he could kill Cruddle, hit the Daimler or hit the Triumph. With the condition of his brakes and the state of the road, he knew he'd have to hit something.

The choice was easy.

Bearing in mind the complexity of the 'Accident Report' he would have to complete for killing somebody compared to that for merely hitting a parked vehicle, and subconsciously calculating the relative trouble-potential of his damaging a Daimler or a Triumph, he aimed squarely at the latter as he stamped on the brake.

*

"Ah! Dahling, there you are!" cried Gloria, as her 'friend' came into the bar.

"This is Rodney," she introduced him to a few of the press who were gathered round her.

"Hey you!" came a shout from the doorway. "What about me fare?"

Rodney ignored the gesticulating taxi driver but Jacob, smelling trouble, detached himself from the bar counter and hastened to pour the proverbial oil on the waters.

"Jusht send your b-bill to the theatre," he said, surprised to find his speech impaired so early in the day – he'd had only a few sherries and some champagne.

"Who are you?" asked the taxi driver.

"I'm the theatre m-manager."

"Trouble?" asked Archie who, like Cracker, wanted no disturbance of the present friendly atmosphere.

"There will be!" threatened the taxi driver. "If I don't get me fare!"

"Something wrong, Alderman?" asked Nora, who had followed Archie across the room.

"Not at all, not at all," smiled the urbane Archie.

"Aye, there is! I haven't been paid!" protested the taxi driver, attempting to push his way between the large bodies of Archie and Jacob to get at Rodney.

155

"You don't bloody deserve to be if that's your attitude!" said Nora, glowering at the truculent upstart. "Are you a registered Hackney Cab?"

"Eh? No. I'm private hire."

"Well I'm the bloody mayor!" retorted Nora. "A socialist mayor! And I don't believe in anything private! So sod off!"

Jacob and Archie, now aiming to keep Nora quiet, manhandled the protesting taxi driver to the door.

*

Cruddle picked himself up from the wet cobbles, his only thought to be on time to collect the mayor. It was one thing to act abusive and argumentative with Alderman Carrigan but quite another to fail in his duty.

The town hall clock chimed the noon hour.

Galvanised into action, the town officer brushed himself down, got into the taxi, released its handbrake and pushed it forward a few yards, thus leaving road space to run the Daimler flush with the kerb. As he did this he didn't notice the taxi driver being jostled out of the pub. And the taxi driver, in his haste to get to the police station after seeing Cruddle move his taxi didn't notice the crashed bus.

Driver 108/Rumley looked around him. There was no one to be seen. Hardly believable – no witnesses to the accident.

In fact, quite a few people had seen the bus veer across the road to smash into the back of the Triumph, but, at that precise moment, what had been a steady downpour became an undisciplined deluge. The sky went black, the colourful riverside cranes faded into the murk. Anyone foolish enough to be in the street was there for a purpose, not simply to subject themselves to a soaking and act as unpaid spies for the bus company. And for most of the sodden population anyone sufficiently fortunate to own a car on a day like this deserved to get it bashed in by a bus.

The bus driver jumped down from his cab to inspect the damage. There was none to the bus but the back end of the

Triumph was badly bent. Then he saw Cruddle at the door of the Daimler.

"Hey, you! This was your fault!" the bus driver shouted, rain running down his neck.

"Balls!" responded Cruddle, who'd tried his damnedest to be unseen. "You just skidded, that's all!"

"Aye! To avoid your flaming posh car!"

"Look," said Cruddle, scurrying over to the bus, "if it's your report you're worried about, just say that an unidentified pedestrian stepped in front of you and you swerved to avoid him. Save everyone a lot of trouble."

"I suppose you're right."

"Well, aye! Nobody saw it." Cruddle looked more closely at the bus driver's face. "I know you, don't I?"

"Yes. I used to work for the council. You don't know whose car that is, do you?"

"Aye, I do. But I won't be saying anything to the bugger."

"Whose is it?"

"The treasurer's. He bought it a fortnight ago."

"Did he?"

"Aye."

The bus driver looked thoughtful for a minute then gave a laugh.

"Aye. Right!" he spluttered as he climbed back into his cab. "Funny, that is! Pity the bastard wasn't in it!"

Cruddle nodded agreement as the bus was reversed slightly before being driven away, then he dashed to the pub.

Driver 108, embittered and much roughened by a period of unemployment after his unceremonial resignation from the town hall and the subsequent horrors of the bus-driving school, felt in fine form. He wouldn't report the accident at all. Life had taught Willie Rumley that conscientiousness got you nowhere.

*

"I'm not going yet!" protested Nora. "I want to enjoy meself!"

Cruddle grunted and went off to get Archie. It didn't take the alderman long to convince the mayor that she'd enjoy herself more if she were to change out of her robes.

"I'll have to keep me chain on, though," she said.

"Yes, yes. Perfectly in order, perfectly in order."

Nora was about to rouse Jimmy from his alcoholic stupor, but changed her mind. He was just a nuisance to her drunk. So she allowed Cruddle to lead her off.

But, after he got her into the car, the town officer realised that he couldn't do his three-point turn. The Triumph blocked access to the opposite kerb.

He fiddled with the ignition key.

"Won't start," he said.

"What?" shouted the mayor.

"Car won't start. Must be all the rain."

Nora cursed, got out of the car and, holding her robes high to prevent them trailing on the wet road, waddled carefully over to the town hall.

The sight of the mayor paddling her way into the seat of Mankley's political power may not have added much to the town's reputation for civic pomp, but it did distract all but one of the treasurer's staff from seeing the damage to Postlethwaite's car as they crossed the road in the opposite direction.

"It's a smashing car, isn't it?" commented Arnold.

"Not bad," replied the salesman.

"Pity it's bashed in at the back."

"It's not. They fixed it last week."

"Oh," said Arnold, not wanting to start an argument.

But just before entering the pub he did glance back at the Triumph to check that the damage was real and not imaginary.

*

Upstairs, at the front of the bus, Mrs Postlethwaite, who up to four minutes ago had been quietly snoozing, picked herself up from the floor. She felt a bit giddy after hitting her head on the front window but not so distracted by pain to forget where she was going and, seeing the town hall disappearing backwards on her right, she struggled to her feet and wobbled down the aisle to descend the stairs and alight.

As the bus stopped, Postlethwaite stepped forward from the shop doorway.

"Glad to see you, dear," he said.

"Oh, yes," his wife replied vaguely, "glad to be here."

"You look shaken."

"The bus braked suddenly and I was thrown from my seat. Silly really," she laughed lightly, "I must have hit my head and knocked myself out for a minute. I usually do that only in your car. Hurts just the same though..."

They walked in single file close to the shop-fronts to gain shelter from the rain, Mrs Postlethwaite in front. Hurrying and not certain of where the pub was, she went past it.

Not her husband. He stopped at the doorway.

"Here we are, dear!" he called after her.

"Oh!" she turned and caught sight of the Triumph parked across the street. Postlethwaite saw her staring at it. He was pleased it had been delivered. From his angle it was impossible to see the newly damaged back end.

"You've noticed the car?" he asked proudly. "It's back. They repaired it quite quickly for me. Bit of influence of course."

"You're satisfied with it?" asked his wife, tearing her gaze from the bent metalwork.

"Yes, yes. Now, let's go in, shall we?"

"Christopher!" cried Mrs Postlethwaite, retracing her steps towards him. "It's just the same. It's exactly as it was!"

"What, dear?" he asked, pushing her into the pub.

"The car! It's exactly as it was!"

"Yes, dear. Just like the day I bought it."

"It's still damaged, Christopher!" she said, tightly shutting her eyes and clenching her fists.

"No, dear, it's repaired now. Very kind of the garage to deliver it really – ah! Hello, there, Councillor!" he called to a scruffy little man busily fastening his flies as he came out of the gents.

The man acknowledged his wave with a curt nod.

Postlethwaite recognised a few others as he moved further into the bar. Those who knew him were surprised to see him there. He was not a renowned socialite.

Archie Carrigan commented on the fact.

"Now, there's a fellow you don't often see spending money!" he muttered to the people nearest him as he raised his glass towards the Postlethwaites. "Charming wife though. Teacher she is, a teacher. Very active in charity work, oh yes, very active."

Impressed, the little group looked over at the treasurer.

And the vicar commented, "Ah, look! There's the man who keeps the rates down! Hello, there, Mrs Postlethwaite, and Mr Postlethwaite of course! Ha! Ha!"

So more faces turned towards the couple. One or two made to approach and pay their respects. It was unusual to see him away from the town hall. Quite a different man he looked. And what an attractive wife.

"You will let me get you a drink, both," Councillor Webster offered politely.

"No, no," replied Postlethwaite jovially. "I'm the one who's buying today. Giving my staff a little treat actually."

Fenwick Fancourt left Arnold's side and squeezed towards the treasurer to give him his car keys. As Postlethwaite took them, his wife caught sight of the staff, smiles on their faces and drinks in their hands.

"There they are, Christopher!" she said brightly.

Postlethwaite looked in the direction she indicated.

"Ah, yes. I expect they'll..." he half turned and hailed another council member who caught his eye. "Good day to you, Chairman! Nice to see..."

His voice faded away and his head spun round to look again in the direction of the staff.

He paled.

"We'll go now!" he whispered, his eyes bulging.

"What?" cried his wife, following his tortured gaze.

The crowd separated and from the midst of the staff, down an avenue of noisily chattering guests strode Paddy Kean, welcoming, beckoning, his hand offered in greeting.

Postlethwaite's eyes and feet continued to point towards the landlord, but his arms, hands and body set off for the door.

"I'm not going!" Mrs Postlethwaite was firm.

"We must!" hissed the treasurer through clenched teeth as his body gave a convulsive doorward jerk.

"I'm not!" She stamped her foot.

Paddy had almost reached them.

With eyes still bulging, Postlethwaite's lips drew back in a macabre parody of expressed mirth, then, with an involuntary animalish howl, he leapt backwards, knocking aside Councillor Webster, terrifying the retreating Fenwick, and with arms and legs flying like some giant stick insect, rampaged out of the pub and across the High Street.

Driver 108/Rumley, now on his return journey to Lemington, couldn't believe his day. By almost standing on the brake he missed Postlethwaite by a millimetre.

More aware of the rush of wet wind than the fact that he had narrowly missed a messy death, the treasurer stumbled and fell against the back of his car. His hands felt along its battered outline. He rose to stare at it, the blood again draining from his face. With an even more animalish howl he bounded into the town hall to his office where he slammed the door behind him and leaned against it panting, his eyes flashing round the room.

Kean was everywhere. Always happy.

There must be an answer, said Logic, forcing its way into the tangle of Postlethwaite's consciousness.

And it came, in a flash of cerebral tomfoolery. Of course. Local government finance officers were never happy, even when retired. The only ones that were were in prison. Paddy had been at it. He'd been on the fiddle.

Logic, having been momentarily banished, pushed in again. But how, it asked, when Paddy hadn't been seen to lift a finger to do anything other than twirl a pencil?

"The pencil," Postlethwaite muttered, and swung open the door to the outer office.

"THE PENCIL!" he shouted.

Birstin, leaning back in his chair, his feet resting on the desk, instantly crashed backwards to the floor in surprise, a mouthful of condemned chicken pie plugging his throat.

"THE PENCIL!" screamed Postlethwaite again, exultantly.

Preoccupied in coughing up bits of half-chewed chicken, the auditor didn't answer. Postlethwaite sprang at him and yanked him to his feet by the lapels of his jacket.

"The pencil! Where is it?"

Birstin struggled – he'd had enough of physical violence for one day.

"What pencil?"

"Kean's pencil!" ranted Postlethwaite with a knowing look. "He pinched it, didn't he?"

"So what?" protested the auditor, shrugging off the deranged Postlethwaite.

"So I'll have the little swine in court! Ruin his reputation!"

"You'll have a job! His pencil's in the cabinet drawer. He got a receipt for it when he left. He insisted."

Postlethwaite stepped back with hands aloft, then turned and flew up the office to wrench open the cabinet. Paddy's pencil lay there, the wood worn from years of twirling.

The treasurer sagged visibly. He seemed to age ten years. With shoulders hunched, he returned to his own office.

Outside, the heavy sky gave out no light and, somehow, Postlethwaite approved its leaden greyness.

*

Mrs Postlethwaite stood stock still as Paddy came near. This was the first time she'd seen him at close quarters. He didn't look the man to whom her husband had attributed all his problems and failures. He didn't look lazy, incompetent, menacing. If anything, he looked rather friendly, and very handsome.

Yet, she thought, coldly ignoring the outstretched hand, here before her stood years of lost weekends, lonely evenings and loveless nights; for even Postlethwaite's impotence she laid at Paddy's door.

"Couldn't he stay?" asked the landlord, without a hint of malice.

"I don't think he's feeling well," she replied.

"Can I get you a drink?"

"Yes," she said, suddenly wondering why Paddy was here. "A gin and tonic. A very large one."

The landlord escorted her to a high bar stool at the extreme end of the counter from where she had a clear view of the whole room. Hitching herself up and displaying far more leg than was necessary she looked around her.

She was going to get drunk.

*

Nothing much happened in the pub for the next hour. For councillors and businessmen it was an opportunity to initiate deals, form new liaisons and grant favours, and it was invigorating to contribute to the heady atmosphere created by the presence of the media and the actors.

The world of entertainment provoked discussion.

At one table Jacob Cracker sounded off to Elton Fish, an impressionable young reporter from *The Mankley Courier*, who had unwittingly suggested that the future of live theatre might well rest in the hands of local authorities. "What? Never! They don't know their arts from their elbows! C-c-can't even run a d-d-dance without fifty bloody committees!" spluttered the theatre manager. "Theatre's a business, n-n-not a bandstand! Give them a week and the whole place'd b-b-b-be plashtered with green tiles and the shtaff'd be knocking off work at half past five!"

At another table Archie Carrigan sounded off just as vehemently, though with more political astuteness – he knew the value of being overheard accidentally by the right people at the right time.

"Never had a lot of time for theatre, meself," he said blandly to the theatre critic of *The Lemington Globe* but for the benefit of councillors standing nearby. "Interesting museum, that's all. Television! – that's where the future of entertainment lies. Spent a night down South once, in Birmingham. Ever been to Birmingham? Hideous place, hideous. All concrete and adenoids. Nothing much to do there at nights. The hotels are dry, y'know! Not a drink to be had. Merry as a Sunday in Auchtermuchty. Aye. Well. Anyhow. Nothing to do, as I said, so this fellow, this fellow suggests we go theatre-ing y'see. It was hardly a theatre as I understand the term, mind you. Hard seats, black-painted walls, smelly teenagers. Sat there for two hours watching a couple of homosexual plumbers pouring buckets of paint over a naked girl! Nice looking girl, mind, but I had a feeling I was missing the point of it all; didn't get the significance, the significance!"

At yet another table, Gloria too had her audience; a constantly changing one demanding autographs for nephews and nieces. And people called her 'Gloria' as if they had known her all their lives. Rodney, Bill and Karen sat with her, but only Gloria talked – in a strange mid-Atlantic accent she had developed *à la* pop singers and evangelists. It had the advantage of saving her from having to remember which country she was in when pissed.

And Jules, watching from the bar counter, had a feeling that it wouldn't be long before she was just that. But, he decided, he wasn't going to worry about it yet. He was more absorbed in attracting the interest of Dodie Ochiltree, whose eye he had caught and in whom he sensed a kindred spirit.

He gathered up Winston and smiled at the tight-trousered television personality.

The only obvious 'group' in the pub was the staff of the Treasurer's Department. In their charcoal grey suits they were less well dressed than everyone else. Enjoying their drinks at Postlethwaite's expense, they had hoped for something more extreme from his confrontation with Paddy Kean. A fight would have satisfied them, even a stand-up row. Postlethwaite's exit had had its amusing features but worthy of only a titter, not the belly-laugh for which they had geared themselves. And, with Mrs Postlethwaite sitting within earshot, they could hardly joke too loudly about it.

On the edge of the group hovered Arnold and Fenwick, awaiting the arrival of their friends from the metalworks.

It was Giuseppe who first appeared, but after a glance in their direction, he promptly vanished.

Arnold pushed through the bar to the entrance.

"What's wrong?" he asked the Italian.

"We can't go in there!"

"Why not?"

"Look at the way we're dressed," answered Midnight, indicating his overalls and heavy industrial boots. "The girls can stay, but we can't. We'd feel embarrassed. We'll go to The Clock instead."

Marjorie and Joan shoved through into the bar.

Arnold was disappointed.

"Are we going to start meeting here again on Fridays?" he asked.

Midnight looked down on him kindly.

"Aye," said the big Negro, "this week, eh?"

"Aye," said Arnold, feeling happier as Giuseppe and Midnight went off.

"It's a good pub, isn't it?" enthused Fenwick as the girls joined him.

"Arse deco," sniffed Marjorie, looking around.

"Aye, it's smashing," replied Fenwick, going to buy some drinks.

Gradually, with Arnold forming a link between the staff and his friends, the two groups merged, pulling two tables together for all to sit at, close to Mrs Postlethwaite on her bar stool.

She didn't join them. Various people who knew her came to talk and buy her a drink – the vicar, a few councillors – but conversation with these was limited to the flimsiest of superficialities. She was feeling increasingly angry. Angry that her life had been marred by Paddy Kean. As she watched him circulating, a friendly word for everyone, she resented his obvious popularity. She noted the esteem in which he was held.

She still didn't know what he was doing here.

*

In the town hall, Malcolm Birstin, now in a state of microbic stability after eating his chicken pie, was champing at the bit to get back to his audit. He wondered if the inspector in charge had overtaken him. After thinking for a minute he knocked on the treasurer's door. There was no answer. He knocked again, waited a moment, then entered.

Hunched over his desk, with head in hands, Postlethwaite sat motionless in the half-light.

Malcolm coughed politely.

"Is it convenient for me to get on with my audit, now you're back?" he asked.

He was ignored.

"I want to finish it today," he continued.

There was only the sound of the rain outside and the faint sigh of Postlethwaite's breathing.

"So I'll go then," the auditor said, matter-of-factly leaving the office.

Less than five minutes later he was on his rounds again, back in the ladies' – but this time the attendant was on duty.

"I hear you had the police here this morning," she said.

"Well, somebody did," grunted Malcolm. "I didn't ask them to come."

"I know," the woman replied, idly wiping one of the washbasins. "That's the funny thing. Nobody knows who did."

"It was probably one of the women who came in," grunted the auditor as he attacked another coin box. He didn't really want to talk about this morning's happenings. It brought back painful memories.

"That's what I thought at first," said the woman, "but it wasn't! The police got here before she made the street. She's going to charge them with assault. They knocked her over, y'know!"

"Oh?" muttered Birstin, counting pennies.

"And, anyway, I went over to the station and asked the copper there who'd told them – 'cos I was curious, like – and he said it was a bloke who phoned. It wasn't a woman! It was a bloke! Funny, isn't it? The copper said he had a peculiar croaky voice an' all. And he was laughin'. And he knew exactly what was going on. And he didn't give his name. And the sergeant wants to know who it was so's he can charge him with wasting police time."

"Is that right?"

"That's what the copper said."

As he completed checking the cash and prepared to leave, Birstin was thoughtful. It was impossible for a bloke to have known he was in the toilets. It could have been only two or three minutes between the big woman flattening him and the police arriving. Just time really for her screams to have attracted the two women from the street. And, in any case, what man would go into the ladies'?

He crossed the road then turned and looked at the lavatory. Beside it he saw the iron stairs leading to Cruddle's flat. A croaky voice the woman had said. Birstin's suspicions were aroused. It had to be Cruddle.

The auditor ran back across the road, up the iron stairs and pounded on Cruddle's door. The town officer, of course, wasn't there to open it. Birstin was furious. He hated the violent little freak and was impatient to get him charged with wasting police time. Besides, the auditor wanted to ingratiate himself with the policemen he thought had been so charming.

Again he pounded on the door. Getting no reply he returned to his office and took from the safe a large bunch of duplicate keys. Back at the top of the iron stairs he tried them one after the other until Cruddle's door swung open.

As he entered he saw the telephone. That fitted with his suspicions. He tried to estimate which part of the room formed the ceiling of the ladies'. Knocking cats aside and trying to ignore the sickening stench of boiled fish and cat's pee, he worked it out. But he still couldn't imagine how Cruddle could have known what had actually happened below that morning.

Puzzled and disappointed, Birstin made to leave. The easel caught his eye. He studied the photographs pasted there. At first he had difficulty in deciding what they represented. Some were of groups of people, but central on each of them was the same strange figure – a man with his back to the camera holding wide his coat whilst others gazed with astonishment, surprise or admiration at whatever was being revealed.

Birstin didn't try hard to keep the revolting realisation out of his mind. He didn't battle desperately to attribute to the photographs some innocent explanation. With a rare half-smile on his pallid face he again made for the door. But something else distracted him: a kitten in the corner of the room pushing up the carpet with its claws. The carpet folded back a little and Birstin thought he saw a chink of light coming through the floor.

With the look on his face he had meant to save for the day he exposed his first embezzler, he sprang across the room.

There was the answer.

Cruddle's knot-hole.

*

"What do you mean, you want to make a complaint?"

"They nearly killed us!" the woman shouted tearfully. "They were like animals! Knocked us flyin', they did! D'you want to see me bruises?"

"You were obstructing the police in the execution of their duty!" the policeman yelled back.

"Execution of their duty!" the woman sneered. "I'll give the buggers an execution! If my husband had seen what they did he'd have knocked their bloody heads off!"

"Now you're using threats!" The policeman's face was going red; this was getting out of hand. "Another remark like that and I'll charge you!"

"Right!" said the woman, poking a finger in his chest. "You do! You charge us! Go on! I'll have you out of your job!"

"All right, all right." The policeman attempted to introduce an element of reason into the conversation. "Don't let's get worked up."

"Worked up? Me?"

"Just complete the form and take it to the sergeant. He'll sort it out," the policeman sighed.

"Oh, I see! Passin' the buck now, are you? Well, I'm not filling in any form! You're not gettin' me on your records."

"But I've told you!" yelled the policeman. "If you want to make a complaint you have to see the sergeant!"

"Come on, come on!" yelled the taxi driver. "I've been waiting here for twenty minutes. Get on with it!"

"You keep your mouth out of it!" bullied the woman. "I was here long before you!"

"I've got a living to earn, you know!" The taxi driver tried to justify his impatience.

"Aye!" intervened a second woman. "A bloody good one, an' all! It's a disgrace what you charge these days!"

"You're right!" said the first woman. "A flamin' disgrace! I paid six bob last week, just to Windy Nook! Six bob!"

"It's terrible, isn't it? Have you seen the house he lives in? Like a palace!"

"A palace."

The policeman leaned over the counter.

"This isn't a tribunal on taxi fares, missus," he joked heavily.

"Don't get cocky wi' me, young man!" the woman rounded on him.

"Excuse me," said Malcolm Birstin, in an attempt to be noticed – the excitement of discovering Cruddle's knot-hole was bursting his chest.

"Shut up!" said the taxi driver.

"Shut up!" said the woman.

"Wait in the queue!" said the policeman.

Malcolm sat quietly in the corner next to a little lad.

"I've lost me dog!" the boy confided.

"So, come on then!" yelled the woman. "Where's this sergeant you're so bloody proud of?"

The policeman, fed up, battered his truncheon on the counter. Everybody went quiet as Sergeant Goodenough appeared through a door.

"That's him!" whispered the woman. "He was the ringleader!"

"Eeh, aye!" said her friend, staring at the sergeant.

"They want to make a complaint, sir," said the policeman.

"Ha! Ha! Ha! This way, ladies," laughed Goodenough.

He raised a flap at the end of the counter and the two women filed through to follow him nervously into his office.

The policeman turned to the taxi driver.

"Right! What's your problem?" he asked.

"Theft, assault and somebody moved me taxi without consent!"

"Oh, aye? And when did all this happen?"

The taxi driver told his tale.

"I'd just write it off to experience if I were you," advised the policeman, trying not to laugh. If this bloke thought for one minute that all the police existed for was to go around arresting town officers, influential aldermen, theatre managers, mayors and friends of internationally known film stars, he had another think coming.

"Have you got a licence to drive that cab of yours?"

"That's nowt to do with it! I'm here to make a complaint!"

The policeman stuck his face over the desk, close to that of the taxi driver.

"Listen, kidda! 'Let him who's without sin cast the first stone', saith the Lord! – and just you fuckin' remember it! I want to see your licence and insurance documents here within five days. And I hope that cab of yours is in bloody good nick!" The policeman gave a dismissive wave towards the seats. "I'll get somebody to attend to your allegations. Who did you say was in the pub?"

"Gloria Lessingdale," said the taxi driver with a feeling he wasn't being believed.

The policeman shook his head and laughed to himself. It took all types, he thought philosophically.

"Next?"

Malcolm Birstin at last stood up to approach the desk, but was knocked aside by a frantic woman in curlers and headscarf who swept wailing and howling into the police station.

"It's me son! It's me son!" she cried, tears rolling down her cheeks. "He's been blown up! Lost everything he had, poor bugger!"

Florrie Moon, blind drunk, aimed to lean her elbow on the desk, missed, and fell flat on her face.

*

By the time the mayor returned to the pub the atmosphere had changed. Gone was any hint of the self-conscious formality of what her presence had made a quasi-civic event. The consumption of much alcohol had loosened tongues and brought forth personalities where none might have been expected to be dormant. It was noisy. Intense conversations were in full swing. Even little Jimmy, now on his fifth pint, was talking – to himself, but talking.

At the end of the bar counter where Mary was pouring her yet another gin and tonic, Mrs Postlethwaite, still on her stool, had kept meaning to talk but hadn't found a suitable opportunity. She was still angry with herself for being drawn instinctively to the dapper Paddy when he had shown her to her seat. It was her Christopher to whom she should be instinctively drawn, she thought; he should be the one to be popular, friendly, handsome and happy. Not this layabout, Kean.

Mary was intrigued at why Postlethwaite's wife, having stayed, should find it necessary to get drunk. Still, it didn't matter, so long as she avoided falling about.

"There you are, love," the landlord's wife smiled.

Mrs Postlethwaite looked up gratefully, her eyes brightening. Here was someone she could talk to. Everybody talked to barmaids.

"You know, I've never had a holiday!" she said, apropos of nothing in particular. "Not a real one, not like everyone else has."

"Aye?" queried Mary apprehensively.

"Do you know that? Never! Not once have I had a holiday. Not once since I married!"

Mary looked at her sympathetically.

"And all because of him!" Mrs Postlethwaite flung out her arm behind her, nearly taking herself with it, then turned her head to follow its meandering arc with ill-focused eyes to blearily home in on Paddy, now chatting to a group surrounding the Vicar.

Mary followed her dull gaze and frowned.

Mrs Postlethwaite's eyes swivelled back to bore inexorably into the barmaid's soul. Mary was used to that look; people in the first stages of depressive drunkenness always looked at you like that.

"Him!" Mrs Postlethwaite repeated, her arm still extended vaguely in Paddy's direction. "Ruined my life!" She gave a sad smile. "You're not interested, are you? I was only talking because I don't know you and you don't know me – but," she said with intense bitterness, "somebody should know about that man!"

"I'm fascinated," said Mary flatly, picking up a glass to dry.

Mrs Postlethwaite leaned over the counter confidentially.

"You think he's only a barman, don't you? But he hasn't always been a barman!"

"Really?"

"No!" Mrs Postlethwaite went on, dropping her voice. "He used to be the deputy borough treasurer of this town. He used to work at the town hall!"

"Oh?"

"No! That was the trouble! He didn't work, that is. No. Wouldn't, I mean. Work." Mrs Postlethwaite struggled to get her point over. "He wouldn't do anything. Not to help Christopher."

"Who?"

"My husband." She laughed ironically. "I'm Mrs Borough Treasurer! Christopher was that man's boss. That man," her arm swung out again, this time fetching Arnold, who had stood up to get some drinks, a glancing blow on the ear "never did a stroke!

Wouldn't work! Refused to do anything! My husband had to work late at nights and at weekends. Turned his mind. Lost all interest in life. But that Paddy Kean had no sympathy; undermined everything Christopher did."

"I'm surprised your husband did nothing about it."

"Oh, he did! But Kean had friends, you see." She tapped the side of her nose with a finger. "The town clerk for one. Wouldn't let Christopher give him any work."

Arnold, standing at the bar, found all this very interesting. So did Anne, now serving him, and Margaret, who had come to help her mother dry glasses.

Mrs Postlethwaite hardly noticed them as she paused to take a sip of her drink. She had gone too far and was aware of a brittle expression in the barmaid's eye. But the lady couldn't stop herself.

"If it hadn't been for him," she sniffed, "I wouldn't have had to work, or join stupid societies. I could have had a real marriage. That lazy, incompetent Kean over there wouldn't know what that is, of course. You should have seen the floozy he was with at the wine and cheese lunch..."

Her voice faded as she realised, too late, that what she'd been saying was not at all what she felt.

Mary, of course, couldn't have known. She didn't see before her a woman who'd been sickening for warmth and love all her married years. She didn't realise that Mrs Postlethwaite had stopped talking because her feelings were confused. Mary saw only a well-dressed, unhappy drunk with more good looks than good sense, attacking her Paddy – and that she was not going to have.

"You know, don't you, that Paddy Kean is my husband?" said Mary icily.

Mrs Postlethwaite's eyes lost their moist intensity. Away went her suffocating search for something to cry about. Her fingers, drawn tight around the glass of gin, relaxed. She was struck momentarily sober, but circumspection didn't come with sobriety.

"You're Mrs Kean?" she asked incredulously.

"That's right."

"You can't have had an easy life!" The words slipped out in a rush.

"What assumption prompts that remark?" laughed Mary.

"Oh!" responded Mrs Postlethwaite. "I didn't intend to be rude... it's just that, if I may be honest, I feel so sorry that your husband should end up working in a pub, in a job so lacking the dignity to which he must have become accustomed as Christopher's deputy!"

That did it.

Mary banged down the glass she'd been trying to dry and the slow fuse that had been lit years ago when Paddy first told her of Postlethwaite's behaviour at last ignited her pent-up anger.

"Paddy had no dignity at the town hall!" she snorted. "His dignity was stripped from him by your damned husband! Paddy had worked in that department for thirty-seven years, seven of them as treasurer, and your Christopher took from him everything he'd built up. It nearly broke his heart! He could well have killed himself he was so distraught! The job was all he had. He valued it, loved it. He cared about this town. Your husband didn't care about anything. He just wanted position and influence to push him on in his career. Can you imagine what it must have been like for Paddy to sit there all those years, with all that knowledge, and have absolutely nothing to do? Just because your husband was terrified of being usurped!"

Mrs Postlethwaite blanched. It all rang true.

"And as for your suggestion that Paddy is less than a perfect husband," Mary continued unabated, "you can forget it! He's faultless! He's superb! He's everything I could have ever dreamed about! And, judging from the state you're in, he's made me a hell of a lot happier than your precious Christopher has made you!"

Mary turned to Margaret, lowering her voice.

"I've got to get back to work, it's nearly two. Give her another gin and tonic – she looks as though she needs it!"

Arnold, with his drinks, returned to the tables. Anne began to serve another customer. Margaret set Mrs Postlethwaite's drink down, picked up a tea towel and carried on where Mary had left off drying.

Mrs Postlethwaite was silent. She was stunned. But this time it wasn't an excess of juniper-flavoured spirit that produced the distant look in her eyes, it was the effect of a far more intoxicating depressant: truth!

Or, at least, truth as she saw it for now. The instinctive liking she'd felt for Paddy on her arrival had made her feel guilty, but curious. How was it, she asked herself, that this failure of a man could appear so fulfilled, buoyant and productive of such loyalty in a wife. Mrs Postlethwaite had never imagined Paddy to be married. Hadn't Christopher harangued her over the years on the man's mental and physical inertia? Hadn't the staff, on the few occasions when she'd talked to them, added corroborative detail? Surely Paddy had always been derided, despised, even hated! Surely he'd had a life of misery.

She wished Paddy had given her time to talk to him. She might have found some answers. But, after he ordered her first drink, he'd politely excused himself, leaving her imagination to come to its own conclusions.

She watched him again going from table to table collecting empty glasses and occasionally emptying an ashtray – it took her a few minutes, a while to ponder, then the terrible realisation dawned on her of what his being a barman meant. Through the mists of alcohol and shock, her natural sensitivity for the downtrodden was aroused. A lump came into her throat.

No wonder his young wife had been so defensive. It had all been a front. That car he had arrived in at Doreen's had been hired, the girl with him probably some local barmaid in borrowed clothes – all to impress his old colleagues. And, no doubt to avoid miserable poverty on his pittance of a pension he'd been forced to accept this lowly job, clearing up after the privileged, to keep himself going in his last years.

How had he hidden his shame? From what vast reservoir of courage had he summoned the will to shrug off the despondent air of the hired menial, straighten his shoulders and stride forward as if he owned the place to confidently greet his old boss? Oh, the cruel beauty of it all, she agonised as a tear came to her eye. And his wife, working with him to ease the financial pressure.

"Young lady!" she called.

"Yes?" enquired Margaret, promptly responding with a smile.

"The old man who so kindly ordered my first drink, and the barmaid who got me this one, did they pay for them?"

"No. But it doesn't matter..."

"No. No," blustered Mrs Postlethwaite, searching haphazardly in her handbag.

"It's not necessary, I assure you," smiled the girl, uncomfortable in the face of what she knew to be an awful misunderstanding.

"I insist! Here's ten shillings. Just leave the change on the counter, I'm sure I'll find a use for it..."

"Look, are you sure about this?" pleaded Margaret. "I'm sure Dad would prefer it if you..."

"Dad? Who's Dad?"

"Mr Kean. It was my mother you were talking to."

"You're his daughter?" Mrs Postlethwaite was flabbergasted.

"Yes." Margaret's smile broadened; she was happier to be nearer a normal subject of conversation.

"Well, I'd never have guessed!" Mrs Postlethwaite returned the smile, then suddenly became intense. "Tell me, do you like working here?"

"Of course."

"You'll need the money, I suppose?"

"Oh," laughed the girl, "we're not getting paid! We're merely helping out, my sister and me. It's just that Daddy asked us, this being the opening."

This was quite ghastly, thought Mrs Postlethwaite, it made her romantic notion of an impoverished Paddy eking out a miserable existence as a barman even more poignant, more redolent of tragic circumstance. To ensure that his new job got off to a good start, his family was working for nothing. God, these common people stuck together.

Poor Mrs Postlethwaite had always clung to romantic notions. That was why she'd been driven to join so many diverse organisations. Her notion of Christian idealism had driven her to the Church, her concern for the care of animals to the RSPCA, her apolitical loathing of government to the Anglo-Soviet Friendship Society, and her love of beauty to studying Italian. All but the last, and that only by its recent development, had left her preferring her notions to the organised realities. And today was not to prove an exception to the rule.

"I suppose you know who I am ?" she asked.

"Yes. I overheard."

"I daresay if Christopher and I hadn't come to Mankley your lives would have been a lot happier."

"Oh, no they wouldn't!" cried Margaret.

"Happiness is one thing, of course," Mrs Postlethwaite philosophised more to herself than to Margaret, "illusory but satisfying. But education, travel, awareness of opportunities – these are the building-blocks of fulfilment. None of these will have come your way, not on a deputy's salary. We can hardly exist on the money Christopher earns. Your father's can have been only two-thirds of that. And he's brought up a family. It must have been hard."

Mrs Postlethwaite was determined to hang on to her obsessional romanticism.

"Oh, I don't know," Margaret mused, beginning to enjoy the conversation, "we've managed. Mother always worked, of course..."

"How awful..."

"... but only part-time, at lunch times, in The Golden Eagle at Dunston. She and Daddy had better things to do at nights."

"Terrible."

"No, it wasn't!" the girl insisted.

Mrs Postlethwaite gave her a pitying look, as if to say, 'It's all right, dear, I understand you want to be brave about it all.'"

"Look!" said Margaret firmly, "I think you're under a few misconceptions. In the first place, Dad inherited an absolute fortune from his parents. From the day they died he had no need to work. That was why it was so tragic that your husband took away his job. You see, he is really very stuffy and not at all outgoing. He would have made a poor philanthropist, but he did have a talent for financial management. He saw such work as his best means of serving society. And, so far as education is concerned, he gave us the best that money can buy. We travelled the world. Your husband always gave Dad the worst weeks on the holiday list, but this was marvellous for us because then we could see places as they really are, not as the tourist sees them. Oh, we've been to Brazil, Japan, New Zealand, round the world twice actually. We had a wonderful time. You see, Dad had nothing but us to care for. He had nothing else to occupy his mind. He only married Mam in a fit of drunken depression – he'd have been too embarrassed sober! – because she listened to him when he was so unhappy about the way he'd been treated at the office – and he took us on too. And we were from the most awful background. I think he's the finest man in the world. We all love him very much. He'll never know how much. We had nothing before he came along. Now we have everything. We're grateful to your husband for coming to Mankley, Mrs Postlethwaite, very grateful!"

Mrs Postlethwaite felt faint. She tugged nervously at a thick gold chain she was wearing round her neck.

"And now that Dad's retired from the town hall, he's been able to enjoy himself a little," Margaret went on. "That's why he bought the car. He'd always wanted a Jaguar. He only passed his driving test four weeks ago, after three attempts. And he did enjoy the 'Cheese Do' – he'd always been invited, every year. Seeing the faces of the staff amused him; because they thought he was such a drag on the department. It pleased my Dad to show them there was a bit more to him than they thought..."

"But surely he cannot need to work as a barman, if he has all this money you speak of!" Mrs Postlethwaite interrupted – she might be drunk but she wasn't stupid; this was the prattling fiction of a schoolgirl. "That is," she added, looking Margaret straight in the eye, "if you're telling the truth!"

"Oh, yes, Mrs Postlethwaite." Margaret was now very serious. "The fact is that Daddy is working here because he owns this pub! He bought it! For cash! You can have as many gins as you want – on the house!"

Mrs Postlethwaite's eyes dropped, her romantic notions scattered to the winds.

She resented it.

Then, oddly, her countenance brightened, became radiant with spite.

"And I suppose that gives him the right to play the show-off!" she said accusingly. "The right to have another woman behind your mother's back! I saw him with a girl – a young, attractive girl – at the cheese thing last weekend. She wasn't the kind of girl he could claim as his niece, you understand? Not at all!"

Mrs Postlethwaite placed a well-manicured hand over her glass and stared at Margaret, waiting for a spluttered defence.

But the girl merely looked back at the lady warmly.

"You mean my sister?" she laughed.

And Anne, who'd been standing nearby, struck a pose, pouted and stretched her arm up the tall drinks cabinet.

Mrs Postlethwaite had played her last card – and lost! She cast an appreciative glance over Anne. It was obvious that here was the girl in the Jag.

It was also obvious to the staff. They gave a little cheer, and Anne curtsied sweetly. And Mrs Postlethwaite realised that, for a long time, all the staff sitting near her had been listening to everything she and Margaret had been saying.

"Oh... shit!" she said to herself, despondently knocking back her gin and tonic.

It should have been a moment of disgrace and embarrassment, a cue for a hasty exit, but the lady was made of kookier stuff than that. She spun round in her seat, smoothed her skirt to emphasise her shapely legs which she then crossed elegantly, and in full view of everyone, clicked her fingers at Paddy.

"Barman!" she called, with an amused expression on her face. "Drinks for all my friends!" Then, as the landlord, smiling quizzically, came towards her, she raised her glass to him, meanwhile winking at the staff and nudging Arnold's shoulder with her elbow, causing him to drop his sandwich.

It was something that only an exceedingly beautiful, well-groomed and intelligent woman could have got away with. That point was lost on no one – except Arnold, who was busy trying to fish his sandwich out of his beer.

*

In the town hall, the borough treasurer was still at his desk. His body had slipped from its former seated position, so he now almost knelt.

The sky outside remained dark, heavy with cloud, but he didn't see it. His hands tightly covered his face, and his mind was as dark and heavy with cloud as the sky.

He'd heard Birstin come in and talk, and heard him go. Vaguely he'd been aware that some time later someone had visited the outer office. He'd heard the telephone ring there a few times. Occasionally, an indistinct voice had echoed through the tiled foyer.

But none of it had touched Postlethwaite. His eyes were closed. If he'd been able to close his ears he would have done so. He craved sensory deprivation like an insomniac with a hangover.

*

Not far away, in the police station, Sergeant Goodenough screwed up pieces of paper and nonchalantly threw them at the waste-paper bin. He missed, but he didn't care.

Swinging his boots onto the desk and gently bashing his truncheon against the leg of the chair, he addressed the three constables lined up in front of him.

"Right, Griffiths! You investigate that woman! See if her husband's got a car. Get the bugger stopped every time he goes out in it! We don't want complaints against the police to take too long to sort out, do we?"

"No, sir!"

"Ha-ha!" the sergeant chortled. "That's right! Then get your arse along to the hospital. Find out about Moon. The bugger'll likely be malingering, but you'd better go through the motions. That's something he won't be knowing about for a bit, if his mother's telling the truth! Eh? Ha-ha! Incidentally, did you charge her with drunk and disorderly?"

"No, sir."

"You're slipping, lad, you're slipping. Right! Off you go!"

"Sir!" Griffiths donned his helmet and went.

The sergeant perused his notes and looked thoughtful. He shook his head and sniggered as he read Shawe-Iskay's report of the taxi driver suggesting that upright citizens like the mayor, the alderman and the theatre manager had committed assault, to say nothing of the idea that a world-famous film star was in the local pub. The fellow was off his head.

But this town officer bloke might have moved the taxi. And Birstin mentioned the same fellow. And the perverted sexual overtones – pretty heady stuff this knot-hole in the floorboards.

Goodenough took a little book from his desk. On the cover was printed 'Deviants – Mankley'. He flicked through its pages. No 'Cruddle' to be found, nothing under 'Town Officer' either. To be on the safe side, however, for future reference, the sergeant wrote the name under both headings.

Drawing in his cheeks, he sucked, whistling slowly inwards through his teeth, and glowered at the two remaining constables.

"Your ankle all right, lad?"

"Yes, sir!" replied PC Johnstone.

"We'll have to look into Birstin's allegations. His father's a JP."

"Yes, sir!"

"You'd better come along with me."

"Yes, sir!"

"Shall I come, sir?" enquired PC Shawe-Iskay.

"If you must," grunted the sergeant. "Incidentally, you interviewed the taxi driver didn't you?"

"Yes, sir."

"What did you charge him with?"

"Well, nothing, sir!"

"Might have guessed. I sometimes wonder if you should be in the police force, young fellow; might be better if you took up hairdressing or something," the sergeant muttered wistfully as they left the station with Birstin, who had waited eagerly to join them.

Goodenough was a lot less wistful when the auditor let him into Cruddle's flat.

"Cats!" the sergeant exclaimed. "Hundreds of the buggers!" He'd been right to include Cruddle's name on his list of deviants. Everybody knew that perverts liked cats.

Birstin indicated the photographs.

"Disgusting!" pronounced Goodenough.

Then the auditor went to the corner and lifted up the carpet.

"Open and shut!" The sergeant clapped his hands.

"Just a moment, sir," said Shawe-Iskay, extending himself on the floor. "I don't think it's possible to see anything through this hole."

"What?"

Shawe-Iskay wriggled about but his helmet, knocking against the skirting board, prevented his eyes coming anywhere near the knot-hole.

Goodenough, loath to be thwarted, kicked Shawe-Iskay aside and threw himself on the floor. So did PC Johnstone. As Shawe-Iskay rose to his feet they scuffled about, their helmets banging together.

Meanwhile, Shawe-Iskay went to the easel and copied some words from a banner that appeared on each of the photographs just above the assembled groups of people.

A few minutes later, back at the police station, with Birstin now off to his next public convenience, the sergeant changed into civvies. This Cruddle business disturbed him. Ordinarily he would have had the pervert locked up, but Goodenough was wary of putting away public servants, however lowly. They had a nasty knack of knowing troublesome types – like solicitors and town clerks – and, up to now, there was nothing really positive to go on.

So, he decided as he straightened his tie, now that he was off duty he would take a look at this new pub. Make himself known to the landlord. A bit of public relations never did any harm.

*

Chocolate sidled around and out of the town hall foyer and sniffed the air. She was near, but not in the post office.

He loped to the corner. There was nobody about to confuse the issue – Jess's scent was stronger. Trotting down the side of the town hall, however, he sensed it weakening.

Confusing.

Chocolate stopped, lifted a leg to the wheel of a parked car to remind himself of how far he had gone, then retraced his steps to the corner.

He padded along the High Street. This was more encouraging. But, after he'd passed the police station, the scent faded again. Then came a whiff of blue serge. He snarled. Then a whiff of something more familiar. It was too much. He needed to think.

Retracing his scent to a shop doorway he lay down and rested his muzzle on his paws. From here he had a view of three streets. Jess had to come along one of them. Every so often he gave an involuntary twitch as the bitch's scent became temporarily stronger.

And that other scent.

And both mixed heavily with blue serge.

Chocolate's patchy brown forehead puckered up.

*

Mrs Postlethwaite was now at ease. She conversed entertainingly with Paddy, the staff and Arnold's friends. Arnold, seated next to her, was captivated. The others stood in a rough circle – they could relax better standing, and hold more beer.

Behind them various working members of the public and some of the guests began to drift away – back to add their two penn'orth of inebriated inefficiency to the nation's ailing economy – but the noise-level didn't diminish with their departure. Those who remained were mostly seasoned drinkers; the more they drank the louder they became.

"It's a pity Midnight and Giuseppe didn't stay, isn't it?" remarked Arnold to Fenwick.

"Aye," was the disinterested reply.

"Are they your friends?" Mrs Postlethwaite asked Arnold.

Shyly, he mumbled a 'yes' and stared into his beer. Mrs Postlethwaite looked down at him warmly.

"Your husband's got a really impressive name," Joan remarked. "Christopher Oates Postlethwaite – sounds dead right for somebody in his job."

Mrs Postlethwaite didn't want to be reminded of her husband's existence at this moment.

"I see it on our rate demand every six months," Joan went on.

"Well," Mrs Postlethwaite interrupted, "he gets his 'Christopher' from his grandfather," – a wicked smile appeared – "but I don't know where he gets his 'Oates'!"

"Probably after Captain Oates," said Joan, missing the pun, "of the Antarctic Expedition."

"That will account for his cold feet." Mrs Postlethwaite would have expanded on this but she noticed Stan and David looking at their watches, then at each other.

"Best be getting back I suppose," David muttered.

"Oh, no!" cried Mrs Postlethwaite. "You've no need to return until closing-time – you've got another hour yet! I'm sure Christopher fully intended you to stay!"

And that's how Postlethwaite's staff didn't return to the town hall until much, much later.

*

That's also how Malcolm Birstin, at five minutes past two, having at last completed his audit of the town's public conveniences and returned to finalise his figures at the office, didn't remain there.

He wasn't going to be the only one working; not when everybody else was out enjoying themselves, and when the deranged Postlethwaite might at any moment leap out and attack, and with the phones to answer and enquiries-window to attend. 'Stuff that,' he thought, slinging his clipboard on to his desk, 'what's good for the goose is good for the gander...'

Thinking of poultry he felt hungry, so decided to slip along to the Health Department to grab a bite to eat.

On the way, just to add malicious interest to his day, he paused to talk to Harriet, who usually did Postlethwaite's typing.

"They're all over at the pub," he said, "drinking! I see you weren't invited!"

And Harriet, upset, developed a migraine and went home.

Then he popped his head round the door of the rates collection office and expressed surprise that the staff there were not at The Bone Idol with everyone else, resulting in their displaying for the rest of the afternoon an even more than normal mood of belligerent mediocrity towards the public which paid their wages.

But Providence exacted retribution on Malcolm Birstin – where it hurt. When he arrived at the Health Department, where up to an hour ago had lain a heap of condemned goodies, there was now a locked cabinet with 'CONTENTS CONDEMNED – KEEP OUT' emblazoned across its doors.

Only barely hiding his panic he entered the adjoining office. A few young public health inspectors were lounging about reading motoring magazines and discussing torque and oversteer. They ignored Malcolm.

"Audit!" he announced officiously.

"Sod off!" suggested one of the young men good-naturedly.

"Where's the delivery note for that new cabinet in there?"

"Ask the boss; he'll be back from holiday in two weeks."

"Where's his deputy?"

"On the sick."

"Right!" snapped Birstin. "Until I see a delivery note I'm confiscating that cabinet. Two of you can carry it along to my office!"

The young men laughed him into an embarrassed exit – a casual though justified act of rudeness which was to earn their future expense claims to the Treasurer's Department a remarkable degree of scrutiny.

But Birstin's immediate problem was free food and where to get it. It was obviously to be denied him in the Health Department. His only recourse was to join the staff at the pub. Smith could buy him something from the money Postlethwaite had handed out.

Malcolm quashed his distaste for untainted edibles and set off pubwards.

*

Florrie Moon moaned and opened her eyes. The pretty policewoman smiled.

"Feeling a bit better?" she asked.

At the sight of the uniform Florrie forgot the pounding of her head and sat bolt upright.

"Is this prison? He said they'd put me away. 'Don't trust them bastards', he said!"

"No, love. It's not prison."

Mankley's police would never arrest Florrie – so long as she was at home they knew where to find the other Moons!

"We just put you in here to sleep it off. Here's a cup of tea."

"Ta." Florrie took the hot brew gratefully. "Have they found out who did it?"

"They're investigating now."

Florrie slurped her tea and burped gently.

*

"Is that him?" asked PC Griffiths, inclining his head towards Ernie Moon encapsulated in tubes, drips and plastic.

The doctor nodded.

"And he hasn't told you who did it?" the policeman frowned disbelievingly.

The doctor shook his head.

"Nothing? Nothing at all? Not a word?" Griffiths persisted.

"No. He has groaned once or twice, tried to form words, but he's very ill. One can attach no significance to the sounds he makes..."

PC Griffiths cast a cynical eye over the blankets outlining what was left of the lower half of Ernie's body and decisively snapped shut his notebook.

"Probably praying," he sniffed, to the doctor's disgust.

*

Postlethwaite was praying.

The idea had occurred to him only as a last resort; because he had already slipped from his chair into a kneeling position, his eyes were already closed, his hands already covered his face – and it cost nowt! And, in extreme circumstances, even a creative local government accountant can appreciate the directness of a non-committee dictatorship. Besides, anybody capable of coining a phrase like 'creative local government accountant' and believing in it, is equally capable of believing that God has nothing better to do than hang around like some out-of-season Father Christmas waiting only for a word from a man with qualifications to instantly respond with a flash of divine garrulity. Though, from God's point of view, it may be reasonably imagined that a few words from Postlethwaite must have had at least novelty value. A wry smile might have come over the divine countenance.

After all, here He was, coming to the end of the Jesus campaign with its sign-in-the-red-box-and-don't-worry-about-the-small-print free offer, with damn all to show for it but a wider variety of bigots, all having paid their deposits and not kept up the instalments, and out of the blue, up pops Postlethwaite, not a squeak from him since birth – your genuine, died-in-the-pig-swill prodigal!

So Postlethwaite was heard.

God, of course, interpreted the treasurer's plea for Kean to be struck by lightning while visitations of the plague descended on The Bone Idol as a subconscious desire for self-confidence, so, after weighing the pros and cons, after checking the terms of the once-and-for-all Jesus offer, He gave Postlethwaite the benefit of some Fatherly advice, deliberately using the same words He had put into the mouth of the town clerk years before.

As Postlethwaite knelt, hands pressed hot to his forehead, having exhausted his knowledge of Biblically-inspired disasters to befall the pub across the road, through an ocean of amazing warmth, he heard, "Mr Kean is a fair man. Go to him and apologise. Tell him you made a mistake. Flatter him. Beg his help."

Postlethwaite's fingers dug deep into his sweating brow. Could these be the words of God? God, the Just? God, the Powerful? The Avenger? Who went round knocking off your firstborn and burying Egypt under a mountain of frogs?

"Aye!" God struggled through the static of Postlethwaite's questioning. "But all that stuff's in the small print! All we're bothered about just now awhile is the free offer!"

Postlethwaite heard Him not. Instead of listening respectfully, he raised his voice and entreated, "Well, if that's what You want me to do, give us a sign, as it were! Give us a light! A light so's I know it's You! That's what I want! A light to show the way! A Sign!"

"I can't do that!" roared God, almost deafened by Postlethwaite's spiritual cacophony and rapidly losing interest in the demanding borough treasurer. "I'll put you on to the other fellow. He's better at party tricks than Me!"

But again Postlethwaite heard Him not.

Frothing at the mouth and babbling incoherently, he continued to call for a sign, a light, a brilliant manifestation of God's power.

*

Gloria's Rodney, bored with the chatter of the actors, having an eye for a pretty woman, and his resolve strengthened by some rather splendid malt whisky, had worked his way into the bunch surrounding Mrs Postlethwaite's legs.

Gloria, after a moment, noticed where he was and, recognising competition when she saw it, crossed the room to be by his side.

Alcohol is a hallucinatory drug, a creator of fantasy, and because Gloria was a star, those in the company did nothing to indicate that they thought any less of her than she did herself. She wobbled slightly as she stood; a strand of hair straying raggedly over her brow, her make-up smudged, one false eyelash loose, but, inebriation bringing to its highest expression the self-delusion that festers so virulently in the breasts of thespians, she thought she was beautiful. Worse, she thought she might have something to contribute to the conversation.

But Gloria was no match for the lady on the bar stool. Gloria, away from a script and clever lighting, was hardly a match, physically or intellectually, for a cardboard cut-out.

But most of those near her were happy to be at such close quarters to so famous an actress. They quizzed her politely about her films. She replied with quotes memorised from press handouts and favourable reviews.

She was complimented on the roles she had played.

"I'll never forget that one about the dying opera singer – I cried right through it, I did," said Joan.

And she too was favoured with the star's famous smile.

Mrs Postlethwaite, privately resenting the actress's intrusion, said little but listened politely.

In the opposite corner of the room Dodie Ochiltree and Jules Federman sat at a table. An understanding had been reached between them but conversation was stilted. They were keen to be alone together now. There was little they could do in the bar to further develop their relationship.

Out of boredom, Jules showed Dodie how clever Winston was: how he could beg, offer a paw, and catch thrown pieces of cheese in mid-air.

Then, seeing that Gloria was occupied in conversation at the end of the bar counter, he gigglingly demonstrated Winston's latest trick.

"Been dying to show you this," Jules said to Dodie, then leaned down to whisper in the dog's ear. "How did Gloria

Lessingdale get to the top, then?" And Winston threw himself on his back, widely separated his back legs and panted.

Dodie and Jules sniggered together in the corner. They occasionally touched one another as if by accident and drew apart, feigning embarrassment.

Of the forty or so people still gathered only two were alone – little Jimmy Slattery and Jacob S Cracker. Jimmy was contented enough – oblivion had come with his eighth pint when he had inconspicuously keeled over in his chair, an amused smile on his shrunken face.

But Jacob wasn't contented. He'd tried previously to join in conversation with the circle of council members gathered round the mayor – now loudly spewing forth her views on the town clerk and his pettifogging rules about use of the council Daimler – but his speech had become so impaired nobody had had the patience to listen and, little by little, he was squeezed out of their company. So now, though still seated where he'd sat for the past hour, he was obviously not part of the loud, self-opinionated crowd immediately to his left.

Archie Carrigan had occasionally come to keep him company but Cracker got no joy from that. As the theatre manager had become more drunkenly morose, Gloria, then still at the charming stage of her inebriation, had spoken to him.

"I meant to say to you earlier, dahling, what a beautiful old theatre you have. Of course, you won't have gone civic yet..."

It was then that Jacob remembered what the alderman had said at their first meeting: "Be grand if I were able to persuade council to bail out the old place, eh, Jacob? Save it for the borough! Be grand, wouldn't it?"

Jacob looked about him at the chattering councillors. There'd be nothing grand about it, he thought. He could see it now. Councillors, officials, clerks – all stage-struck and tumescent with civic pride. There'd be no room for the touches of self-expression the theatre manager had always known – like getting pissed with the press. It would be goodbye to his little empire.

"The council would keep you on, of course," Archie had continued breezily, "probably pay you a bit more than you're getting now an' all!"

Jacob sighed. That was the trouble. They'd keep him on all right, but only as their stooge. He resolved to go to London that week and discuss the matter with his bosses. Surely if they'd been going to sell his theatre to the council he'd have been the first to know. He'd think of new ideas to make the place more profitable. He'd prepare a report to convince the directors that a little investment might just tip the scales. But, as he thought, he knew he'd not do these things. And even if he did, he knew it would make no difference.

The voices in the bar were becoming louder. Paddy turned up the volume of the background music.

He bumped into Archie.

"Everything all right, Paddy?" queried the smiling alderman.

"Yes," said Paddy, looking around him, "but not many folk came in off the street. Did you advertise in the newspapers?"

"No need!" laughed Archie. "After tonight's television your pub'll never be empty, never be empty! Advertising costs money – we got the television for nowt!"

Paddy, convinced and impressed, wandered away; and Archie heaved a relieved sigh – he'd forgotten about the public, they'd had no part to play in today's scenario. He ordered himself another drink and took one to Cracker.

"You look a bit down," Archie remarked.

"N-n-n-spashl fidle..." answered the theatre manager.

"Aye," said Archie, "well, there's another drink. Let's go and chat to people shall we?"

He helped Jacob to his feet and guided him to where Gloria was regaling the town hall staff with advice on how best to act in films.

"Y'know," she was slurring in her mid-Atlantic accent, "y'must dramatise everything, y'know. Y've gotta vitalise the screenplay that the director's definitised. Y've gotta emotionalise the drama, dramatise the emotion, sympathise the audience, internationalise the appeal..." – feeling a sudden need to urinise the bladder, she broke off in mid-Atlantic mid-sentence and, with glass unsteadilyised in front of her, tottered off to the ladies'.

"Where's she gone?" asked Arnold, innocently glancing up from his pint. He'd been listening to Miss Lessingdale's soliloquy with interest.

"Probably to ecstacise her clitoris," muttered Mrs Postlethwaite.

"I thought her dog was called Winston!" said Arnold.

Herklitorus seemed a funny name for a dog.

Sounded Greek.

Time was getting on. The braying clamour of talk and laughter was deafening to anyone who hadn't taken a drink, and the background music at its increased level blended the individual sounds into a cacophonous whole; yet the words of the song were discernible if one listened carefully:

"Istanbul's not Constantinople now,
It's Istanbul..."

But nobody was listening carefully, or even at all. The music was just there, like the walls or the carpet.

Paddy continued to circulate, a word for everyone. He was glad to see expressions of enjoyment on the faces filling the place. Of course, those with a sense of sobriety or with firm commitments had left by now. Those Paddy saw were hard-core boozers, regular I'll-go-when-he-chucks-me-out types.

Some there should have left long before. The girls from the metalworks, for instance, who were thoroughly settled in – Joan dreamily impressed with everything and everybody, and Marjorie cynically storing up what she could understand of Mrs Postlethwaite's wit for future use.

Fenwick Fancourt also remained. He was amazed at having met a real film star – even if she was a bit tatty.

And, of course, all the councillors were there – those few who had jobs would tell their employers they'd been to a civic function.

It was as Paddy was chatting to Jules and Dodie that the stalwart figure of Sergeant Goodenough strode purposefully to the bar counter. The landlord hadn't expected customers from the street so late in the day. And, a few minutes later, in came Cruddle, clad once again in his mackintosh.

"I've come for me measuring rod and I thought I'd have a pint to celebrate your opening," the town officer gabbled, gyrating an eye over the pack of councillors. "I see that lot haven't shifted yet! They'll be here for ever if you let them!"

Archie Carrigan, seeing Cruddle arrive, felt it diplomatic, bearing in mind this gentleman's previous remarks about Nora, to steer the mayor away from the centre of the room and usher her over to talk to Dodie and Jules.

"Ooh!" exclaimed Jules. "A real mare! If I pull your chain, will you flush?"

Nora laughed like a drain and flopped down beside him.

"Cheeky little bugger!" she cackled, coughing and spilling her drink as she slapped a ham-like hand on his knee.

Jules nearly fainted. Yet, in an odd way, Nora warmed to him and, after a while, he showed her Winston's trick.

"Eeh! That's clever," she screamed, "and all you have to do is say 'Gloria Lessin'dale'?"

And Winston, again, flipped over and spread his legs, panting – tireless little pooch.

Returning from the ladies', Gloria, overhearing her name being used, smiled across at the mayor, and Nora smiled back, neck and cheeks blotchy with excitement.

It was then that Malcolm Birstin arrived. On seeing so many elected members gathered there, his initial reaction, as a local government officer, was to flee; but it occurred to him that here might be an opportunity to impress. Judging from Postlethwaite's present mental condition, the treasurership could well become vacant at very short notice, and maybe it was time for auditors to be considered suitable material for such high office. It would be a smack in the eye for his father if Birstin got promoted. His father had never wanted him to be an auditor.

"Any damned fool can go round checking on other people!" Birstin Senior had said.

But if Malcolm became borough treasurer, it would be a different story.

With that thought in mind, he adopted the attitude of the nonchalant professional and posed in a superior fashion beside the table nearest the staff. Nobody noticed him. They continued to listen to Mrs Postlethwaite. Then Malcolm spied Jacob. The theatre manager looked important. Trying hard to be the gentleman, just as his father had done so often at events such as this, he smiled, held out his hand and leaned forward slightly.

"How d'you do," he said, "I'm Birstin."

"Spuddlub... bytightly olgrost..." muttered Jacob.

Discouraged, Malcolm turned his attention to Archie Carrigan, now leaning across the bar counter.

"How d'you do," the auditor announced himself.

"What's that?" asked Carrigan, more concerned with catching the eye of the barmaid.

"I'm Birstin."

"It's the chemicals in the beer," replied Archie, at last attracting Anne's interest and instantly losing any in the auditor's possible physical discomfort.

Then Birstin saw the sergeant. No need for introductions here, he thought, and confidently attached himself to the big policeman.

But Goodenough's mind was occupied. Within the assembled company he had savoured a whiff of pooffiness emanating from the corner where the mayor was sitting.

Now the sergeant knew that mayors were never pooffy, and he was pretty sure that such a quality was rarely found in women. So his suspicions fell on Jules and Dodie. He wasn't entirely sure whether or not television personalities were regularly pooffy, but he did know that people who looked like television personalities invariably were. And that fellow near the mayor looked remarkably like a television personality.

While the sergeant mulled over these points of logic, he became aware of Birstin chuntering about something. He looked down at the auditor.

"What is it, lad?"

"Look!" whispered Birstin. "There's Cruddle!"

The sergeant straightened his shoulders and surveyed the town officer with a narrow-eyed stare.

One of Cruddle's eyes swung round to stare back, but it wasn't looking at the sergeant; it was looking at Malcolm Birstin, and Cruddle was wondering how it was that the auditor was here in the pub instead of being beaten with steel rods in the cellars of the police station. He was also wondering how it was that Birstin and the sergeant were standing together in apparently amicable conversation after the punch-up in the ladies'.

Anyway, thought Cruddle, there was no way anyone could have discovered who had telephoned the police that morning. All he had to do now was ensure that Birstin was under no illusions about the right of the town officer to have a pint in his free time.

He scurried over to face the auditor, one eye aimed directly at the sergeant's left shoulder and the other scanning Mrs Postlethwaite, madly gin-popped but still regaling the staff.

This resulted in the sergeant suddenly screwing his eyes down left in a frantic attempt to see what was wrong with his shoulder, while Mrs Postlethwaite ceased her flow as she tried to recall where she had seen a face like Cruddle's before – she knew it was recently but the memory wouldn't come clear.

Meanwhile, Birstin, not knowing what the weird little figure in front of him was doing there, simply felt uneasy – especially as he recalled Cruddle's dexterity with the heavy-duty mole wrench.

But when the town officer spoke, Birstin had no doubt that he was the object of the little man's interest.

"Listen, you!" Cruddle snarled croakily. "I started at six this morning, kept at it till twelve, took the car to the garage, filled in your stupid logbook and stamped your fuckin' invoices, so if you've got anything to say about me havin' a pint after all that, you can fuckin' say it to the town clerk, not me!"

Birstin, sickeningly embarrassed – just as Cruddle intended – tried to formulate a reply, but before he could do so the town officer had scuttled off to join the mayor at her table with Jules and Dodie.

Thoroughly put out, Cruddle flapped an arm in the direction of the auditor.

"There y'are, Mrs Slattery!" he said. "That bastard over there – he's the one that stops you gettin' a ride in the car!"

Nora consoled him.

"Aye, I knew it was nowt to do with you, Emlyn, pet. You sit here now and enjoy your drink."

Then she turned to Jules.

"Show him your trick with the dog, son."

Jules obliged.

So did Winston.

Cruddle was disgusted.

"All you have to say is 'Gloria Lessin'dale'!" Nora coughed up phlegm in enthusiasm.

Cruddle wanted to vomit, not at Mrs Slattery – though, God knows, the sight of her in her present state was cause enough – but at the thought of a dumb animal being made to do tricks. People should pay more respect to animals. Anyway, he'd never heard of Gloria Lessingdale.

If the sergeant had felt earlier in the day that the mixture of the knot-hole in the floorboards, peculiar photographs, and hordes of cats was pretty heady stuff, his feelings after seeing Cruddle in the flesh gave him the intuitive conviction that here was a villain of the first order.

Intuitive conviction was something in which the sergeant was something of an expert. In fact, quite a few of the less privileged in Mankley's society, thanks to Horace Goodenough, had a string of intuitive convictions a mile long. Especially those with a squint or those who didn't have blue eyes or who walked with a provocative gait – oh, yes – intuitive conviction was what policing was all about. The sergeant just had to look at a football crowd at St James's Park to pick out the baddies: 'Look at that!' he'd say, 'Born to be hung!' or 'Now, there's a rogue – see the shape of that nose!' or 'Touch of the tar-brush there! Watch the bugger! Badness in the blood!'

Goodenough didn't know what was in Cruddle's blood, but it hardly took a Scotland Yard detective to tell that a hook nose, eccentrically mobile eyes and a dirty mackintosh combined in the person of one who kept cats and peculiar photographs spelled a man unlikely to contain a wholly normal moral attitude to life.

"Well, well!" Archie Carrigan interrupted Goodenough's thoughts, and again ignored the presence of Birstin. "If it isn't Horace!"

"Afternoon, Alderman." The sergeant politely touched the place on his forehead where his helmet would normally have been.

"Having a tour of inspection at the ratepayers' expense, are you?" quipped Archie.

"Well, sir, it's as well to look over public houses now and again, though, as you see I'm off-duty at the moment."

And Archie and the sergeant got down to a fine old chinwag. A couple of the press joined them and the sergeant discovered that the somewhat faded lady to his left was in fact Gloria Lessingdale, and that there had been a quasi-civic celebration that day; and his mind, for want of a more suitable term, was put more at ease when he learned that the man in the corner was actually Dodie Ochiltree and not a pooffy look-alike.

The sergeant decided not to call immediately for reinforcements. He would watch a while. His instincts were never wrong. Mr Ochiltree, being a respected television personality, might not be pooffy, but that colourfully dressed, skinny creature next to him probably was – he kept touching Mr Ochiltree. Funny that Cruddle should make for that table. And there were theatricals in the bar. They were always suspect. The sergeant had once heard an actor say that hanging was immoral. Dangerous people, actors – and he wondered what that dog was doing, constantly throwing itself on its back.

It was half past two as Paddy reached the seat where little Jimmy was spread-eagled. Here was somebody who had no need of polite conversation – he was out cold.

"By hell!" spluttered Big John, the Laughing Postman, bustling through the door from the street, shaking raindrops from his heavy coat and momentarily reviving Jimmy as a result. "It's terrible out there! As wet as your beer! Ha! Ha!"

Paddy grinned a welcome and offered his hand as little Jimmy stretched, yawned and went back to sleep.

"Nice of you to call in, John."

"What? I wouldn't have missed this for anything! Couldn't come earlier. Shift didn't finish till two. It's a suspicious occasion is this, eh, Mr Kean? Ha! Ha! But you should put your front lights on! Can't see a hand in front of you out there!"

"Blast!" cried Paddy, furious with himself. "I forgot about my neon sign! Thanks John, I'll switch it on right away!"

The landlord pushed his way behind the bar counter. No wonder there'd been so few in from the street. He pulled a big tumbler-switch, and a broad swathe of light cut across the road to bathe the town hall in a lustrous radiance.

*

The babbling, God-struck Postlethwaite sensed rather than saw the floodlit vividness of his office.

He took his hands from his face, tears dimming his vision, then sprang to his feet, raised his arms to heaven and called, "A sign! A light!" – then, distractedly muttering: "Go and apologise... Beg his help... Flatter him..." the glow of blind faith shining in his eyes, he tore open the door and pranced through the foyer, consumed with an impulse to cross the road towards the dazzling manifestation, his hands extended high above his head.

Driver 108/Rumley, chugging along on his last run of the day, stared with red-rimmed horror through his misted-up windscreen at the jabbering treasurer. Once again, this time with both feet, he jumped on the brake.

But a bump was inevitable.

*

Having established the time of Ernie Moon's arrival at the hospital, PC Griffiths continued his investigation at ambulance headquarters where he interviewed the most senior officer available.

"Week past Saturday, you say?" the divisional superintendent asked, a strange look of dying hope about him.

"That's right. At about eleven o'clock at night."

The superintendent fumbled through a card index.

"I might have known!" he suddenly exclaimed, looking up. "Not your day, Constable!"

"You're right there!" agreed the policeman, thinking of his sore ankle.

"You're not going to believe this, but the blokes who picked up your Mr Moon disappeared last Monday!"

"Why?"

The superintendent's voice betrayed a wild, surprised sadness.

"Oh, they were always doing queer things, them two. Like the night I caught them shifting furniture in the ambulance. Wouldn't have been so bad except there were two patients in there as well – a heart attack and a woman in labour! Found them under a table and a bookcase, and these blokes thought it was funny! Always dropping people they were. Got a pile of complaints here. Glad they've gone. One poor sod thought he was having a seizure, phones for an ambulance, up come these two Johnnies and by the time the bloke reaches hospital he's got multiple fractures, a burst liver and he dies the next night. Funny thing – after the autopsy, we learn that all he had originally was wind and a fish-bone stuck in his throat! It was them fellows dropping him!"

"So where do I find them?"

"Well, I've got an address here, but it'll be out of date."

"I'll take it down anyhow."

"Proper cowboys they were," the superintendent muttered, "never filled in reports or anything."

He handed the card to the policeman without seeming to be aware of what he was doing.

PC Griffiths noted down an address and, as the superintendent had predicted, it was out of date.

The house was abandoned.

*

Florrie Moon had a desperate thirst on her. The tea had gone down well, but something a bit stronger would go down a hell of a

lot better, she thought, swinging her legs and rocking to and fro
on the hard bench.

"What's the time?" she asked suddenly.

"Twenty-five past two," the policewoman replied.

Florrie began to fret. Only thirty-five minutes to the pubs and
off-licences closing. Stupid that off-licences closed at the same
time as pubs – that was when they should open.

The sides of her throat felt as though they were sticking
together. She had to have a drink. But she could hardly just up
and go. Not when she was supposed to be concerned about her
son. What would that nice policewoman think?

Florrie racked her brains.

She would give it another ten minutes.

*

That was long enough for PC Griffiths to have returned from
his fruitless investigation at the hospital and ambulance
headquarters.

As he arrived at the station, a little boy ran in after him and
tugged at his wet cape.

"Have you found me dog yet, mister?"

"What?" The policeman spun round suspiciously.

"Me dog!"

"When did you lose it?"

"This mornin', mister. I came here this mornin' an' all, but
everybody was too busy to see us, an' this drunk woman came in
an' fell over an'…"

"Shut up!" yelled Griffiths, giving the child an insight into why
the British bobby is loved, admired and renowned throughout the
Commonwealth and the world for his tact and good manners.

'Get the buggers terrified when they're young', the sergeant
was always saying, 'and they'll stay that way for life!'

Griffiths walked to the end of the passageway and opened a
door, through which could be seen a flight of stairs descending
into darkness.

"Constable Cyril!" he called roughly. "Have you got a lost dog down there?"

"Are you fucking joking?" came an echoing response and the clunk of a bolt being withdrawn.

There was a crescendo of snarls, yelps, howls, slaverings and scrapings and a scream of pain.

After a shout of, "Down, you bastard! Get out of it!", up from the gloom there emerged a policeman with a finger missing, his ripped uniform covered in dog hairs, bloodstains and excrement, and smelling like a cesspool. He gave a distracted glance at the little lad while Griffiths, chortling maliciously to himself, disappeared into the sergeant's office.

"What's its name?" the luckless Cyril enquired, none too enthusiastically, as he reached for a report form.

"Jess!" said the boy.

"Have you got a licence for it?"

"Me mam said you'd ask that."

"Well, have you?"

"Aye."

"And what's it look like?"

"Just a bit of brown paper!"

"The dog, you cheeky little git!"

"White an' fluffy an' about my height an' it's got a collar on with a disc with me mam's name and address on it an' me mam says you should have brought it straight round to the post office where we live if you've found it 'cos that's what we pay rates for, an she's a bitch..."

"She sounds it!"

"... an' she's in heat..."

The policeman seemed to lose his sense of reason.

"So that's your fucking bitch is it?" he ranted, wild-eyed. "It's got that lot down there in a bloody frenzy!"

"... an' me mam says that it'd better not've been got at by any dogs or she'll send the pups to the chief constable..."

But the tattered policeman had gone, back to the savage-sounding darkness down below.

Two angry shouts, a squeal and the noise of kicking later, and Jess romped up the stairs to be reunited with her young master. In her enthusiasm, she knocked him over and licked his cheeks; while he, obviously delighted to see her again, played boisterously with her on the floor.

Meanwhile, in the blackness below, Constable Cyril fought for his life with three Alsatians that had gnawed their way out of their crates in lustful excitement at seeing Jess set free.

In time, however, his good hand covered in blood and saliva, the demented guardian of the law returned.

"You'll have to sign a receipt," he shouted at the pair rolling about on the floor. "Come on, come on, pack it in..."

Florrie had a brainwave!

"Eeh!" she gulped. "I forgot to draw the bairns' family allowance!"

The policewoman looked up.

"The post office isn't far away. Why don't you pop out now and collect it? I'll make us another pot of tea while you're out."

It took Florrie a moment to adjust to the calm response. Her boys had always told her that once 'they' got you in, you didn't get out till 'they' said so.

"Er... right!" she eventually found herself able to say "I'll be back in a minute."

"Okay," smiled the policewoman.

Florrie walked from the interview room slowly, quickened her pace when she was out of sight, and had started to run by the time she made the enquiries desk. So she tripped over the dog and the little boy!

*

Chocolate raised his muzzle for the umpteenth time.

The fur on his brow wrinkled.

This was it!

Jess was in the open!

202

Canine senses strained to their limits, eyes narrowed, the savage call of the wolf-pack was strong in his veins. In one movement he was on his feet and away Jesswards without a care for anything but the urge to be first.

Like a bullet he sped, looking neither right nor left. Lust drove out all fear of the bus careering towards him – he had been weaned on dodging trams – and certainty of purpose precluded even a tinker's cuss for the God-squadding Postlethwaite whose path the dog intersected.

Yet Chocolate probably saved the treasurer's life.

108/Rumley loved dogs.

Five feet from hitting Postlethwaite face-on with the bus radiator, he realised that the Jess-bent Chocolate would also cop it. He heaved on the steering wheel in a suicidal effort to avoid the animal. The bus skidded, and Postlethwaite received only a minor thump from the front mudguard.

Mind you, a minor thump from the front mudguard of a ten-ton bus at twenty miles an hour is not exactly equivalent in sensual pleasure to a lifetime of oysters and champagne – it was enough to send Postlethwaite flying into the street at the side of the town hall, down which he wandered mindlessly.

Half relieved and half furious, Driver 108/Rumley came to a halt, lowered himself from the cab and looked around. No sign of the dog. No sign of Postlethwaite. He shrugged, then drove on. He was getting used to the nightmarish quality of this day.

Twenty minutes later, his shift ended, he was parking his bus in a corner of the depot and assisting his conductress in gathering together her bits of equipment and bag of cash.

"You won't be saying anything about me hitting that car earlier, will you, love?" he asked hesitantly.

"Mmmmmm! I don't know about that..."

"Aw, come on, love. You wouldn't?"

Rumley was pleading – he had built up a good record with the bus company and didn't want it spoiled. He would never get another job – not if references were sought from the town hall.

The conductress looked at him thoughtfully.

"No. And I won't say anything about you trying to kill that tall, skinny bloke running across the road either," she said.

*

Chocolate burst through the door of the police station. But the sight that met him was far from what he expected. Ravishing Jess was not going to be the simple end-product of normal healthy lust. It would require skill and adroitness, neither of which attributes come easily when procreative instincts are aroused. And dogs, incapable of intellectual resistance to the fact, are essentially creatures of instinct. So Chocolate found his back end pulsating instinctively against Jess's cavorting rump, his tail wagging instinctively at the sight of Florrie, while his lips writhed back instinctively to expose his fangs at the rank smell of blue serge. Then, sensing an attitude of playfulness about the little boy, he rolled instinctively on his back for his tummy to be tickled.

That was unfortunate.

Jess was not into sexual athletics. Struggling to get her back off Chocolate's stomach, she began to howl. And, in sympathy, so did a dozen lost pooches in the dog compound below.

Constable Cyril had had enough. Seven months duty looking after strays had shortened his temper, to say nothing of one of his fingers, and he was not going to see his career totally ruined by a fracas in the police station. God knows where he would end up if he was demoted again.

It might be thought that the constable would have gained something of an insight into doggy reactions from his experience in the dog compound.

But not a bit of it.

Cyril was as much a creature of instinct as Chocolate, and probably with even less ability to exercise intellectual resistance.

Sad.

Wielding a truncheon and bellowing obscenities, he leapt from behind the counter to separate the writhing bodies.

He would have got away with it if he'd grabbed the child and hit Jess, but by grabbing Jess and hitting Florrie, he couldn't have done more to enrage the highly-charged Chocolate.

The dog's mixed feelings were already expressing themselves bizarrely in four physical directions at once, though with a singular lack of achievement in any of them, so the opportunity to channel his energies into one outlet came as an immense relief.

He lunged at the blue serge so temptingly close to his muzzle and, with a satisfying crunch, clamped his jaws on Cyril's testicles.

Any howls emitted by Jess and the sex-maddened pack in the dog compound paled into musak-like insignificance against the policeman's coloratura arpeggios of agony.

"What the fuck's goin' on?" PC Griffiths yelled above the din as he burst from the sergeant's office.

"What on earth are you doing?" screamed the pretty policewoman running towards the mêlée, concerned to see Florrie lying on the floor.

"God Almighty!" exclaimed the horrified taxi driver, who at that moment arrived to present his driving documents – and promptly disappeared, shaking, to spend the remainder of the day telling his customers how he'd seen the police setting dogs on suspects, "one of them just a little lad of eight!"

Eventually Jess freed herself from Chocolate's grasping front paws and shot into the street. Chocolate, after a final sideways jerk to Cyril's crotch, gave chase – Florrie and the boy in hot pursuit.

Jess, threatened by the big brown dog, terrified by the truncheon-wielding policeman, and in urgent need of a friendly, protective human, knew exactly who she wanted to be near: the big warm man who'd cuddled her as a snuffling pup in his greatcoat and had taken her on long, early-morning walks, who had nurtured her first litter, tended her sore paw, at whose knee she'd so often lain, brown eyes gazing up undying loyalty, confident of approval and security – Jess wanted Big John, the Laughing Postman.

Her nose, four hundred times more sensitive than a human's, told her where he was. She ran towards the place, her path undeviating – up the back lane, through the muddy patch of grass, along cobbled Argyle Street and into the High Street – unslowed by the gathering weight of her rain-drenched fur.

The panting Chocolate was at her heels and, behind him, a parched and battered Florrie heading with as much directness of purpose as Jess for the nearest pub, the wind whistling ultrasonically in her curlers, causing Chocolate to cock a confused ear from time to time and shake his head in distraction as he ran.

And behind Florrie – a long way behind – came Constables Griffiths and Cyril.

"I'm goin' to get that bastard dog and wring its bloody neck..." vowed the near-castrated Cyril.

"Charge the... charge the woman with... with assaulting a... a p'lice... a p'lice..." grunted Griffiths, losing his breath.

"Station?" suggested Griffiths. "You can't... can't... can't assault... assault... a... a... p'lice station... can you?"

"I don't know," replied Cyril, out of his depth.

*

The background music at The Bone Idol was louder now:
"Istanbul's not Constantinople now,
It's Istanbul... "
"Go on, Stan!" urged Doreen, slapping his back encouragingly. "Do your elephant dance!"

"No, no." Stan held up a deprecatory hand.

"Ah, go on!" pleaded Ethel. "It was great when you did it at Doreen's!"

Mrs Postlethwaite, who up to that moment had been listening to the staff, lost interest and turned to Arnold.

"And what do you do with yourself when you're not slaving away in Christopher's financial forcing-house?"

"Pardon?"

"Do you have any hobbies, interests?"

"Not really," replied Arnold, resisting the urge to quote from his Midnight-inspired curriculum vitae and blushing. "I like music."

"Really? Do you have an instrument?"

"Pardon?"

"Do you play anything?"

"Oh, well, yes, I play the piano and sing a bit, you know, in the church choir..."

"We must talk again someday. Perhaps you would like to join the Choral Society. I sing in it, every season..."

Mrs Postlethwaite then turned her attention to Rodney, still hovering admiringly despite obvious hints of disapproval from Gloria flashing hot, damaged-looking eyes across the room.

"And what about you?" Mrs Postlethwaite asked. "I dare say you have a fascinating job in theatre?"

Rodney cast a desirous eye over her and moved close so as not to be overheard.

"You know," he said softly and, he imagined, persuasively, "I think you are the most beautiful, exciting and desirable woman I've ever seen."

Mrs Postlethwaite gave him an arch glance.

"Yes, well," she replied, "we don't want any of that sort of talk, do we?"

She inched down her skirt and turned from the ardent Rodney. A wave of dizziness swept over her. She knew she wouldn't be able to stay upright for much longer.

"I mean, it's Eastern music!" Doreen continued to urge the reluctant Stan. "Go on, just a few steps?"

"Oh, all right," Stan gave in.

So, to the rhythm of the song, he danced his elephant dance.

Rodney didn't watch. Peeved at being rejected by Mrs Postlethwaite he rejoined the bored-looking Gloria.

Arnold watched but his mind was elsewhere. Fancy being invited by the boss's wife to go with her to the Choral Society. Perhaps he'd meet with a more civilised crowd there. People like him and Mrs Postlethwaite.

"Even old New York was called New Amsterdam..."

Stan danced on, his audience encouraging his efforts with hand-clapping and cheering.

Mild stuff, however, compared to the wild guffaws wafting from the increasingly large circle forming round Dodie, Jules and the mayor.

Gloria wondered what the attraction was.

Rodney, who guessed, distracted her with sweet talk and another drink. There would be murder done if she discovered what Jules had taught Winston.

It was better to have Miss Lessingdale drunk than angry.

"May I ask who that is, sir?" The sergeant indicated Mrs Postlethwaite who, remarkably, looked as attractive now as when she'd first arrived – despite the gin inside her.

"Aah!" responded Archie, following Goodenough's frankly appreciative stare. "Charming lady, charming! Wife of our borough treasurer..."

"Is he here too?"

"Well, er, no, actually – had to dash off. Interesting man though, one way and another," Archie bubbled on, "Yorkshireman, he is. Came here years ago..."

As he was speaking, it occurred to the alderman that earlier today had been the first occasion he had seen Postlethwaite other than at council meetings and the annual mayoress's garden party. It also occurred to him that, for a treasurer, Postlethwaite had behaved somewhat eccentrically as he'd left the pub. Archie made a mental note to enquire the cause of that.

"Yorkshireman, you say?" The sergeant's jowls quivered as he interrupted Archie's chatter and thoughts.

"Aye, that's right, from West Yorkshire as I recall, Heckmondwyke or somewhere."

"Never liked Yorkshiremen myself," sniffed Goodenough – for him, decadence started at Scotch Corner. You could always judge the moral fibre of a region's population by the quality of its beer; and, in the sergeant's view, Yorkshire ale was the worst of the lot.

"Accidents of geography, really," mused Archie, "accidents of geography."

"Bloody accidents, I'll give you that, sir," chortled Goodenough immoderately.

Archie chortled too. So did Birstin who was still standing there – but he stopped when the two big men looked at him.

"Mustn't be uncharitable, Horace!" admonished Archie, glancing at the sergeant in mock censure and realising that here was an opportunity for a bit of homespun philosophy. "It's very easy, you know, to dismiss the Yorkshireman as a pompous know-all with never a good word for anybody or anything; the temptation exists in us all…"

"Aye, too bloody true!" agreed Goodenough, optimistically imagining that Archie had finished.

But Archie was just beginning.

"… yet, at his best, at his best – with his mouth shut and without a sneer on his face – he could pass as a human being! Not at all the mean, narrow-minded, destructive, cynical cretin the world acknowledges him to be…"

"Has this place got a licence for singing and dancing?" Goodenough interjected, his ever-vigilant gaze on the cavorting Stan.

"What?" Archie was none too pleased to be interrupted again. "Oh, aye. No, y'see, it's just that Yorkshire, or most of it, is made up of high, barren hills enclosing ugly valleys and dismal towns…"

Two members of the press who had been standing nearby wandered off – they had heard Carrigan's 'Yorkshiremen' monologue more times than they'd had hot dinners.

"… I mean, it's different in Northumberland: climb a hill in Northumberland and you get something for your effort, for your effort – a view, a sight of the sea, the snow-clad Cheviots! But not in Yorkshire, not in Yorkshire…"

"There's something going on over there!" the sergeant grunted, attracted now to the opposite corner. He couldn't be sure, but as a few councillors moved to one side he saw two men touching each other and, amid gales of laughter, he thought he heard a pooffy remark. And the suspect Cruddle was among them.

"... and, in any case," Archie went on doggedly, "in Northumberland the valleys are so bloody lovely nobody wants to get out of them. But not in Yorkshire. Oh, no! Everybody there wants to be away, away to something better..."

"Afternoon, Alderman!" laughed Big John, clutching a pint. "Damn sight drier in here than outside, eh? Ha! Ha!"

'Aye, John," faltered Archie. "Nice to see you, lad."

And John shoved his way boisterously towards the noisy corner, the source of Goodenough's discomfort.

"Have a look at that!" The policeman again distracted Archie from his monologue.

"Eh?" Archie was becoming impatient.

"That table over there! I don't like the look of it..."

Archie cast his gaze at the rollicking crowd. He didn't like the look of it either. The mayor, Jules and Cruddle, in close proximity spelled sure trouble, but it would be madness to encourage Goodenough's suspicions, whatever they were.

"It's all right," the alderman said, "they're just enjoying themselves!" – he laid a restraining hand on the sergeant's arm in anticipation of a cornerwards lurch and the possible loss of his audience – "Anyhow, as I was saying, they all want to be away to something better. Well! Who wouldn't? Living in Yorkshire, eh? Ha! Ha! But, y'see, if you climb out of one of them hideous valleys of theirs, when you reach the top of the hill and look around, all you see is another valley! Equally bloody hideous! Just like the one you've left! I tell you, a few hundred years of claustrophobic hill-walking can soon put a sneer on the face, a sneer on the face! To say nothing of developing a nice line in cynical philosophy! Eh? I mean, thumping your way breathlessly upwards for miles to meet nothing but what you've left behind soon teaches you to 'know what you like and like what your know'. Eh? It soon drums home the message that 'every silver lining has a cloud'. Eh? I mean, being underwhelmed, being underwhelmed is a Yorkshireman's mode of existence! It comes from generations of exhausted disappointment!"

"Aye," grunted Goodenough, unimpressed.

His eyes were fixed on the corner.   Peculiar things were happening there, he was sure of it.

His nose twitched.

Stan finished his dance but, at the insistence of Doreen and Ethel, Paddy rewound the tape to the same song:

"Istanbul's not Constantinople now... "

and now both Stan and David began to dance, their shirt-tails over their trousers, scraping their feet in a mad, suggestive sand-dance.

Realising that so far as the sergeant was concerned his 'Yorkshiremen' monologue had been something of a lead balloon, Archie, in pique, turned to the white, greasy-looking Birstin, who at least had appeared attentive.

"So, young fella! I've seen you around the town hall a few times, haven't I?"

"Oh, yes," stuttered the auditor, grateful to be spoken to, "as a matter of fact, I..."

"What was the name, lad?"

"Birstin, Malcolm Birstin. I was..."

"Used to know a bloke called Birstin," muttered Archie, frowning, "used to be on the bench..."

"My father," said Birstin hesitantly.

"Fine judge of character as I recall," said Archie.

"He's a Yorkshireman!" pointed out Malcolm spitefully, thinking to cast doubt on his father's impressive local reputation.

"Aye, that's as may be, but you can never generalise – anyhow," Archie glowered, "that's a bloody awful thing to say about your own father! What's your job?"

"I'm the auditor."

"Auditor! I wasn't told we had one of them!"

"A lot of councils have got internal auditors these days..."

"Wouldn't have thought there'd be the need..."

"Oh, yes..."

"I mean, we've got the district auditor, haven't we?"

"Of course, but..."

"Anybody caught pinching and we call the fraud squad anyhow – don't we, Horace?" Archie nudged the sergeant.

"Pardon, sir?"

"Call the fraud squad, I said."

"It's the bloody vice squad we want here!" grumbled Goodenough, now in a dilemma. If he were to arrest that pooffy lot in the corner he'd also have to take action against the two obviously unpooffy, shirt-tail-flashing dancers now heaving their buttocks at each other. The sergeant's temper was fraying.

Aware of that fact, and knowing Goodenough's predilection for acting rashly, Archie racked his brains for a diversion, but something Birstin was saying caught his attention.

"... so I'm here to avoid trouble with the district auditor and the fraud squad, and with cash-control and cost-cutting I can save the council..."

"The cost of your own salary?" asked Archie shrewdly.

Birstin flushed.

"Well, er, yes, ultimately, I suppose..."

"Rubbish, lad! All you'll do is add to the cost of running the borough! The systems you'll encourage'll cost a bloody fortune! Don't you kid yourself, or me. You're a burden on ratepayers like meself!"

"Oh, er, I, er..."

"Mind you, I can tell you a way to ease that burden, if you want!"

"Oh, really?" Birstin looked eagerly at the alderman.

"Aye. I'll have a whisky, a large one, without water! – do you want one, Horace?"

"Oh, thank you very much, sir!" replied the sergeant, distracted at once from watching the 'puffs'.

"There y'are, lad!" Archie grinned at the open-mouthed auditor. "Do a bit of cost-cutting for the sergeant and me!"

Birstin, who'd never bought anything for anybody in his life, was taken completely off-guard – but there was no way out, not if he wanted to impress, or if he wanted to become borough treasurer after Postlethwaite got confined to the funny farm.

"Er... right!" he said, trying to smile. And, with a flourish, he whipped out his wallet.

It was the flourish that did it. That was what caught the attention of the staff. Creative local government accountants are not renowned for their flourishes.

"Mine's a pint!" shouted a jubilant, perspiring Stan, still dancing madly.

"And mine!" added a panting David.

"Two vodka and limes!" called Doreen.

"A pint!" came a cry from Arnold, "and a gin and tonic for Mrs Postlethwaite."

The lady paled at the thought but smiled bravely.

"And a pint for me!" yelled Fenwick, joining in as if he had the right.

"Whisky and ginger!" Marjorie followed his lead.

"And a sweet sherry!" Joan called.

"Drambbl... shchawagh..." spluttered Jacob, raising his chin from his chest, the effort nearly killing him.

Birstin's eyes wildly scanned the happy, expectant, challenging, drink-sodden crowd and, breathing malevolence, turned to the barmaid. There was no escape. But he vowed that what he planned for the public health inspectors would be as nothing to what he would inflict on the members of his own department.

Just wait until he was treasurer!

The main cause of all the laughter and commotion in the corner was Jules, telling theatrical anecdotes.

"... and, anyhow, I says to him, 'Well, where's the sets and cossies, then?' and he says, cheeky as anything, 'They're all in the boot of the car!'"

At this the company roared, even Cruddle with his blackened teeth.

"And they were!" screamed Jules, hooting more hysterically than anybody. "I couldn't believe it! Tattiest show I ever worked! 'Course, he's laughing all the way to the bank! Fills the theatres with sticky-fingered schoolkids at two bob a time;

teachers don't care – anything for a break from actually teaching the little prawns – I mean, if it's theatre it's got to be educational, hasn't it? Stupid cows!"

He took a sip of his drink and fondled Dodie's leg.

"Anyhow," he laughed again, "he's written this show but he's short of time so he needs an assistant. Of course, he doesn't want to have to pay anybody, so he phones the Arts Council, doesn't he? He says, 'Have you got any students what need a bit of practical experience as part of their training?' Y'see! Well, the Arts Council claps its communal hands! I mean, it's got students by the thousand camping out halfway down Piccadilly, all turgid graduates thinking they're God's gift to the performing arts, wanting to prove themselves; I mean, the Arts Council doesn't know what to do with them all, so he's a godsend..."

By now Jules' hand was on Dodie's buttocks, blatantly feeling the television interviewer's behind.

"... and they send this dreamy bitch along, failed pianist with a degree in mathematics, full of creative zeal, and the first day she starts, he says to her: 'Right, sweetheart! I've written a new production of 'Red Riding Hood' so get your backside along to Woolworth's and buy loads of red crêpe paper for the cossies!' Well, when she gets back, she says, 'I've got the crêpe paper but they didn't have red, so I got green!' and he replies, quick as a flash, 'Never mind, love, we'll call it 'Robin Hood', eh?'"

Jules screeched again in infectious hilarity and poured the remainder of his drink down his throat.

Those of his audience who'd been listening were equally hysterical. The mayor, spluttering and having difficulty with her teeth, turned a curious shade of purple. Dodie preciously pressed closer to Jules. And Emlyn Cruddle, even without the stimulus of alcoholic irresponsibility laughed till tears came to his eyes. So did Big John, but only because he did all the time anyhow. He'd missed most of Jules' story.

But it wasn't so much the story itself that amused; it was Jules. The high-pitched, openly camp, permanently surprised voice, the outrageous hand movements – the acceptable face of homosexuality. It was new to Mankley.

"Funny little bugger, that!" one of the onlooking councillors observed.

"He's one of 'them'!" was the reply.

"He's all right, though," the first man said tolerantly.

"Bet you wouldn't let your daughter marry one!"

"Eh?"

They wandered off to watch the sand-dancers.

Bill and Karen had joined in the laughter along with everyone else – it didn't matter to them that they'd heard it all before. They liked Jules.

Perhaps more than any other profession theatre absorbs the most diverse of physical, genetic and emotional absurdities and gives them stature. There could be nowhere else for Jules. Only theatre, with its kaleidoscopic relationships and attitudes, always ahead of popular opinion and essentially all-embracing, could take him in, turn him around, and present him as a facet of creativity.

It was the probability that today Jules might not live up to such presentation, however, that caused Bill's and Karen's laughter to be a little more muted than it might otherwise have been. It didn't matter too much that Jules was drunk – 'the body' and 'the butler' could probably get away with it – but as company manager, he should really have done more to keep the star sober.

The two actors glanced nervously at Gloria, leaning heavily on Rodney's arm, admirers gathered round, her make-up like a battlefield, streaks of mascara caked in her wrinkles, voice slurred but strident and, more nerve-racking than anything, her confidence undiminished. There was no doubt about it, Gloria's condition would be more than obvious in tonight's show.

"Oh, God!" groaned Karen, looking at Bill pathetically. "Not again!"

"Looks like it," replied Bill, "and I think tonight was her last chance, too."

Their eyes searched the room for the theatre manager – ultimate responsibility was his. But, when they saw him, any last hope they might have entertained that he might save the situation died a dull death. Jacob, slouched against the bar counter, was plainly beyond recovery.

"Jules will have to ring the office when we get back to the theatre," said Bill. "They'd better be warned."

"Oh, God!" groaned Karen again.

As people moved around, some to get drinks, others to sit elsewhere, Big John plonked himself next to the still laughing Cruddle.

"Why, it's little Emlyn Cruddle, the postman's friend! Ha! Ha! Ha!"

Cruddle's laughter dried up.

"Listen, you," he croaked, swinging round and grabbing the big man's lapels – sitting down, Cruddle was taller than John – "any cracks about pillar boxes and I'll have your balls off!"

"Now, now, it's only a joke," replied the postman, removing Emlyn's hands and glancing about the table. "Good do, is it?"

"Not bad," said Cruddle, turning away.

Mrs Postlethwaite scanned the corner's occupants, her view from the high bar stool uninterrupted.

She gave an involuntary giggle. What a horrible collection: Nora Slattery, puce and disgusting; Jules, skinny and simpering; Dodie, like a tailor's dummy; Cruddle, inhumanly hideous; and now John, gross and loud.

Back came the vague memory that had struck her when first seeing Cruddle. It troubled her that she couldn't recall the event or place.

But she spent little time thinking.

Waves of nausea were drowning her.

"Christ!" exploded the sergeant when he saw Jules nibbling Dodie's ear. "Now, look at that!"

Archie looked, guessed that trouble was now a breath away and disappeared to talk to Cracker.

"Nearly time to go, I suppose," said the alderman.

Cracker was incapable of even an uninterpretable response.

"Oh, hell," muttered Archie, giving the theatre manager a black look and turning to Mrs Postlethwaite.

"Enjoying yourself, my dear?" he asked pleasantly.

"Splendidly, thank you," she replied, smiling.

"Pity your husband couldn't stay," the alderman muttered.

The lady's smile froze slightly but she made no reply.

"Thought, perhaps, he wasn't well, actually," the alderman continued, examining his fingernails.

"He's perfectly well, thank you," came the cool acknowledgement.

"Thought he looked a bit strange when he left..."

"He jusht had to attend to shomething, that'sh all," Mrs Postlethwaite slurred, hanging on to her loyalty rather better than her diction. "He's a busy man, you know." With an immense effort of will she pulled her tongue together. "And from what I've heard, there could be nothing stranger than the speech your mayor gave!"

"What?"

"I'm told it was nothing less than a public disgrace!"

"Not at all!" defended Archie.

"I don't see why you had to drag the poor old hag here in the first place. What have you got up your sleeve?"

The alderman's eyes popped in false innocence.

"Now, Mrs Postlethwaite, I hardly think that's fair," he spluttered, avoiding the question. "Mrs Slattery's a fine lady, a fine lady. Honest. Candid. Salt of the earth..."

Mrs Postlethwaite laughed lightly.

"I suppose that's as good a euphemism for pig-ignorance as any!" she said, and sat back a little on her stool, feeling sicker by the minute.

Archie made for Gloria and Rodney.

"I'd like to be in the fraud squad!" said Birstin, assuming that as he'd bought the sergeant a drink he was entitled to a bit of attention.

"Not tall enough, lad!" replied the sergeant – as far as he knew, his drink had been purchased by Archie Carrigan. Anyhow, he was deep in thought. The disgusting scenes around him demanded action, but he wasn't inclined to do anything himself, not with all these councillors in the room. He'd get some uniformed boys in off the street. Let them carry the can if there was a comeback.

Birstin, squashed again, let his gaze wander the room to the corner. No wonder the sergeant kept looking over there. What an ugly mob – especially Cruddle, with that vast, veined nose, weird cylindrical body, and that unbelievably flat head...

The auditor suddenly shook with excitement. He pulled hard at the sergeant's sleeve.

"Look! Look! Look!" he stuttered, rapt enlightenment pervading his pallid features.

"You and I are going to fall out, lad! What is it?"

"Look!" the auditor repeated, pointing at Cruddle, who, for some reason had stood up with his back to the room.

"What about him?" Goodenough demanded to know – he was beginning to worry that Birstin might have flipped.

"His head!"

"What?"

"His head!"

The sergeant blankly viewed the town officer's truncated cranium.

"See?" babbled Birstin.

"See what? It's just his head!"

"It's flat! It's flat! It's flat!" Birstin was frothing at the mouth.

"It's not the shape of his head I'm interested in!" bullied Goodenough. "It's the shape of his twisted fucking morals!"

"But with a head that flat he'd be able to see through the knot-hole!"

"What the hell are you bleating on about? Fucking flat heads and bastard knot-holes! We all tried to see through the bloody knot-hole..."

The sergeant stopped speaking and riveted his idiot-blue eyes on Cruddle's hairy plateau. The implication at last filtered into the pedantic fissures of his mind.

"Rrrrrrright!" he erupted, and the veins stood out on his brow as he charged for the door to find a bobby.

But the sergeant was not to reach the door.

And the bobby was to find him.

There is about many theatre people a certain smooth outward friendliness and, provided one chooses not to interpret it as patronising, which it invariably is, it can charm and stimulate the ego.

So it was with Emlyn Cruddle. Once recovered from his disgust at the performing dog, he felt a rapport with nine-bob-note Jules, and a genuine liking for Dodie. Conversation came easily. Emlyn confided some of his personal history, interests and hobbies – and ignored the vulgar Nora and her interruptions.

"Big John's got a hobby as well!" she bellowed, after half-hearing a snatch of Cruddle's conversation. "He collects stamps!"

A few near her gave a titter, but Jules, Dodie and Emlyn didn't even look up. They continued to talk in low voices.

"Well," exclaimed Jules, looking at Emlyn in disbelief, "I've never heard of anyone doing that!"

"Neither have I," drawled Dodie.

"I'll show you, if you like," enthused Cruddle.

"Ooh!" "Really?" "Oh, do!" came voices, and those at the table stared at him expectantly.

So he stood up, unbuttoned his long mackintosh and positioned himself where everyone in the corner would have a good view.

"What's he doing?" hiccoughed Gloria, joining those watching.

"He's goin' to show us his hobby!" Nora cackled obscenely.

Rodney blanched – he was sure that anyone who looked like Cruddle would be unlikely to have normal hobbies. He turned to say as much to Alderman Carrigan, but the alderman had disappeared.

"Are you Gloria Lessingdale?" asked a councillor who had arrived late.

Winston threw himself on his back.

"Yes, yes." Gloria tried to smile but her mouth wouldn't work properly. She wondered what Winston was doing.

"Can I have your autograph?"

"Shurrup, man!" shouted Nora. "I want to see Emlyn's hobby!"

Gloria looked vaguely at the piece of paper the councillor handed to her. She realised that she was beyond signing autographs. The room was spinning a little. She frowned, trying to guess how long it was until curtain-up, and a weighty premonition came over her.

"My wife and I really enjoyed you in that picture about the opera singer," the councillor said.

Again, Gloria tried to smile, that special smile she kept for people who remembered that particular film, but it was no good – her face merely twitched peculiarly.

"Come on, Emlyn!" yelled Nora.

Bill looked nervous. Karen turned away her face. But Jules and Dodie stared hard at Emlyn's middle.

"Right!" announced the town officer, whipping open his mackintosh and holding it wide. "Get a load of that!"

There were gasps and groans and cries of amazement.

"Eeeeeeh! It's lovely, pet!" screamed Nora deafeningly. "I didn't think you had it in you! You should win a prize!"

"Very impressive," said Dodie, putting on his spectacles.

"My God!" squeaked Jules. "I've never seen one like that before!"

They were the last intelligible words he was to say in public for some time.

"AAAAAAAGH!" – a scream of animal torment broke from the lips of Sergeant Goodenough in his headlong charge for the door.

"AAAAAAAGH!" – the scream came again as, with eyes bulging sideways on Cruddle, he tried to change direction, miscalculated his footwork and slammed full-tilt into the door frame.

These preliminaries dispensed with, however, he got down to business.

Gone were reasoned considerations of uniformed men carrying the can. Gone too were fears of onlooking councillors and their like – 'Caught in the Act', that credo for successful conviction rang stirringly in his simple brute soul.

He sprang at Cruddle from behind and battered the little man to the floor.

Nora, outraged – and maddened with drink anyhow – went berserk.

"Yer rotten sod!" she shrieked as she tore off her chain of office and swung it at the sergeant, her teeth loosening with the effort. "Yer dirty-minded ignorant shitshchshch..."

The glue holding together her top set gave way – one half shot forward to stick crookedly out of her mouth, the other jammed solid between its mate and her bottom set. In fear of a dislocated jaw, she promptly thudded back, gurgling, to her seat.

Jules, awe-struck, murmured, "It's all too much," and went into a major fade.

Dodie, always aware of his public image, tried to become invisible.

Big John laughed, as much from embarrassment as habit, but nevertheless heartily.

As people milled about to get a better view of the goings-on, Mrs Postlethwaite, again, studied the grotesque faces there, tunnel vision adding a black-bordered memorability to the scene. She fought to make sense of it. People weren't meant by God to be like that. Ugliness wasn't part of Nature's master plan. It must be man-made. People couldn't choose to look like Nora, or behave as she did. She must have been made that way by external influences. Lack of breeding, opportunity, education, encouraging companionship – perhaps these were the restraints that made her as she appeared to be. These, then, were her prison, her manacles... her horse collar.

"Gurning!" Mrs Postlethwaite announced suddenly, eyes bright with intellectual achievement. "It's a gurning competition!" and, smiling, she rested her head on the bar counter and slept.

"LAST ORDERS GENTLEMEN PLEASE!" called Paddy through the loudspeakers.

Interest in Goodenough and Cruddle waned, the sand-dancers broke from their gyrations, there was a stampede to the bar counter.

Concerned that he might be tricked into buying another round of drinks, Malcolm Birstin suppressed his natural desire to see Cruddle killed and, pausing only to pocket a few curled-up sandwiches from the floor, wandered off, back to the town hall.

Archie, frantic to escape any connection with the fracas in the corner, yet unwilling to leave unaccompanied, first attempted to rouse Cracker then, failing in that, noticed Arnold. Their eyes met; Arnold's veiled by bland innocence, Archie's by rheumy scepticism, but both haunted by incipient wisdom.

"Emergency exit," said Archie, this being the only way he could think of to avoid the corner.

"Aye," replied Arnold, slipping from his chair.

They left.

The sergeant was having difficulty getting a firm grip. Every time his fingers closed on the capacious mackintosh Cruddle gave a wriggle and seemed to slip further out of it. The women were appalled at the brutality.

"Do something about it!" Karen urged Bill.

"Do something about it!" Gloria urged Rodney.

The only one there who would have been happy to do something about it was Nora, but she was busy using a fork to dislodge her teeth.

Rodney looked at Bill. Bill shrugged hopelessly.

At last, Goodenough got a good hold and prepared to drag his victim to his feet when, to his surprise and fury, his arms were seized and pinioned behind his back, and he himself was forced upright.

The sergeant saw Cruddle wriggle under the table, so kicked him in the kidneys.

"Now, look here!" began Bill.

"That's quite enough!" snapped Rodney in the tones of a petulant oboe.

Roaring like a rutting rhino, the sergeant threw off the two men and rounded on them.

"See that!" he bellowed, shaking a five-pound-hammer fist under their noses. "That's going to smash you bloody senseless if you touch me again! And see that!" he continued, whipping out his police identity card, "That's going to ensure you get six fucking months for it!"

"Aah! Oh! Yes!" stuttered Rodney, stepping back a pace or two.

"Oh, well, yes, of course," added the more eloquent Bill.

"Now I'm going to arrest that bloody pervert," the sergeant went on, pointing at Cruddle, "and chuck him in the cells! And nobody's going to stop me! Get it?"

Bill and Rodney backed away, almost bowing.

"Nobody!" roared the sergeant, leaning across the table and staring hard at each of its silent occupants in turn.

Now imagining himself more in control of the situation his face assumed a less challenging expression. Straightening up, he looked quite majestic, a picture of decision and firmness – then he was felled by Jess who leapt rain-sodden and panting from the street and into the pub. Executing a high jump onto the table and scattering drinks and empty glasses, she skidded across its surface to her protector, Big John.

The sergeant staggered, tried to save himself, tripped over his own feet and crashed to his knees, his proudly jutting chin hitting the table-top with a sickening crunch.

Cruddle, under the table, seeing the sergeant's undefended loins so enticingly close, promptly rolled over and kicked, repeatedly and without mercy. Little legs have advantages in confined spaces. At the same time, a volley of fork-propelled false teeth hit the sergeant in the eye.

He might yet have escaped serious injury except that Nora, free of her teeth, immediately leaned forward, wrapped her chain of office round the back of the sergeant's neck and pulled, forcing his Adam's apple hard against the edge of the table.

"Now, yer dirty-minded agent of the State!" she slavered, covering his face with spittle from her loosely flapping lips. "You just stay there and bloody gasp while I tell you…"

But the mayor's opinion of the sergeant was cut short by Jess shaking herself, fluffy white fur rain-drenched, soaking the company with two gallons of dog-tainted water.

Nora spluttered, let go her hold on the fainting sergeant and tried to protect herself from the shower.

Then, closely followed by the eight-year-old boy, came Chocolate.

Without pausing to assess what further inconvenience his mangy dripping presence might inflict on those around, he hurled himself up after Jess, knocked the mayor's teeth into her lap, shook another two gallons over everyone, and attempted copulation.

The crush at the bar counter eased a little, thanks to the energetic efforts of Anne, Margaret and Paddy to quench the communal pre-war-prices thirst, and people again began to look over at the noisy corner – except the dancers, for whom the music inspired more sweaty action. Doreen and Ethel were joined by Fenwick, Joan and Marjorie as they lurched about in imitation of Stan and David. As the song continued monotonously they formed a ragged line to conga round the room, others joining in as the fancy took them.

Twisting and jerking and stamping their feet, they passed the corner, laughing at the crumpled-up, tortured Goodenough, cheering the triumphant Cruddle, cackling at the copulating dogs, shouting 'Yah' at the two newly-arrived dithering constables now standing bemused and panting in the doorway and, in their passion to keep moving, continually obstructing the desperate Florrie Moon as she tried to get to the bar counter.

"Bloody hell!" exclaimed Constable Cyril, feeling in his pockets for his notebook.

"You can say that again!" said PC Griffiths. "The sergeant would hit the roof if he saw this lot!"

"I think he's just landed!" observed Cyril, his eye on the familiar, heavy-jowled features pressed into the carpet in agony.

With the help of the constables, Goodenough struggled to his knees.

"Arrest the bastards!" he winced through gritted teeth. "Especially them queers! I want them all in my care until morning! All of them!"

The effort was too much. He sank to the floor holding his crotch and going white.

Now Constables Cyril and Griffiths had often heard the sergeant speak about queers. They'd even had certain citizens of the town pointed out to them as queers – the vicar, for one – but, despite Goodenough's contention that there were 'millions of the fuckers', the constables' direct experience of the genuine article was, to say the least, devoid of a rough edge. Only one thing they remembered from the innumerable lectures and outbursts, and that was that queers 'disport themselves in women's clothes'.

Their eyes flitted to Karen – but she looked altogether too wholesome. Then they gave the once-over to Nora, sloppily fitting her three-piece teeth back where they belonged – but the heaving acres of bosom ruled her out. Then they saw the dishevelled Gloria in her heavily spread make-up – and, as one man, they pounced.

Gloria screamed.

Rodney intervened.

"I say, do you mind! This lady is Gloria Lessingdale!"

Winston, programmed like a Pavlov protégé, threw himself on his back.

The sergeant again raised himself on his elbow to speak weakly.

"All them fucking queers... in the cells... I'll clean up this town if it kills me... they're everywhere... dirty, filthy perverts, ruining the lives of decent people..."

Chocolate barked.

Winston lay panting, waiting for a pat from Jules.

Chocolate barked again, louder.

Winston looked around, saw that Jules was out of touch with events, sprang to his feet and barked back, his head cutely on one side.

That did it.

Chocolate, still in mid-copulation, let forth a terrifying series of growls and snarls. Jess, almost deafened, had finally had enough. She scrabbled away from under Chocolate and down onto Big John's knee, sending him crashing backwards into the table behind.

Chocolate went insane. With hair on end, he launched himself at the poodle. Winston shot under Dodie's seat. Thwarted, the big dog then went for everything in sight. He savaged the sergeant's ankle, ripped Rodney's trousers, chased Cruddle from under the table – then flew at the constables in a frenzy.

Down went Griffiths with a screech of terror, leaving Gloria to sink gratefully into a chair – and out went Cyril, leaving the whole ridiculous mess for the safety of a telephone box to call for a van and reinforcements. He reckoned he'd done his bit for law and order as far as Chocolate was concerned.

"TIME GENTLEMEN PLEASE!" bawled Paddy through the loudspeakers.

For the last time he rewound the tape.

Florrie Moon burst through to the bar counter, her money hot in her hand.

"A bottle of sherry to take out," she called.

"Sorry, love, we've finished serving," said Paddy, concerned about the presence of the police.

"It's to take out!" she pleaded.

"I'm sorry, love," Paddy insisted gently.

Florrie, at screaming pitch, looked around at the mayhem in the corner – her eyes locked on those of her sister Nora.

"Even old New York's now called New Amsterdam... "

The conga dancers swept on, round and round the room.

The van arrived and, suddenly, the doorway and corner were filled with policemen, all trying to avoid Chocolate now astride the prone, gibbering Griffiths.

But Chocolate knew when he was outnumbered and, after a last few minor acts of savagery, raced away to lie in the calm of the post office. Jess had to come back there sometime.

But Jess was first in the van, her young master soon to follow.

"The little lad and the dog, sir?" asked an amazed policeman who'd come to Mankley from another force.

"Under-aged in licensed premises, you fool!" snapped Goodenough, some of his old spirit returning.

The policeman whistled unbelievingly and took the boy's hand.

"Come on, son," he said, "I'll give you a ride in the van."

Elton Fish pocketed his journalist's notebook and mingled with those in the corner, and as Bill and Karen were escorted outside he tagged along. This might make something of a story.

Jules came next, the proximity of so many big uniformed men sending him into another fade, but he went willingly, almost squeezing Winston to death in excitement.

"Your sergeant," he said, "powerful man, isn't he?"

"Oh, aye," replied Constable Cyril, the light of hero-worship in his eyes, "clever, too! Caught the 'Mankley Wanker', y'know!"

"I don't believe it," whispered Jules, the fade coming over again.

"It's fuckin' true!" snarled Cyril, going red as he pushed Jules into the van.

Then came Dodie, threatening all the horrors of legal action.

Then John, still laughing.

Then Cruddle, hopping mad.

Then Rodney and the ladies.

"Are you really Gloria Lessingdale?" asked Constable Cyril.

"Yes, believe it or not."

The policeman searched his pockets for some paper as he assisted her into the van.

"Can I have your autograph?" he asked, pathetically holding out a grubby old payslip and a pencil stub.

Gloria eyed him in silent amazement.

"It's just that my wife thought you were marvellous in that film about the dying opera singer," he continued.

"You stupid bastard!" Gloria stamped her foot. "It wasn't me! It was..." A false eyelash detached itself and slipped down her cheek like an electrocuted hairy caterpillar – then she vomited.

Nora was the last to be taken to the van, but not before a row with Florrie.

"What are you doin' here in your curlers, you bloody slut?" the mayor bellowed across the room.

"Aye. Too well off and stuck up to speak to your own sister..."

"You look a right clip!"

"Don't want to know the likes of me, with all your posh friends around you..."

"Get back to your midden!"

It developed in volume but not in variety.

Four policemen held Nora back until, with the help of two more, they got her to the doorway. She kicked little Jimmy as she passed, and he followed.

"What's been goin' on?" he asked, yawning.

"Nowt to do wi' you!" replied the mayor.

"Where's your chain?" he asked,

"Eeh! My God! I've lost me chain!"

Nora looked back into the pub, but the policeman pushed her on.

"You're always losin' your bloody chain!" Jimmy muttered, yawning again as the van doors slammed shut behind him.

'I see she got her sister in on the act, despite all her promises," a councillor observed after Nora had left.

"Aye," replied his mate, "Archie'll have some explaining to do on this one."

And they supped up their drinks.

Paddy cast his eyes about the bomb-hit pub. Morosely finishing the last of their drinks, its few occupants looked drained. The music blared.

Goodenough and Griffiths dusted each other down and hobbled away, each with a supportive arm about the other.

When they'd gone Paddy took a bottle of sherry from the shelf and handed it to the vacant-looking Florrie, standing there humming tunelessly to herself. She offered money. Paddy smiled and shook his head. Her eyes flashed gratitude and, grabbing the bottle, she hurried off.

Paddy's glance then lighted on Mrs Postlethwaite, curled up at the side of the bar, and he motioned the girls to take her upstairs to the flat.

Then he looked at the riotous members of the treasurer's staff leaping about mindlessly to the music, their clothes awry, singing at the tops of their voices.

The last few councillors had left, carrying a gobbledegook Jacob S Cracker between them.

Paddy turned up the music to its maximum setting – it fair boomed out:

"Istanbul's not Constantinople now,
It's Istanbul... "

The singing, roaring, drunken dancers at last headed for the door like members of a bellicose aboriginal tribe.

"Even old New York,
Was called New Amster... "

"Damn!" they chorused stupidly, "Singing Nellie put your belly next to mine!"

Now alone, Paddy was revolted by the behaviour of his guests and customers. He sighed. This wasn't as he'd planned it – not the violence, police, and them blasted dogs. A weight settled on him. He was tired. He doubted if it was worth all the effort.

The girls returned from depositing Mrs Postlethwaite upstairs.

"A drink, Daddy?" asked Anne, smiling at her stepfather, a concerned vertical frown adding warmth to her smooth forehead. "You deserve one."

"Aye, I suppose I do," replied Paddy, tearing his eyes away from the doorway and summoning up something of a smile.

"Despondent?" asked Margaret, ruffling his hair.

"A bit."

"Everybody enjoyed themselves, you know."

"I suppose they did."

"Mam'll be home soon, she'll cheer you up," said Anne.

"Aye, she will," replied Paddy, "I'll just pop upstairs to look out for her coming."

To help dispel his depression he took the stairs two at a time, so arrived breathless in the bedroom. On the bed Mrs Postlethwaite dozed silently, her skirt rucked up to reveal frill-bordered thigh. Paddy stole past to pull aside the curtains and look through the window.

Below him in the street he saw the last of the staff conga unrhythmically around Postlethwaite's Triumph and into the town hall. In the office that was once his he saw Malcolm Birstin standing near the door, a clipboard in his hand. The treasurer's enclave was empty and in darkness, but the pub's neon sign lit it sufficiently to make out the desk to which Paddy had once aspired, the green leather swivel chair in which the old borough treasurer had died, the black fireplace and its fireguard with the dead leaf motif.

Mary now appeared in the town hall entrance. Preparing to fasten her coat against the weather she glanced upward at the now clearing sky and saw Paddy. She flashed a smile then trod warily across the shining, slippery cobbles of the High Street.

Strange, thought Paddy, that his life should have changed so dramatically in just a few short weeks. Strange that of all the pubs Mary might have persuaded him to have taken, he should end up with this one, back at the place where he'd spent all his working life. Yet, there was a rightness to it, a naturalness. He was part of this town, for all its inanities and deprivations, and he knew and understood it. For years he'd worked to maintain its ordinariness, its regular pattern of existence. Now, he realised as he pondered the day, here he was, at its centre, introducing change; unintentionally but actively forging a new pattern in its life.

Mrs Postlethwaite stirred in her sleep.

Paddy turned his head to look at her. His features brightened with amusement as he wondered what Postlethwaite would think if he knew that his wife was in his ex-deputy's bedroom, how he'd feel when he discovered that his former deputy had a floodlit view

of the town hall offices. Paddy turned back to the window and an expression of pain came over him. His eyes glazed, his hands reached for the top of the frame to support himself, his knees sagged and a tight fullness tortured his chest. His grip weakened, his palms squeaked flat down the glass and his body folded to the floor.

He could no longer restrain himself. Beating his fists on the carpet, he laughed; loud, hard and long – like the Devil at a disco.

EPILOGUE

For Paddy Kean the day could be seen as a sort of ending to a story – a triumphant ending. But really, for him and everyone in Mankley, it was more a beginning. As repetitiously a beginning as every other event in the world's history. Anything that happens alters life for ever. The opening of The Bone Idol was no exception to the rule.

Even as Paddy fought to control his mirth as he rolled about on the bedroom carpet, the clouds of accountability, recrimination, guilt, embarrassment and sober contemplation were gathering all over town.

*

"...singing Nellie put your belly next to mine!" Stan yodelled, leading the dancers drunkenly through the town hall foyer to the outer office of the Treasurer's Department.

"Whoa!" he shouted, holding up his hand.

Those behind him tumbled into his back, laughing, singing and falling about merrily.

Facing Stan was Malcolm Birstin, holding a watch and a clipboard.

"Three fourteen and twelve seconds – S Scrimshire," the auditor dryly announced as he made a note.

Stan stared blearily for a moment before bursting into renewed laughter.

"Ah! Ha! Ha! Ha!" He turned to the staff. "He's clocking us in!"

The staff, following his lead, hollered and thumped their fists on the wall.

"Anything for a laugh, our Malcolm," chuckled David, grinning stupidly as he attempted to tuck his shirt into his trousers.

"Three fourteen and twenty-one seconds – D Smith," the auditor intoned, making another note.

The sounds of hilarity dried up.

Marjorie, Joan and Fenwick slunk away, back to their places of employment.

"You're joking, aren't you, lad?" asked Stan uncertainly.

"I'm bloody not!" snarled Birstin.

"We brought you your beers like we promised – didn't we, folks?"

Stan looked for encouragement, but the others were already weaving towards their desks.

A fiendish expression came over the auditor.

"That's bribery, that is!" he said. "It's a criminal offence to bribe a local government officer! And that'll go in my report along with your bad timekeeping!"

So everyone sat down and thought about their superannuation until home time.

*

In the Black Maria the mood was less restrained.

"Aw, God! Somebody's been sick in here!" yelled Nora Slattery as the van doors clanged shut.

Nobody answered.

"It's bloody awful, this!" she continued. "The stink's terrible!"

"For heaven's sake, shut up, woman!" snapped Rodney. "We've all got problems!"

"Aye, but you don't have to sit in them!" protested the mayor.

"Just shut up!" repeated Rodney, more loudly.

"Who said that?" blustered little Jimmy, getting to his feet with his fists raised and promptly being restrained by two policemen.

"I did!" said Rodney.

"Nobody talks to my wife like that!"

"If it weren't for your wife trying to strangle the sergeant we probably wouldn't be here!" responded Rodney, the presence of the police giving him the courage.

Again Jimmy jumped to his feet. Again the policemen nearest made to restrain him, but just then the van jerked into movement and its occupants were hurled sideways. Little Jimmy, fists flying, shot towards Rodney.

But Rodney, for once in his life, was ready. He caught Jimmy on the chin, knocking him down.

"The rotten bastard!" screamed Nora as policemen thrashed about trying to restore order.

"Who?" enquired Gloria vaguely.

"Your flamin' Rodney!" retorted the mayor.

"Oh, him," muttered the star.

"Well, we'll see if the bugger fancies his chances wi' me!" threatened the furious Nora, hurling a policeman to one side and, with surprising agility, diving for Rodney.

It was at this point that those policemen who were new to Mankley gained something of an insight into why the regular town force had so jaundiced a view of the local population.

Nora missed Rodney and hit Big John, Big John, laughing, missed Nora and hit Cruddle, Cruddle didn't aim for anybody and hit everybody – and out came the truncheons and handcuffs.

By the time the van pulled up outside the police station, its inhabitants showed all the signs of battle, not least the eight policemen who urged their captives across the pavement to the door.

All except Jess, who padded home to the post office.

*

A few streets away Chocolate, too bored and hungry to wait for Jess shambled to his feet to set off elsewhere and, yawning massively, looked about him. He perked up – his mistress, Florrie, was wandering towards him. Giving a bark of pleasure, he ran to meet her. She was aiming for the police station to continue her vigil there for news of Ernie's attacker, but as soon as she saw Chocolate she changed what was left of her mind, guessing that, somehow, the dog would not be welcomed with open arms by the police.

"Howway, me bairn," she said, turning on her heel, hiccoughing and staggering slightly against the wall. "We'll go home."

And together they went across the stretch of derelict land surrounding the ghetto, Florrie stumbling occasionally and pausing to take a swig from her bottle, while Chocolate contentedly splodged about in the clarts.

*

The policemen lined up, gave their names and numbers one by one and PC Shawe-Iskay booked them into the van for a trip to the hospital where they would be given tetanus injections, treatment for shock or a thorough medical check-up, according to the frequency or duration of their recent exposure to Chocolate or the mayor.

"Here's a list of charges," said Sergeant Goodenough as he hobbled past the young constable, "and I want them all charged, d'you hear? Every bastard one of them!"

"Well, I'm not sure..."

"It's a fucking order!..." the sergeant's knees buckled as his voice rose, great waves of pain throbbing from his swollen testicles.

"I'll see," replied Shawe-Iskay, coolly outstaring the sergeant.

Goodenough banged his fist on the desk, struggling to produce intelligible speech, but the effort was too much. He reeled from the station to board the van.

When he had gone, Shawe-Iskay cast his eyes sadly down the hastily written pages of scribble that constituted a charge sheet, sighed heavily, then lifted the handset of the telephone and dialled a number.

Thirty minutes later a large, black Wolseley 6/110 saloon swept up to Mankley's unimposing police station and a number of high-ranking officers emerged.

After some discussion with Shawe-Iskay and the pretty policewoman, the prisoners were released, a great fuss being made of them. There were apologies – grovelling apologies – and much explanation; and Elton Fish wrote it all down verbatim in shorthand. Then taxis were ordered and charged to police funds.

Sergeant Goodenough couldn't believe it when he returned from the hospital.

"You let them all go?" he asked incredulously.

PC Shawe-Iskay looked at him coldly.

"Instructions," he said.

"Whose fucking instructions?"

"I was asked not to say."

The sergeant blustered and threatened but got nowhere. He went home a dispirited, nervous and highly suspicious man.

It was quite late in the evening when the telephone rang.

"Hello?"

"Hello, there, Horace," came a smooth voice. "How are you?"

"George!" exclaimed Goodenough. "I mean, Chief Superintendent, begging your pardon, sir."

"Always George to old mates, Horace."

"Very good of you, sir."

"Mmm... tell me, can you come to see me tomorrow morning at ten?"

"Well, actually, sir, I had a little trouble earlier today and I'm not feeling too well – might take a few days sick leave..."

"Come on, Horace," wheedled the voice, "what would you do if I told you that at ten tomorrow the 'Mankley Wanker' would be up to his old tricks at the convent?"

Goodenough almost clicked his heels.

"I'd be there to apprehend him, sir!"

"Of course you would, of course you would, old boy. Good old-fashioned coppers like you always put duty first... so, see you at ten?"

"Yes, sir. Of course, sir."

Goodenough slept well that night. He had almost forgotten about his old friend George Sammen getting promotion.

He wondered what the meeting would be about.

*

While for most connected with the events of the day the improprieties had been public and at the prompting of strong drink, Postlethwaite's had been solely at the urging of his own imagination.

It was long after Paddy and Mary had dropped off Mrs Postlethwaite at home that the treasurer got there. In fact, it was long after his wife had gone to bed.

Postlethwaite's search for a sign from God had proved fruitless and had ended in St Aloysius' Church graveyard where a priest, halfway through an interment ceremony, had nervously observed the demented treasurer sauntering through the grounds.

The priest paused in his oration to whisper aside to two hefty gravediggers standing nearby leaning on their shovels.

"Go and see what he's doing!"

"Who?" a mourner interrupted, looking up curiously.

"Pardon?" whispered the priest.

"Get on with it, it's pissing down!" said the undertaker.

"Ah, precisely," said the priest.

As the gravediggers approached Postlethwaite they diagnosed his condition – he was a nut. A quiet word from the two burly men, however, and the vibrant glow of dementia left the treasurer. He became himself again and walked from the graveyard.

"Always works with nuts," said one of the gravediggers.

"You're right, it does," said his mate.

"Cured hundreds like that."

"Have you?"

"Oh, aye. But you've got to look serious when you ask them which mound they would like to be under – and you've got to hold the shovel as if you intend to use it!"

It was a long walk from St. Aloysius' to the town hall, but Postlethwaite didn't care. With every step of the way quasi-normality reasserted itself. It was an iron-willed treasurer who opened the door of his car, side-stepped fifty gallons of accumulated rainwater and drove home. Gone were thoughts of popularity, little books of jokes and a new image. The green eyes, always mirthless, were now soulless too. The events of the past three weeks were blotted out, as if they had never happened. His dalliance with superficial humanity was over.

It was dark when he got home, so he didn't see the state of his scorched lawn until morning.

*

Arnold had walked part of the way to his house in the company of Archie Carrigan, fascinated by the alderman's observations about people and the world. At first, so much free opinion about those in high places gave Arnold a sense of unease, but he knew everything said was in confidence. Archie, curiously, had no doubt that Arnold would treat it so. He trusted and liked this half-formed youth and recognised in him qualities that set him apart from the rabble usually obvious in Mankley.

Parting at the Co-op offices, Arnold almost ran the hundred yards to his home. He rarely talked there, or indeed anywhere else, but today, no sooner had his parents come in than the verbal floodgates opened.

His mother was delighted – fancy her son meeting councillors and aldermen and the mayor and that nice Dodie Ochiltree off the television, and Gloria Lessingdale. She could hardly believe it.

Arnold's father, more simply, didn't.

"It's a pack of bloody lies!"

"It's not!" protested Arnold.

"It's rubbish! You're telling your mother all this because you took the afternoon off work!"

"Honest, Dad!"

"You'll get nowhere! Why the hell can't you just stick in at your job and earn an honest living?"

"Listen, Dad," pleaded Arnold seriously, "it's true! All the staff were there! We did meet Gloria Lessingdale. She talked to me!"

"It's not bloody true! It's lies! And I won't have it!"

Arnold tried to recall some convincing corroborative detail.

"She had a dog!" he said.

"What kind of dog?" his father asked sceptically.

Arnold faltered for a moment.

"A Greek dog!" he stuttered uncertainly.

"There's no such thing as a Greek dog!"

"There is!" cried Arnold. "She had one! It was called Herklitorus!"

His father's face went crimson and he clenched a fist threateningly.

"Shut up! Bloody filth! In front of your mother an' all!"

Arnold didn't know what his father was talking about. He was simply frantic to convince the man that what he was saying was true. He became mildly hysterical.

"It's not filth! Honest, Dad! She did have a Greek dog! And it *was* called Herklitorus! It was little and thin and woolly..." A confused memory of canine breeds filtered into his mind and he brightened. 'It was a Troy Poodle!" he blurted out triumphantly.

*

The effects of the nature of the day were most dramatically immediate, however, at a more esoteric aspect of Mankley's communal life. The Royal Gaiety Theatre was probably the most inappropriately named theatre in the world. It was as gay as a death certificate. But it had class: the fading genteel class of association with great names and moments. Its peeling auditorium echoed in heavy silence the applause, laughter and delight of a hundred years or more. Warm rather than vibrant, oppressive rather than dominating, it gave the visiting artiste a degree of tradition and a feeling that this was *real* theatre.

Unfortunately, Gloria Lessingdale was real drunk and in no condition to play that night.

Jules telephoned head office.

Up from London flew the managing director of the production company to be met at the airport by the theatre's assistant manager and whisked by taxi to the stage door.

For the cast it was a moment to be recalled with horror for years to come. The show was cancelled until the Wednesday, when another 'name' would take over.

Miss Lessingdale, not unexpectedly, was sacked on the spot and told she would never work again.

"Ha!" she replied. "Phooey! I've been told that by the best in the business! The greats! The biggest studios in Hollywood've told me that, y'know!"

And she clicked her fingers contemptuously as she spoke.

It didn't occur to her that each time it had been said another slip down the ladder of fame had followed. And she was incapable of admitting, even to herself, that rock bottom was a piss-in-the-wind away. There was nowhere lower for her to go and still be in work. Professionally she was dead.

Gloria had risen to the top too quickly, too young, too unthinkingly. She had no bedrock of legitimate theatrical experience, no hard core of professional goodwill on which ageing film stars so often ultimately rely. Soon she would be broke and willing to take on any job anywhere, doing anything compatible with her desire to eat and have a roof over her head. Hollywood would never call, the West End would survive without her.

Nothing quite so tragic happened to Jacob S Cracker.

His evening was only marginally abnormal. He had something of a problem climbing the stairs to his office, but the councillors assisted him; and when they got there they relieved him of the intricacy of pouring the drinks.

It was five o'clock when Jacob fell asleep and the councillors departed to the nearest pub. A theatre manager to his fingertips, however, he awoke at precisely five to seven to buzz his assistant to open house. And his assistant had no difficulty at all in interpreting his chief's garbled speech as an indication that Jacob would be unlikely to be functioning for a while.

So he went to the foyer, exchanged the tickets of the seventeen paying customers for another evening of their choice, then dealt as politely as possible with the disgruntled mob, some four hundred strong who, clutching their 'comps' were there to paper the house.

Then he gratefully went home to his wife and kids, and the stage door keeper locked up the theatre.

Jacob awoke again at nine o'clock wondering what the time was. But he was locked in for the night. It didn't bother him. He sank half a bottle of vodka and collapsed to sleep fitfully until morning.

*

For some whom the day had affected, the dawning of the next was a time to put things right, establish a basis for a new start. For others, however, such action was out of their control.

It came as a shock, for instance, when Goodenough reached headquarters to find his old pal, George Sammen, in the chair of what seemed like an investigative committee – and a disturbing revelation to discover PC Shawe-Iskay as one of its members.

But it was when the sergeant saw his little book marked 'Deviants – Mankley' lying in front of the chairman that the single, hard-backed, vacant chair facing the committee assumed in his mind its rightful significance – he was to be the sole subject of the morning's deliberations.

Wincing as he hobbled across the uncarpeted floor, his savaged ankle competing for attention with his bruised testicles, lacerated neck and black eye, he at least felt that his conscience was unscarred – and that was what mattered to him, he had never failed in his duty.

This was a self-delusion which was to give him little comfort during the next two hours, though the meeting began amicably enough.

"Pleasant drive down, Horace?" enquired the chief superintendent, glancing up from the single sheet of typed paper in front of him.

"Very pleasant, sir," said Goodenough, wincing again as he eased his oversized rump on to the hard chair, but reassured by the conversational tone. "A bit busy coming through Prudhoe, with the roadworks and that, but..."

"Made good time, did you?" interrupted one of the two senior officers whom the sergeant did not know.

"About thirty-five minutes, sir..."

"Not long, in a car," mused the officer, his eyes narrowing a little on the sergeant's face.

"Quite a long time in a locked cell, though!" the other officer snapped accusingly. "For a little boy of eight!"

"Oh, I wouldn't say that, sir!" the sergeant blustered.

"Wouldn't you?" The chief looked up, a frown darkening his brow.

"Not under the circumstances..."

"You'll get an opportunity to explain the circumstances later, Sergeant," the chief cast a steely glance over Goodenough, "but first I'd like you to think back to last winter..."

Goodenough's spirits plummeted. For a moment, at the mention of the little boy, he had hoped that the meeting was to deal only with the events of yesterday where he felt justified in the action he'd taken. Indeed, he felt his injuries made justification more than self-evident.

Shawe-Iskay, seemingly indifferent to the sergeant's presence, now gave a little cough, opened the first of seven grey box-files stacked on the table and passed its contents to the chief. From a door to Goodenough's right came a shorthand writer who took her place, pencil poised between red fingernails above her notebook, as the sun, having hovered behind a cloud for most of the morning, emerged as if at the flick of a switch to shine through the tall windows, full, bright and remorseless into the sergeant's eyes to blur his observation of those in front of him.

But he heard the voices clearly enough, and intermittent wavelets of unease washed over his mind.

It didn't show.

In fact, the sergeant dealt capably and straightforwardly with the hundred-odd public complaints made against him and his men over the preceding eight months. He blustered and parried, occasionally admitted partial lack of foresight or, perhaps, the odd untypical hint of over-zealousness but, largely, his effusive reasoning rang true – his heart was in it.

And that was a difficulty for the three senior officers. The sergeant might well lack circumspection, judgement, knowledge of the law, the most basic of diplomatic skills – but so did most of the force. And Goodenough's record of arrests was mighty impressive. It was in the primitive instincts of his inquisitors to approve all the man had done. After all, Mankley was a tough patch.

But the mood of the times was against such reasoning, and they wouldn't be senior officers now if they had not adapted previously to the changing moods of the times. There were plenty lily-livered Shawe-Iskays gaining influence today, both in the force and the Home Office. Poor old Horace was out of date. He would have to be made an example of.

The last boxful of letters dealt with, the senior officers were no further forward. Goodenough still confronted them, a potent uniformed animal undaunted by the flood of public outrage.

But after the tea break there was a change of emphasis. Instead of box-files of unsupported letters, the chief had before him Shawe-Iskay's report, well-researched, carefully compiled, thoroughly corroborated by signed statements, photographed and tape-recorded evidence. It was indisputable.

"Do you know the correct procedure when a member of the public approaches you with a complaint?" asked the chief,

"Yes, sir."

"But you don't approve its implementation at Mankley?"

"Well, sir, it's just that my way is simpler," said the sergeant. "Same result in the end!"

The chief frowned again.

"But I do expect you to go through the motions, Sergeant! We don't take statements just to tear up and throw away in the hope of a retraction..."

"They always retract their complaints at Mankley, sir!" asserted Goodenough, a vicious smile of certainty playing on his lips. "I just anticipate it a bit..."

"You mean you terrorise the families of the complainants?"

"So?" The sergeant couldn't see why the chief should object to that.

"So it's got to stop!" came the reply. "I gather that a Mr... er... er..."

Shawe-Iskay leaned sideways to whisper a name to the chief.

"... er... Matthew McDonnell, the husband of the lady who complained to you only yesterday morning, was booked seven times for offences against the Road Traffic Act by six o'clock last night!"

"Bugger probably deserved it," muttered the sergeant.

"Do you know what Mr McDonnell does for a living?"

"No, sir."

"He is the senior driving instructor for a nationally known driving school!"

"Oh, I see, sir," Goodenough sounded a trifle contrite.

"He claims you attacked his wife!"

"No, sir. She was blocking the entrance to the scene of an affray. It was an accident, sir."

"But you didn't apologise?"

"No, sir. Weakens public confidence in the force, sir."

The chief gave the sergeant an exasperated look.

"You were going to tell us earlier about the little boy..."

"On licensed premises, sir."

"You were going to charge him?"

"Er... yes, I think so, sir."

"That is what you instructed Shawe-Iskay to do..."

"Yes, sir."

"And you were going to throw in 'assaulting a police officer', 'keeping an unruly dog' and 'causing an affray' for good measure, I see!" The chief said this in a tone of considerable bewilderment.

"Quite a formidable little boy, Sergeant, especially as his headmaster says he is shy, his Sunday school teacher says he's timid, and his doctor claims that he is of a nervous disposition! You know, of course, that his father was killed three years ago..."

"No, sir."

"Knocked down by a police car..."

"I didn't know that, sir..."

"Obviously not! Now, what about the postman?"

"Postman, sir?"

"That's right! He too was arrested on your orders. A man with a faultless record and two police commendations for bravery!"

"I can't remember a postman, sir," the sergeant faltered.

"Well, he remembers you, Sergeant! And if I were in your shoes, having seen the size of the man, I wouldn't go about too often where he might find you! He's a family friend of the postmistress, mother of the little boy we were referring to a moment ago."

"I see, sir."

"You also arrested a Mr Rodney Pratt together with two actors from the local theatre..."

Goodenough brightened.

"Ah!" he said. "Yes, sir! I did! They attacked me! I remember that, sir!"

The chief superintendent paused, rubbed his chin with his hand, then, with a wave towards the box-files, said, "There are forty-odd letters in those boxes from people whom you claim attacked you, Sergeant. In no case did we dare prosecute and, had we done so, in no case do I believe we would have secured a conviction. Do you?"

"We can all make mistakes, sir..."

"I think you've made more than your fair share, Sergeant! People don't like being charged and thrown into cells! It wastes their time, upsets their families and, in the case of those who can read and write, gives them an insight into just how pointlessly vindictive our police force can be. And the local hospital is complaining about the constant stream of multiple fractures arriving at its doors by way of your police station. And, in the end, it's all trouble for me!"

"I understand, sir."

The chief looked surprised at that but, with gritted teeth, he went on.

"You arrested the mayor yesterday?"

"She should have been locked up, sir!"

"Well, she wasn't," the chief sighed, "thanks to the intelligence of Shawe-Iskay and my subsequent intervention!"

The sergeant gave a sneering gasp of amazement. But the chief ignored it.

"And, in my view, you are damned lucky I didn't let you charge her! Attempted murder! Grievous bodily harm! Resisting arrest! Cruelty to animals! Carrying an offensive weapon – her chain of office, I presume? The mayor of the borough? You certainly pick 'em, Sergeant!"

"Well, I, er..."

"And what about her husband?"

"Aiding and abetting, sir..."

"Protecting his wife, Sergeant!"

"Mmm, I, er, well..."

"And Miss Gloria Lessingdale?"

"The situation became confused, sir..."

"You were going to charge her with 'incitement to riot' and 'drunk and disorderly' among other things!"

"Yes, sir, the lady *was* a little tipsy..."

"Have you seen this morning's newspapers, Sergeant?"

"No, sir."

"We'll show you them later. Now, what about Mr Ochiltree? Did you happen to see his evening newsround on television last night?"

"No, sir."

"His face wasn't its normal shape, Sergeant!"

"He's a puff, sir! So was the other one! Even his dog's a puff!"

"Pouffes, as you call them, Sergeant, are members of society..."

"What?" Goodenough nearly fell off his chair.

"... and as I understand it, Mr Ochiltree, as a result of his experiences at your hands, is..."

"He hasn't had any experiences at my hands, or anything else I've got!" yelled the sergeant, horrified.

"... shortly to put together a documentary concerning police attitudes towards homosexuals. Mr Ochiltree, incidentally, has made it clear to me that, while he is a perfectly normal male, the subject is one that interests him – sufficiently, I gather, for him to have invited me to take part in the televised discussion. That, of course, is by the way, but a Mr Elton Fish, also arrested by you yesterday, will be taking part. Do you remember Mr Fish?"

"No, sir."

"He wrote this morning's newspaper reports."

The sergeant groaned under his breath as the chief continued.

"He named you and five constables. He also states that you tried to kick to death a certain Mr Cruddle..."

"Yes, sir! And rightly, sir!" Goodenough stood up, he was on firm ground now. "He's a peeping Tom, sir!"

"A peeping Tom?"

"Yes, sir! He's got a hole in the floorboards above the ladies' toilets, sir..."

At this, Shawe-Iskay intervened, leaning towards the chief, "Actually, sir, it is simply a knot-hole."

Goodenough flushed at the policeman's interruption.

"Aye! It's a bloody knot-hole all right!" he sneered. "And the dirty, misshapen little sod looks through it at the women havin' a pee!"

Shawe-Iskay came in again, "The knot-hole, sir, is only an inch from the skirting in a corner of Mr Cruddle's studio-apartment. A constable, the sergeant and I, all attempted to see through it, but it proved impossible..."

"'Cos you had your helmet on!" bawled Goodenough.

"... and, later," Shawe-Iskay continued without pausing, "with Mr Cruddle's permission and without my helmet, I tried again – equally unsuccessfully!"

Goodenough laughed, madly and triumphantly.

"'Cos you haven't got a flat head!" he roared. "That's why! Cruddle's got a flat head! Y'see? His head!" Goodenough pointed to his own as if nobody there had seen one before. "It's flat! Flat! Flat..."

"Sit down, Horace!" snapped the chief.

Goodenough ignored the order.

"... flat as a pancake! It's all the evidence we need to convict! Anybody who goes around looking like Cruddle should be inside anyway..."

"Sit down, Horace!" the chief repeated. "After reading Shawe-Iskay's report I'm convinced that Mr Cruddle is innocent of any crime!"

The sergeant's corned-beef complexion took on the colour of something that should have been condemned as a risk to public health and his idiot-blue eyes festered in it like mould.

"Innocent?" he screamed. "Innocent? He keeps cats! He's a raging bloody pervert..."

At a sign from Shawe-Iskay the shorthand writer disappeared, but Goodenough didn't notice.

"... and he's a peeping Tom! And he's a flasher! I saw him do it! Flashed himself!" The sergeant was frothing at the mouth. "Waved his bloody great hampton round the pub he did! Two inches it was!"

"Two inches?" exclaimed one of the listening officers in amazed disbelief.

"From the ground! Bloody enormous! I've got witnesses..."

"You arrested them all," muttered the chief disconsolately.

"... everybody in the pub saw it! Hell! He even keeps photographs of himself doing it!"

As suddenly as he had stood up, the sergeant sat down. He realised he had gone too far. He shouldn't have exaggerated.

There was a long silence.

The chief leaned slowly towards Goodenough and spoke quietly.

"Tell me, Horace – ever studied Greek?"

"Uh?"

"Greek, Horace. Quite a few policemen seem to have studied Greek nowadays." The chief seemed sad as he said this. "Just wondered if you'd dabbled at all..."

"No, sir," replied the sergeant unbelievingly as he passed a weary hand through his hair and wondered if he was going mad.

The chief took a photograph from the table and passed it over.

To the considerable surprise of his inquisitors, as soon as he looked at it, the sergeant's face lit up. It was a photograph removed from Cruddle's easel. On it the town officer was holding wide his coat, the onlooking crowd was wide-eyed and the banner with the indecipherable writing on it was clearly visible.

"It's the words on the banner, you see," the chief smoothly continued, "ΔΙΑΓΩΝΙΣΜΟΣ ΔΙΕΘΝΟΥΣ φΑΝΤΑΣΤΙΚΟΥ ΓΙΛΕΚΟΥ. 'Ο ΝΙΚΗΤΣ' ΕΜΛΙΝ ΚΡΟΤΟΛ. It's the title of the competition and the name of the winner..."

"Some filthy foreign contest, is it?" The sergeant met the chief's mild stare with a lascivious smirk. "A flashin' contest? Fuckin' hell! Cruddle's worse than the 'Mankley Wanker'! This is all the proof we need!"

"Proof of what, Sergeant?" asked the chief.

"That he's a flasher!" yelled Goodenough. "Look at it, man! It's a flashin' contest!"

The chief leaned even further towards the sergeant to look closely into his eyes.

"It's a fancy waistcoat contest, Horace. That's what it is. It's Cruddle's hobby. He designs fancy waistcoats. Member of an international club of enthusiasts. He won the competition in Greece last year."

The sergeant wasn't listening. His day was over and he knew it.

The chief superintendent looked calmly at his watch, then smiled at his colleagues. It was lunchtime.

"We'll inform you of our deliberations, Horace," he said, gathering up his papers. "Enjoy your sick leave."

*

It was probably just as Horace Goodenough was leaving home to drive to County Headquarters that Christopher Oates Postlethwaite was subjected to the intellectual processes of two of the sergeant's men.

"Black magic, sir! No doubt about it!" said PC Griffiths.

"What do you mean, black magic?" whined Postlethwaite scathingly.

"The feathers, sir, mixed with ashes."

Postlethwaite looked down at the charred turf.

"Feathers?"

"Yes, sir! Somebody's been sacrificing a chicken, I'd say."

"Well, find out who it is!" snapped Postlethwaite. "And, seeing as you people are incapable of protecting my property, you might like to suggest a way by which I can do it myself!"

The policemen looked at the high walls surrounding the garden.

"Broken bottles set in cement, I'd say, sir! That's the cheapest way."

Postlethwaite grunted, dismissed the men and went into the house.

"Says it's black magic... somebody sacrificing a chicken," he muttered.

Mrs Postlethwaite stifled a strange bubbling in her throat and disappeared to make herself a coffee.

Postlethwaite sighed and set off for the town hall. He was late, he had to deliver his car back to the garage, there was much to do, he was in no mood to be upset by trivialities.

The first triviality to upset him on his arrival at his office was its occupation by Malcolm Birstin and, resting in the centre of the *Financial Times*, a half-eaten, mouldy egg sandwich. By half past nine, the auditor, convinced that Postlethwaite must have by now been committed to a lunatic asylum had decided to move into his chief's room to get the feel of the place.

The second triviality was a large brown envelope, addressed to the Chairman of the Finance & General Purposes Committee, which fell from Birstin's shaking hands as he backed away, babbling an unintelligible explanation for his presence there.

"What is this, may I ask?" the treasurer interrupted, stooping towards the envelope.

Birstin made a wild-eyed, lugubrious rugby tackle for the subject of Postlethwaite's interest, but the treasurer deftly snatched it from between the fumbling auditor's outstretched fingers and placed it out of reach; then, in silence, coolly regarded the embarrassed, frightened interloper retreating with mumbled crass apologies.

Trivialities continued for most of the morning.

For instance, when David Smith came for the mail, Postlethwaite was treated to an improbable explanation for the events of yesterday afternoon, about which the treasurer had previously known nothing and the essence of which bore no relation to the various alternative explanations offered him later by each of the staff who, on some pretext or other, found their way into his office – except Arnold, of course, whose conscience was clear. Due to his having been in the company of Alderman Carrigan at the time of the post-pub confrontation with Birstin he wasn't subject to any fear of the auditor's threatened report.

Trivialities became more absorbing when Postlethwaite got round to reading the contents of the Birstin's brown envelope. Enclosed was a draft of a statement, meticulously compiled, that would have undoubtedly produced a reaction from the chairman. How often, Postlethwaite wondered, had a chairman of committee received from a junior member of staff a formal intimation that the borough treasurer was a pencil fetishist and homicidal maniac? To say nothing of his having encouraged the staff to lewd, riotous and drunken behaviour, resulting in their being absent from their place of work for the periods listed in 'Appendix E' and their having attempted to bribe the internal auditor of the borough by the offer of two bottles of Newcastle Brown Ale.

The appendices were also interesting: 'A' listed the full names of the staff, their addresses, dates of birth and length of local government service, 'B' gave their grades and current incremental points on the salary scale, 'C' detailed their accumulated superannuation contributions, 'D' their terms and conditions of service, 'E' recorded how many hours, minutes and seconds each had been missing from the office, 'F' itemised the notional cost to the borough of such absences, 'G' gave Birstin's full curriculum vitae, and 'H' listed every local authority in England and Wales to have promoted its internal auditor to the position of borough treasurer within the last five years.

Postlethwaite tapped a finger on his desk as he considered his best course of action. Carefully, he examined the reverse sides of Birstin's hand-written sheets for evidence of their have been in contact with carbon paper. Finding none, he came to that form of conclusion which so identifies the public servant as a proper repository for the aspirations of those who pay his salary – he would do absolutely nothing. It took less than five seconds to tear up the sixteen pages of foolscap which Birstin had laboured overnight to complete, and even fewer to dismiss the whole matter from his mind, at least for a couple of hours.

He had work to do.

First, he telephoned three building firms for written estimates to top his garden wall with concrete and broken bottles, then he phoned the sales manager of the Monk Garage to complain that the Triumph hadn't been repaired.

"That's funny!" said the man, who was genuinely surprised.

"Not in my view!" replied the treasurer.

And the sales manager promised to get to the bottom of the matter.

Then, with an energy that would have done credit to one whose income depended upon effort, Postlethwaite plunged into the financial affairs of the borough.

*

"What are you having, Stan?" asked Paddy, already oozing the *bonhomie* of the experienced landlord.

"Bloody palpitations!" replied the day's first customer. "That bugger Birstin clocked us all in yesterday afternoon. Accused us of bribery. Put a report in to Postlethwaite!"

"Did he, b'Jove?"

"Aye." Stan fumbled in his trouser pocket for some loose change. "I'll have a pint."

Paddy pulled thoughtfully at the pump as Stan turned to acknowledge the arrival of David, now sheepishly approaching the bar counter.

"Hello, you," muttered Stan. "What you having?"

"A nervous breakdown," replied David. "Has the chief said anything to you about Birstin's report?"

"No. Do you want a pint?"

"Well, I er... only came for a sandwich really..."

"That's a good idea!" interrupted Stan. "I'll have a sandwich an' all. The food looks a bit more wholesome here than in the canteen. You don't get the feeling you have to eat it before it eats you."

"That'll be two pints then?" enquired Paddy, inexpertly sliding the first along.

"Yes, please," confirmed David.

Others drifted into the pub to wait for service as Stan and David made their way to a table.

Then Ethel and Doreen arrived.

"Well, it's not as if we're really going for a drink, is it?" Ethel was prattling. "Not with Mr Kean being here..."

*

Arnold was leaving the office.

"Where are you going?" asked Birstin.

Arnold hesitated. These were the first words the glum-looking auditor had uttered all morning.

"Home for lunch."

"I'm not staying here on my own!"

There was a quiver of fear in the auditor's voice and his eyes flitted nervously towards the heavy oak door of Postlethwaite's office.

"That insane bugger attacked me yesterday!"

"Oh," said Arnold expressionlessly.

"He did!" protested Birstin.

"Why?" asked Arnold.

"I don't know."

The auditor looked confused for a moment, then sick. If Postlethwaite had been violent yesterday without cause, God knows what he would do today after reading that malicious report.

"He's mad, you know!"

"Oh?"

"Or up to something! Fiddling the books or something. The worry. Sending him round the bend!"

Arnold's lips displayed the shadow of a disbelieving sneer. He wasn't daft. People in Postlethwaite's position were always honest. Besides, Arnold doubted if Postlethwaite had enough imagination to fiddle.

"It's not unknown for treasurers to help themselves, you know," Birstin went on confidentially, as if he'd guessed Arnold's thoughts. "The opportunities are limitless when you think about it..."

His voice trailed off and his eyes popped like a prawn's as the oak door banged shut behind the treasurer who proceeded to stride down the office towards the two young men.

Thankful for a diversion, Arnold promptly scarpered, leaving Birstin to his fate.

"Your report," began the treasurer, "is it completed?"

Birstin backed away, casting about him for something to use as a defensive weapon.

"Well?" barked Postlethwaite. "Have you completed it?"

"I've got friends in the police!" Birstin blurted out as his back came into contact with the wall.

"What are you talking about? I'm not interested in the police!"

"They'll be interested in you if you lay hands on me..."

The treasurer struck a pompous pose.

"Mr Birstin! Are you drunk? Is your behaviour the result of too heavy a workload?"

"Anyhow," Birstin frantically interjected. "I wrote that report while under severe emotional strain. I'd been beaten up in the ladies' by this fat woman..."

"Be quiet, man!"

"... and then the police beat me up!..."

"Birstin!"

"... accidentally, of course, I mean, they didn't understand; they were quite right to beat me up really..."

"Get a hold of yourself!"

Postlethwaite moved towards the auditor.

"Don't try it! Don't come any nearer!" Birstin raised his arms to protect his face.

"Silence!" the treasurer shouted. "Just give me your report on the public conveniences audit, then you can go home and rest..."

"One step nearer and I'll, I'll... what?" The auditor lowered his arms and stared witlessly at Postlethwaite.

"It's Tuesday, Birstin! Sub-Committee for Parks, Cemeteries and Public Conveniences meets at three! Where... is... your... report?"

"What?" the auditor repeated like an idiot.

"Your report!" Postlethwaite shouted, banging his fist on the desk.

"Oh... yes! It's here!" Birstin shot to his drawer, a picture of penitent humility, and handed his chief a manila folder. "It's okay. There were no discrepancies!"

"Good."

"I thought at first you were talking about that other report." Birstin felt sick but forced a distraught little self-deprecatory snigger. "I thought you might have wanted to see me about it, clear the air and that..."

Postlethwaite raised himself to his full impressive height and looked down on the auditor as if there had appeared on the office floor a particularly slimy form of insect life.

"There *is* no other report, Mr Birstin!" he said meaningfully, then returned calmly to his inner sanctum.

Birstin's eyes followed the tall figure until the door thudded shut. Heavily, he sank into his seat. His feelings were mixed. Relief, gratitude, appreciation of Postlethwaite's apparent big-mindedness, all flickered among them, but suspicion natural to the career accountant predominated. There was nothing big-minded about the treasurer. He was either weak or up to something. Or both. The auditor's spirits rose. Of course. Postlethwaite was frightened. That report to the chairman had terrified him. Now he was trying to ingratiate himself. And the only reason Birstin could imagine for Postlethwaite to do that was because he had something to hide. Something where a liaison with the internal auditor might prove to be of value.

In the office cabinet there was a complex 'Abstract of Accounts' which listed every aspect of the work of the department. Birstin crossed the room and removed the heavily embossed file which contained it. Methodically he examined the main headings, looking for those with obvious control weaknesses where embezzlement might be most likely to have occurred. He was undaunted by the mass of detailed material which backed up the orderly columns of analysis. Even if it took him years, he intended to get through it all. Get something on Postlethwaite and the road to the treasurership would be clear.

Meanwhile, he decided, he would press home his advantage. He wanted an assistant, a car allowance, and a key to the 'Condemned Food' cabinet.

Without pausing for further consideration he rapped confidently on the heavy oak door and entered.

Now, during the course of the morning Postlethwaite had come to a few conclusions of one sort and another. Naturally, after perusing Birstin's damning report to the chairman, it had been the treasurer's intention to cut off the auditor's future by assigning him either no work at all or, at best, the dregs of arithmetical tedium, but an accidental glance through the window at The Bone Idol invoked the memory of how just such action in the past had worked to another's advantage, so the treasurer turned his mind to an opposite line of thinking. It was obvious that Birstin was a threat but, judging from that odious draft, it was also obvious that he possessed a keen analytical mind. And, of all the staff, only *he* appeared to be imbued with any genuine ambition to further the power and influence of his profession.

So Postlethwaite decided to extend the hand of magnanimity – 'know thine enemy' he had once read somewhere. And, though unlikely, Birstin might be one of those soft-headed morons who

258

responded to kindliness, so might submit his considerable talent to the furtherance of Postlethwaite's hopes for the department.

Therefore, when the auditor entered Postlethwaite's office Birstin found a willing ear for his tale of yesterday's happenings, and his few suggestions for the improvement of his professional status received easy agreement. It would take time, of course, and submissions to subcommittees and council, but Birstin left Postlethwaite's office properly hopeful that a car, an assistant and a key to the Health Department cabinet would be his.

That convinced him more than ever that Postlethwaite was up to something. Something big. Something well deserving the attentions of an auditor – but not one from the offices of the district auditor. Oh, no. The relationship between borough treasurers and the district audit office was too cosy by half; quite unlikely to secure Postlethwaite's dismissal and imprisonment. Birstin would handle this one alone.

An obsession was born.

*

Arnold Locock's obsession of the week had consisted of looking forward to Friday night and once again meeting with his friends for a drink. And, for once, he thought, as he walked to the pub, he had something to talk about. The opening of The Bone Idol couldn't help but be the principal topic of conversation, and he had been part of it.

But Arnold was to be disappointed. Nobody, in fact, discussed The Bone Idol. Midnight and Giuseppe steered clear of the subject – the Negro because he disapproved the junketings of councillors and public officials, the Italian for reasons unknown. All Fenwick seemed to be able to talk about was how Postlethwaite's car had come to be still bashed in when everybody at the garage knew perfectly well that it had been repaired. And Joan's preoccupation of the evening was limited to squeezing her rounded little body ever closer to the Italian, whose attention she had at long last succeeded in capturing. Only Marjorie gave any indication of having done something different of late – and that only by a minor-key attempt to emulate Mrs Postlethwaite's style of conversation. It showed itself in the down-turn of her mouth and a series of caustic, monotonous clichés which did more for sarcasm than wit.

"I can't understand it!" exclaimed Fenwick. "It had definitely been repaired. All the worksheets were there! I checked them..."

"Aye," muttered Midnight.

"The foreman checked them. So did the panel beater and the painter..."

"Aye?" the Negro repeated.

"I tried to tell you, you know," Arnold interjected, but he was ignored.

"Anyway, the boss said it had to be done again. Says he's goin' to deduct the cost from my commission! That's a laugh!"

"I did try to tell you, though..."

"I mean, what joy would I have got out of smashing up Postlethwaite's car? None! But the boss says that people in Postlethwaite's position didn't get there by telling lies and being dishonest..."

"Oh, I wouldn't say that!" said Arnold, desperate to be heard. "Bloke in our office says that treasurers are always at it! Fiddling and that! Says the opportunities are endless..."

"Is that right?" The bewildered, failed car salesman at last acknowledged Arnold's presence.

"Aye."

Fenwick stopped talking for a while and thoughtfully supped up.

By this time Giuseppe had slipped his hand on to Joan's knee and was kneading it in that slightly over-passionate manner that Latins frequently adopt to live up to their Hollywood image, much to the embarrassment of the more staid Anglo-Saxon. Joan was thrilled, but annoyed that nobody had appeared to take notice of what was happening.

"Stop it!" she giggled rather loudly, hoping to be overheard.

But Arnold, Midnight and Fenwick were now deep in discussion about whether or not the quality of the beer had degenerated since Paddy Kean had taken over the pub.

"Oh, don't!" exclaimed Joan more loudly, her eyes shining appreciation.

Marjorie overheard the squeak of false protest but her only response was to hitch herself in her seat and gaze coolly across the room, blowing cigarette smoke straight ahead of her.

"God, you'll be after the Arabs next," she muttered.

Joan blushed and promptly slapped the Italian's hand.

"They don't take no for an answer, do they?" she remarked, turning to her sour-faced friend.

"You're dead right!"

"I mean, I tried to stop his hand going any further! I told him to stop!"

"You can't stop the wops," Marjorie sneered, "it's in their nature! They can't help themselves. There's nothing you can do about it. It would be like telling a dog not to chase cats, or a kitten not to play with string – it's in their nature. It's just the same with the wops. It's in their nature to feel your legs. You can't tell them..."

Her voice droned on, a source of some annoyance to Midnight, now in the throes of comparing ales produced by various local breweries. He had a morbid interest in the declining standards of British brewing.

"I mean, that's the whole problem with the Eyeties – they can't help themselves..." Marjorie's voice carped on and on. "Telling them to get their hands off is just like telling a sink not to gurgle..."

Midnight was forced into silence. His little audience had turned its attention to Marjorie's infantile prattle.

"... or telling an American not to be ignorant, or telling the council not to waste money, or telling a Catholic not to have kids..."

"Or telling a woman not to be stupid!" snapped Midnight in a rare flash of anger.

*

Fenwick Fancourt spent a lot of time drinking between Saturday morning and Sunday night. Alone too. A sure sign of a man with a problem. And a sure method of getting the wrong answer.

In Fenwick's case, however, by Monday morning, he hadn't found an answer at all. Just a head like fifty and the inability to see anything but what was placed directly before his bloodshot eyes. And his boss lost no time in placing there the morning newspaper opened at 'Situations Vacant'.

But it was an advertisement of a different type that captured the attention of the doleful Fenwick:

> *"A supply of vehicles to the Borough Engineer's Department as listed below... Tenders to be submitted to the Borough Treasurer, Christopher Oates Postlethwaite by 11 a.m. on Tuesday, 9th..."*

The newspaper fell from Fenwick's hands. Sweat beaded his brow. Inspiration came to him with almost explosive force. 'Always at it,' Arnold had said. 'Fiddling and that!' – and didn't Fancourt, that very day, have to deliver to Postlethwaite his twice-repaired car? And hadn't Postlethwaite tried to fiddle the first of those repairs by claiming a faulty gearstick?

After a hair of the dog at The Clock Hotel, Fenwick popped into the Trustee Savings Bank and withdrew every penny he possessed – a hundred pounds – then, calling only briefly at The Crow's Nest and The Jordan, hastened back to the garage to collect the Triumph.

It was with some difficulty that he got it to the town hall, where he parked half on and half off the footway, but somehow it didn't trouble him. After a couple more drinks, this time at The Bone Idol, he crashed into the town hall foyer and tapped on the treasurer's door.

"Come?"

Fenwick found the shiny, brass doorknob something of a trial. His palms were wet with perspiration. Wiping them on his jacket, a slight inclination of his head brought with it nausea and a sense of blackness.

"Come?" came the voice again, the whining tone more pronounced by increased volume.

Fenwick again gripped the doorknob and twisted. The door opened and he lurched through to stand, rather droopily, in the middle of the room. A scent of polished oak and Old Spice aftershave surrounded the clean, lean figure seated smartly behind the large desk; a figure distinctly different to that which had behaved so oddly at the garage and The Bone Idol.

"Ah!" Postlethwaite exclaimed. "The car!"

"Wha' car?" hiccoughed Fenwick.

"The Triumph!" smiled Postlethwaite.

Fenwick blinked. His stomach turned. Of course. Here was his excuse for being there. Grab it and go. Just leave the keys, give a polite touch of the ould forelock and disappear. So easy. No problem.

But his mouth let him down.

"That's not why I'm here," he said conspiratorially.

Then, imagining himself too far away for a secret conversation, he moved towards the treasurer. But he moved a lot faster than his disordered mind anticipated. The desktop suddenly caught his midriff. He creased and his beer-reeking mouth came not an inch from Postlethwaite's immediately suspicious face.

"I'm here to do you a big, big favour!"

With tortuous difficulty Fenwick extracted the one hundred pounds from his coat pocket and slapped it down before the treasurer's horrified eyes, which flitted through hooded lids to the window and, through it, to the window of Paddy's flat above the pub.

"There y'are!" announced Fenwick. "A hunnerd quid! For you! Engineer wants vehicles; I sell 'em! A deal? Eh?"

"Get out," hissed the treasurer, a shadow of fear crossing his features.

"Good deal!" Fenwick urged. "Easy money! Hush-hush! Nobody'd know – a hunnerd quid! All I've got..."

"Out!" Postlethwaite swiped at the bundle of one-pound notes, sending it flying across the office. "Or I'll call the police!"

Fenwick paled. Desperately he struggled for words.

"Hunnerd quid!" he protested weakly. "Just for the order. Need to keep my job going..."

"Out! Now!"

Fenwick's expression, never very joyous, crumpled. He looked about him, then bent to retrieve the crisp, new banknotes he'd carried so hopefully to the town hall.

Postlethwaite strode to the door and opened it wide.

"Out!" he snarled.

A tear coursed down the car salesman's cheek as, humiliated, he stumbled away to what he felt sure was to be a dreadful oblivion.

*

At least, Fenwick had only oblivion to contemplate. Unlike Postlethwaite. He had a conscience. A nasty one. The kind of conscience that manifests itself when being found out becomes something of a certainty.

His first thought was that, for some reason, the sales director of the Monk Garage had wished to ensure the vehicle tender for his company by the offer of money in addition to freely repairing the Triumph. And this Postlethwaite couldn't understand. It was one thing to quietly suggest a gentlemanly agreement, but quite another to offer a blatant bribe. All businessmen knew that. So, perhaps, Fancourt had been working off his own bat – in which case it was a straightforward criminal offence. Bribing a local government officer – good for a couple of months inside, the treasurer reckoned. And the lad was a friend of Locock's. The treasurer's hand hovered over the telephone to call the police. An example should be made. He pursed his lips and began to dial. Then, as if scalded, he dropped the receiver.

Nobody in their right mind would approach a borough treasurer with a bribe unless they had reason to believe it would be accepted. The risks were too great. So the sales director must have talked. And Fancourt might have talked to Locock.

Shaking, Postlethwaite then recalled his attempt to fiddle the repair of his car. He began to pace the room. Something he was to do often over the next few days. But it brought him no relief – only a strengthened conviction that you could never trust anybody.

The Monk Garage put in its tender for the borough engineer's vehicles. It didn't make the shortlist. And, a week later, for twice repairing the Triumph, Postlethwaite received an invoice the like of which he could scarcely believe - but he paid it promptly, in cash.

Fenwick Fancourt, in anticipation of immediate dismissal, resigned his job, thus making himself available on the labour market for a whole new future.

*

Actually, had Postlethwaite called the police to lift Fenwick, it is doubtful if they would have made an arrest. It was out of fashion in Mankley. After grapevine dissemination of the news of Goodenough's fate, there had been a re-think regarding arrests. The drop in the official crime statistics for the recent quarter was consequently staggering.

But the police dealt with other matters – traffic control, helping people find their way, occasionally advising a drunk to 'go steady', and generally keeping in touch with those concerned with current lines of enquiry.

Like Florrie Moon, for instance, whose family, bored stupid by lack of police concern over their habitually criminal activities, had taken increasingly to staying at home where they sat about morosely arguing or bashing the younger ones for diversion. Still, two months later, Ernie's attackers hadn't been traced, and this was a frequent subject of discussion.

There had been a row about it on a night when Florrie was preparing to reverse the gas meter.

"But it could have been an accident, couldn't it?" suggested Anthony as his mother, equipped with her mirror, disappeared down the short passageway to the little cupboard under the stairs.

"'Course it couldn't!" she replied, sucking on her cigarette, which she'd sensibly left unlit while carrying out her delicate and potentially dangerous fortnightly task.

"How could it have been an accident?" she shouted from inside the cupboard. "Nobody gets blown up by accident!"

She disconnected the two pipes and was just about to turn the meter when there was a knock on the glass-panelled front door. Cursing, she extricated her head and looked at the silhouetted shape of a policeman's helmet. She jumped to her feet and tore down the passage to close the door which led to the kitchen where most of the family was gathered. Then, thinking that the policeman might have news of Ernie, she returned to the front door and opened it, ignoring the gas hissing odourlessly from the cupboard.

"Mrs Moon? Mother of Ernest Moon?"

"Eeh, aye!" she cried. "Howway in!"

The policeman entered, carefully shutting the door behind him. He had little to say. Ernie's condition was improving, but his memory was almost non-existent. He hadn't been able to cast any light on the mystery of the accident. Perhaps, after all, the policeman suggested, it had indeed been merely a bizarre mishap.

"That's what our Anthony says," Florrie muttered, "but nobody gets blown up by accident, do they?"

"I don't know, missus," said the constable. "What's that hissing noise?"

"Eh?... Oh! It's something cooking in the kitchen," Florrie replied, blushing.

"Oh, I see. Right. Well, I'll be getting along, then..."

"Aye. All right," drawled Florrie.

The policeman turned to the door, but before opening it he noticed Florrie's unlit cigarette.

"Here, love," he said, flicking a lighter, "you want a light for that..."

The dull bang of the explosion in the passage – releasing the now pressurised gas below it – was followed by a bang that was heard five miles away.

And felt much nearer.

The Moons, however, neither heard nor felt it. Those not buried instantly under the rubble of the house and half of Railway Street were transformed into thousand-miles-an-hour human torches to land one by one, inconveniently and catastrophically all over town.

Harry, following an involuntary but spectacular high jump from his bedroom immediately above the passage, catapulted from the cables of an electricity pylon to clear the security wall of the chemical works and come blazing down into the middle of the propane gas store, producing a blast of thermo-nuclear proportions and sending most of the night shift to a messy and separate end – an explosion matched only a split second later by the arrival of Fred and Frank at the riverside petrol depot. Within minutes the blaze spread, lighting the evening sky, devastating Mankley's waterfront and, in a brilliant display of pyrotechnics, destroying two tankers full of crude which burned for days.

Amid the holocaust, other Moons, kamikaze-like, descended to scatter destruction and terror over a wide area.

*

It had taken Archie Carrigan all his considerable powers of persuasion to get the local amateur operatic society to invite the mayor to its annual performance. Nevertheless, it was only by his having given a signed undertaking that he would escort her throughout and take personal responsibility for all damages that he had succeeded.

These were assurances he wouldn't normally have given but for the fact that it was a theatrical event, for Archie was keen to bolster his already thickening links with the performing arts. True, there were years ahead, but he was determined to be the one man in Mankley seen to be a force when the time came for the

council to purchase The Royal Gaiety – the alderman knew what he wanted from that little deal.

It was at the beginning of the first act, during the singing of a particularly mawkish love duet, when a blazing Moon crashed through the roof to the stage, setting fire to the scenery and testing to the limit the ability of the singers to soldier on regardless.

Archie nudged the dozing Nora Slattery.

"Look at that! Look at that!" he whispered, as the singers, smiling glassily and still warbling inanities, to the horror of the drummer, surreptitiously attempted to kick the smouldering body into the orchestra pit. "There's a thing you don't see twice in one evening, eh?"

Just then another body arrived by the same route to annihilate any few remaining hopes among the players of completing the performance. The curtain would have been lowered if it hadn't already gone up in flames, and the language of the soprano gave a whole new twist to 'Blue Moon'.

*

It was the time of the Finance & General Purposes Committee's quarterly examination of costs (actual) against costs (estimated) and the staff of the Treasurer's Department, thanks to lunchtime drinking and habitual foot-dragging, found themselves working a late Friday.

Arnold was called into the treasurer's office.

"Ah, Locock!" Postlethwaite smiled in welcome.

Arnold hated effusiveness and shuffled awkwardly as he responded with his usual, "Uh-huh?"

"Seem to have omitted to bring my briefcase to the office. Terribly busy. Wondered if you'd kindly pop over to my house and get it for me?"

"Uh-huh," Arnold assented.

"Aah, good! Now, here's my front door key. My briefcase is in the bedroom to the left at the top of the stairs, near the mirror. Get your bus fare from petty cash. Can't get hold of Mrs

Postlethwaite. Dare say she must be studying her Italian. "

*

She was.

On her back.

Postlethwaite had given no thought to where his wife went to study her Italian. If he assumed anything at all, it was probably that she went to 'Catchpenny' Moran's School of Languages in Newcastle. In fact, she had always done just that, but tonight, consequent to her having recently advertised for a native Italian to give her private practice, and taking advantage of the fact that Postlethwaite was likely to be working late, she was reclining on the sofa drinking in the soft-spoken charm of Giuseppe Mescolare, who was guiding her through all the phrases necessary for making friends in Italy.

With the door locked and the phone muffled by a pile of cushions, it hadn't taken long in the cosy atmosphere for Giuseppe to take her hand, nor any longer for Mrs Postlethwaite to entertain the thought of an affair. This young Italian was handsome and he might be physically pleasing.

They kissed.

She felt guilty.

Then she thought of Postlethwaite and the sexlessness of their marriage.

She felt deprived.

They kissed again, more passionately.

"I take you to bed," whispered Giuseppe.

"Yes," she responded, her hands in his hair, "I'll bathe, then join you."

They went upstairs together.

She showed the Italian into the bedroom, then after a thoughtful pause, went to the bathroom and closed the door.

Languidly disrobing she fantasised about the forthcoming liaison. Soon she would again know passion. There would be the foreplay, the gentle words, the probing. She would lie back, part her long legs to allow him entry. Pre-orgasmic waves would crash over her. Her fingernails would drag up and down his back. His loins would begin to pound, and the coital climb to short-lived ecstasy would begin.

She caught sight of herself in the mirror. Her figure was perfect. She liked what she saw. More important, she liked the person beneath the skin – too much for the intrusion of anything unworthy. The body is the temple of the soul.

Postlethwaite loved her. Why should her present inability to love him mean that she should have her body violated by a stranger, someone without any history of emotional intimacy or proven care?

She had never before been unfaithful, and fidelity was a dignity she wasn't prepared to sacrifice. She might be unhappy with Christopher, but that was no fault of his. Cheap tart she wasn't, she thought, locking the bathroom door and running a hot bath to wash herself clean again.

Meanwhile, Giuseppe took stock of his situation and considered himself fortunate. As he stripped naked he already had a mental picture of this glorious woman, unclothed and luscious. Pulling back the bedclothes he felt the resilience of the mattress. This was going to be the sensual awakening of his life.

To reassure himself, he stepped before the full-length mirror and cast his eyes down his balletically proportioned body. Whether it was at the sight of himself or the thought of what was to come, genital hankerings began to produce a physical reaction. He turned sideways-on to the mirror, the better to admire the expression of his virility. Italian it might be, spaghetti it wasn't.

Well, not for a minute or two.

In which time Arnold Locock let himself through the front door and began to thump his way up the stairs to find the treasurer's briefcase.

Now, masturbation might give you hair on your hands and make you blind, but an erection, in itself, by whatever means, doesn't make you go deaf – nor does it mortify the memory cells. And Giuseppe, on hearing the heavy footsteps, and assuming them to be Postlethwaite's, found that memories of running for his life through the back streets of Turin pursued by knife-wielding relatives of violated wives, sisters and daughters burned strong in his will to survive. He hadn't emigrated to England for nothing. And he certainly hadn't done so to be caught *in flagrante delitto*, or something approaching it, with the wife of one of the town's most important people, who might, on the evidence of his public position, have sinister connections with some form of English *'ndrangheta.*

It was on the point of contemplating breaking the mirror and using a shard of broken glass to defend himself, that the Italian, retreat being something of a racial characteristic, decided that a leap into the garden might be more likely to preserve something of a future and, after shooting through the window and slithering naked down the sloping outhouse roof, it was on the point of a roughly-broken bottle topping the garden wall that his sensual ambitions were compromised for a while to come.

Mrs Postlethwaite, on hearing the unholy scream which accompanied Giuseppe's landing astride the wall, turned off the bath tap, wrapped herself in a rather small towel and headed for the bedroom, just as Arnold reached the top of the stairs heading for the same place. The lady, bumping into him, dropped her towel.

Arnold was no more prepared for the sight of the treasurer's wife nude as he was for anything else in life, and his reaction was typically apathetic.

"Oh, hullo," he said, "I've come to get Mr Postlethwaite's briefcase from the bedroom."

"Oh," said Mrs Postlethwaite, wondering whether it would be more dignified to remain standing in full view of this young man or reach down to re-drape herself in the very small towel.

"Are you not cold?" Arnold asked, as Giuseppe again screamed in torment from the garden.

Mrs Postlethwaite turned into the bedroom, Arnold slowly following. The lady, deciding to introduce something normal into the activities of the evening, got into bed and covered herself, as if that was what she had been intending to do all the time.

Arnold, meanwhile, located the briefcase, picked it up and, hearing another scream went to the open window.

"Shall I close it?" he asked.

"Yes. Fine," replied Mrs Postlethwaite, pulling the bedclothes to her chin.

"Hey!" exclaimed Arnold excitedly. "There's a naked bloke sitting on your wall shouting something."

Mrs Postlethwaite, turned on her stomach and, despairingly, began to pound the headboard with her fists.

"You know," continued Arnold, "I think I know him..." He stopped talking as he realised the identity of the tortured figure.

It was too much for Arnold. Without further ado he closed the window, glanced once more at the garden, then at Mrs Postlethwaite and, deciding to forget the whole matter, returned to the town hall.

Meanwhile, impaled on the wall, Giuseppe realised that his position was delicate. The slightest movement brought intense agony, though the sight of Locock at the window gave him some hope that rescue might be at hand.

After ten minutes or so, however, he began to panic. He had been lucky not to have been seen up to now but it would be just a question of time, he was sure of it. Gently, carefully, he eased what remained of his genitals, stiff with congealing blood, from the jagged glass – the bleeding started again so, with a moan, he relaxed back to his original position. It was a cold evening yet he perspired freely, and the salty sweat added to the renewed pain of his lacerations. He prayed for a miracle – and he got one.

On the last syllable of his muttered supplication, Railway Street, the chemical works and the petrol depot went up and, not thirty seconds later, Postlethwaite's back lawn was cratered by two bodies high-diving it to oblivion.

The Italian reeled with shock, put his hands out to save himself from falling and screamed like a stuck pig as he grasped at more broken glass. Lights went on in the surrounding houses and a police car drew slowly into the back lane on its regular beat to guard Postlethwaite's garden.

It was a miracle all right. Giuseppe might have had a harsh word to say as the police, old instincts to the fore, dragged him roughly from the wall with a snarled, "C'm 'ere, y'cunt!", but he maintained a stout-hearted silence as local residents gathered to give garbled explanations for his being there.

"Big explosion..." said a portly man from number seventeen.

"Terrible, it was..." interrupted an even portlier lady.

"I must say," said somebody in tones reminiscent of a university padre, "it's amazing you survived!"

"His two mates didn't!" a man said.

"Holes ten feet deep in that lawn..." exaggerated number twenty-one.

And much, much more than enough to convince the police that Giuseppe was a victim of some hideous accident now vividly obvious in the sky to the north, while Giuseppe, smiling despite his injuries and disappointment, and remembering that *silenzio e d'oro*, passed into semi-consciousness from loss of blood.

It was another good story for the next day's newspapers. Elton Fish excelled himself in maudlin sentimentality. From all the horror and carnage of the explosions and fires, the only news to make the front page of *The Mankley Courier* was:

MANKLEY MAN NAKED SURVIVES HORROR UNSCATHED

Not that Giuseppe would have entirely agreed as he examined his shredded testicles the next day. He would have called himself scathed, quite definitely. And he would have words with that Arnold Locock when he saw him next. That vision at the window of Mrs Postlethwaite's bedroom couldn't have been imagination.

But, for the moment, he'd concentrate on getting better. For the moment, *silenzio* was obviously *d'oro* – there'd be compensation to claim.

*

Amazingly, apart from Ernie, not all the Moons were destroyed in the holocaust. There were, in fact, two survivors.

As it was Friday, Chocolate had been skulking round the hospital for most of the late afternoon and, as there had been no amputations, he'd spent rather longer living in hope than would normally have been the case.

In fact, it was early evening before he finally gave up and headed disconsolately homeward as the sky went black and red and smoky and rained down assorted bits of industrial Mankley and unindustrious man. Had Chocolate not been disoriented by the tumult, he might well have found the odd titbit here and there among the streets but, for the first time since puppyhood, he was terrified and fled to the ghetto.

His feelings on arrival can only be guessed at. There was hardly a house undamaged, and his own was a shambles. Yet he didn't despair. An eye for the main chance drew him inexorably towards the mound of rubble in what had once been his front garden and, undistracted by the clamour of surviving neighbours and the pathetic cries of the injured, he began to dig.

Now dogs are well prepared to cope with loose sand or soil – even clay can be efficiently dealt with. But unidentifiable bits of metal, twisted piping, concrete, bricks and all the gubbins of human domesticity make hard going for claws and teeth. Yet Chocolate persevered. He knew his future depended on his efforts, and, at last, success came his way.

His paws, bleeding and torn, uncovered a section of the front door, its glass panel, unbelievably, still intact, and under it, Florrie, mouthing pithy remarks and spitting out bits of unlit cigarette as she struggled to free herself.

Any self-respecting human, at such a sight, would have covered her up again and pushed off in the firm belief that he'd done the world a favour, but not our Chocolate. After indulging in only the briefest frenzy of barking, he scraped and scratched at the door until he'd cleared a space through which Florrie could put her hand. A moment later, puffing and coughing and feeling in her ripped pinny pocket for her cigarettes and matches, she was out.

"I knew you'd come, me bairn," she spluttered as she lit up.

Then she turned her attention to the devastation around her.

She may have realised that the family to which she had given twenty years of her life were gone but she shed no tears.

Grabbing a length of iron tubing she made for where the kitchen had once been and, with a strength and energy that belied her size, hacked like a demon at the rubble.

It would have made wonderful television for Dodie Ochiltree – so ethnic; and a marvellous picture story for Elton Fish – that skinny, tattered figure battering so valiantly at the immovable debris against the blood-red background of smoke and ashes. Had she a child under there? A crippled mother? Perhaps a memento, a lock of hair, a family heirloom?

Not on your life.

After five minutes solid battering, Florrie found what she wanted – her string bag and, in it, her worn-out, plastic purse bulging with a week's wages from each of seven of her family. Not much of a nest egg, but enough.

Her beady eyes darted around her craftily, then, sure that she'd not been seen, she was off – spindly legs dancing through the rubble and chaos, off down the main road, away from Mankley. Nobody would find her. Nobody.

And Chocolate happily loped along at her side, growling occasionally, standing guard while she called at the off-licence, and matching her stride as she made for the col of the slag-heap and the fields beyond, and beyond them, the hills that would lead to a new life.

*

So nobody knew the real truth of how Mankley came to suffer its calamity. And this led ultimately to the establishment of a remarkable number of investigative committees – all, it need hardly be said, set up at the tub-thumping insistence of aldermen and councillors urged on by public officials; all, it need hardly be said, composed of a selection of those very same personages; and all, it need hardly be said, cluttered up with weighty, defensive policies presented at enormous public cost and to complete public indifference to prove nothing at all except that committees can be more disastrous to a community's long-term well-being than any number of personally inspired Armageddons.

*

Ordinary people, of course, go on doing ordinary things: Mankley's annual dog show was Mrs Postlethwaite's responsibility and, as secretary of the local RSPCA committee, it was not one she relished. She didn't even like dogs, or, at least, the attendant human sentimentality about them. Her concern for animal welfare had more to do with the dignity of God's creatures than their contribution to the wealth or vanity of man.

But her opinions met with little positive response from the controlling interests of the national organisation, absorbed as it was in the 'British Way of Life', with its fox-hunting, horse-racing and pheasant shoots; and met with even less response from the valiant band of local worthies, dog-breeders and soppy old fools that made up Mankley's committee.

"Of course," enthused Major Orne, the regional organiser, whose salary depended upon enthusing, "you'll be having the mayor to do the honours..."

"Over my dead body!" flashed Mrs Postlethwaite, to nods of agreement from a few of those present.

The regional organiser blanched at the strength of feeling.

"Nyah! Nyah! Nyah!" he laughed, in that special way that so endears ex-army officers to those who meet them. "But, seriously, ladies and gentlemen, it is the weight of civic position that rests on the mayor that matters, not the personality..."

"You'd soon change your mind about that if you met our mayor!" Mrs Postlethwaite burst in. "The weight of her personality makes her civic position fade into insignificance!"

"I'm sure she can't be that bad," said the major – he was worried. There had been a memorandum from Major Twist at headquarters only last week to ask that every endeavour be made to involve civic leaders in the events of local branches.

"Don't you believe it!" responded Mrs Postlethwaite. "Nora Slattery's flair for verbal muck-pushing is of a quality outstanding, even for a councillor!"

Councillor Webster shuffled around a bit but Mrs Postlethwaite was unrepentant.

"And if she's invited in any official capacity whatsoever, I'll resign – with a bang!"

"Oh, dear," muttered the major, "I'm sure we don't want that..." Though, in fact, he wouldn't have minded. Mrs Postlethwaite had been a trial to him ever since her letter to Commander Gibson of parliamentary division demanding the lobbying of the House of Commons for a punitive tax to be put on all those who kept gun dogs.

"Can I make a suggestion?" enquired the vicar.

"Grmph, grmph," the chairman mumbled.

Taking this as an indication of assent, the vicar continued.

"Perhaps an idea that might commend itself to you would be to invite a celebrity to open the dog show.

"Oh, yes!"

"Excellent idea!"

"Hear, hear!"

"I wonder, if Mrs Postlethwaite recalls... there was an actress lady visited the town some months ago... a Miss Lessingdale?"

The vicar, being short-sighted, had found the star particularly appealing.

"Splendid suggestion, Vicar!" exclaimed Squadron-Leader Penfold, whose brewery kept the best team of shire horses for miles around.

'Yes," hesitated Mrs Postlethwaite carefully, "it might attract the media..."

The lateness of the hour and the inability of anyone to think of an alternative settled it. Jacob S Cracker was approached to make the necessary arrangements, and Miss Gloria Lessingdale was engaged to make her second visit to Mankley. It said much for her current state of penury that the actress consented to come – Mankley was not her most memorable spiritual home.

Anyway, more then usual interest was shown in the show. The numbers entering their pooches and attending as spectators were greater than for many years. Such a pity that due to its partial demolition in the explosions, the civic hall was not available for use. The Co-op hall was not so spacious. A fact to be remarked upon by Councillor Mrs Nora Slattery when she arrived on the arm of Major Orne and at his personal invitation.

"God!" she exclaimed to a little group of animal lovers gathered in the entrance. "There's not room to swing a cat in here!"

But the size of the venue was only a minor contributory factor in the failure of Mankley's dog show to shine as the North-East's answer to Crufts.

It was nothing to do with the organisation – Mrs Postlethwaite would never allow herself to be faulted on such a mundane achievement – and it was nothing to do with the presence of the mayor, however generally unwelcome that might have been.

What it was to do with was the committee's choice of celebrity. A natural choice, of course. There was no bigger 'name' than Gloria Lessingdale. She had launched The Bone Idol into instant local fame – a talking point for weeks, especially by those who'd seen Winston do his trick. And they had told their friends about it. And they told others. And it was obvious, in a small town like Mankley, that every dog owner would teach his dog the same trick.

So, could anyone be surprised, as the vicar announced, "Ladies and Gentlemen, Miss GLORIA LESSINGDALE!" that every dog in the hall instantly threw itself on its back, parted its legs and panted?

*

The end of Mankley's memorable civic year was drawing to a close and the council meeting droned on. It was the last of Nora Slattery's year of office and the last to be attended and advised by the town clerk after more than forty years of service to the borough.

Nora thought little of her year. She knew it had been a charade, a dismal fulfilling of the Labour Group's policy. Nothing more. But she didn't blame her political colleagues for what had been, at best, an austere twelve months. She knew her limitations as well as they did and, while she was hurt that more faith had not been placed in her, and disappointed that no one, except Archie, had felt able to offer guidance instead of insult, she wasn't bitter. But she was bloody mad that the town clerk had denied her the full use of the Daimler on her one official outing. That had gone down like a cup of cold sick.

Twice during the meeting Councillor Webster rose to speak, twice he was waved down. But, as the meeting closed, he rose again.

"Mayor, Aldermen, Councillors," he began, to yawns and groaning, "I feel sure you would wish it to be commemorated this evening that our town clerk retires after..."

Nora tutted and adjusted her spectacles, then attracted the attention of a nearby clerk with whom she had a brief and, judging by the triumphant expression on her face, satisfactory conversation.

"... we all remember the war years," the councillor continued. Nora banged her gavel.

"... his kindness to us all..."

Nora again banged her gavel, this time louder.

But the councillor ignored her. The town clerk began to look emotional and blew his nose. Some glanced his way as if seeing him for the first time.

"... we are all indebted to him for so much..."

"Councillor!" shouted Nora.

"... so many occasions..."

"COUNCILLOR!" Nora screamed, banging her gavel like a maniac and, this time, some members present joined in a chorus of objection.

At the clamour, Councillor Webster stopped and looked around him. The room went silent. Nora leaned from her high seat, a malicious leer on her face.

"The town clerk has already been congratulated in committee!" she snarled – then, turning to a minion who up to now had been taking notes, she added, "Strike that speech from the minutes!"

Christopher Oates Postlethwaite couldn't help but titter to himself as he left the chamber for his office downstairs. He'd waited a long time to see the town clerk humiliated. In fact, all in all, in the last few months the treasurer had had quite a lot to titter about – amidst the bureaucratic mayhem of investigating committees, working parties, public enquiries, hardship funds, accusations, counter-accusations, headshaking, pomposity and general ballyhoo, he, along with other careerist senior officials of the corporation, had enjoyed open season. Staffing Committee had gone berserk. New appointments went through on the nod. For a spell, there was nothing that wasn't approved – especially when hung on the 'disaster' banner.

Much of this laxity had been due to the imminent retirement of the town clerk. The presence of that simple, straightforward old soul had acted for years as a brake on the aspirations of Mankley's more ambitious officers. Now that he was gone much more would be achieved, though not to public benefit.

Postlethwaite was elated. Already he had got an audit clerk to assist Birstin; soon he would require more clerical staff, adding machines, calculators, new telephones – the list was endless, the future bright.

As bright as the neon sign that flooded his office.

Postlethwaite glanced at it now and frowned. Pulling the Finance & General Purposes file from his desk, however, he consoled himself by examining his 'Estimated Expenditure' for the coming year. All was well – under 'Fixtures and Fittings (Treasurer's Department)' there was itemised: 'Heavy-duty roller blind – £6.14.11d.' That would shut out Paddy Kean's 'Bone Idol' sign – and the associated memories.

In less than a month the annual council elections would take place. New members would take their seats. Elected fresh into the public eye, they would be nervous, easily manipulated by a seasoned chief officer like Postlethwaite. He would make the real decisions. His would be the administrative nerve centre of the town, and his staff would enlarge with increasing financial legislation. Other chief officers of similar ilk would find themselves equally privileged, but the treasurer would hold the purse-strings. His would be the signature on the cheques. A large bottle of green ink figured in his 'Estimates'.

The aldermanic system in English local government ensured a measure of continuity, but many committee chairmanships would be filled by newcomers and, while Postlethwaite had rubbed along tolerably with his chairman of the past three years, he looked forward avidly to a new, less confident leader of Finance & General Purposes.

It was 1961, a new decade, and plans were afoot to revitalise Mankley. No room for fuddy-duddy men in waistcoats – not to deal with the complexities of mass demolition, a new shopping centre, high-rise flats, a riverside walk, the attraction of light industry. The 1960s were to be the first era of the young, vibrant and easily-led. Young voters, tired of the drab fifties, would elect young councillors. Postlethwaite could smell the change in the air, and his rising, phoenix-like, to eminence.

*

So, in May the local elections were held, and exactly as the borough treasurer had imagined and hoped, over half the wards contested returned young Socialists of under thirty. There was indeed a mood of change. In one of the wards, the successful candidate, Mr Festus Molloy, was not only young but a Conservative; in another, Miss Rose Martin, a Liberal, won the seat.

But in the safest Labour ward of all, with what the press could only describe as 'an annihilating majority' was elected the man who in the June of that year would assume the chairmanship of Mankley's Finance & General Purposes Committee – Mr Patrick Kean!